ISSOLA

BOOKS BY STEVEN BRUST

STEVEN BRUST

ISSOLA

TOR®

A TOM DOHERTY ASSOCIATES BOOK
NEW YORK

ISSOLA

This book is printed on acid-free paper.

Edited by Teresa Nielsen Hayden

A Tor Book
Published by Tom Doherty Associates, LLC
175 Fifth Avenue
New York, NY 10010

www.tor.com

Tor® is a registered trademark of Tom Doherty Associates, LLC.

Library of Congress Cataloging-in-Publication Data

Brust, Steven.
    Issola / Steven Brust—1st ed.
        p.   cm.
    "A Tom Doherty Associates book."
    ISBN 0-312-85927-9 (acid-free paper)
    1. Taltos, Vlad (Fictitious character)—Fiction.   I. Title.

PS3552.R84 I87   2001
813'.54—dc21

                                        2001027122

First Edition: July 2001

Printed in the United States of America

0   9   8   7   6   5   4   3   2   1

This one is for Cynthia.

Acknowledgments

Thanks to Dave Shores, University of Minnesota Department of Chemical Engineering; and to all past and present members of W.I.N., whose help cannot be overstated; and, always, to Adrian Morgan, who started it all. For criticism, I am indebted to Teresa Nielsen Hayden, Pamela Dean, Will Shetterly, and Emma Bull. Special thanks on this one to John Robey. Thanks to Terry McGarry for great copyediting. Finally, thanks to Don Hill for showing me how to generate a bit of additional income while waiting for the book to finish itself, and to all those schlimazels who tried to run down my aces.

PROLOGUE

I've heard it said that manners are more complex in primitive societies—that it is easier to give accidental offense in, for example, the Island kingdoms of Elde or Greenaere, or among the Serioli, or the Jenoine, or the various kingdoms of my own Eastern people, than among the more civilized Dragaerans.

You must allow me to observe that it is invariably Dragaerans who point this out. One can imagine finding a Dragaeran who will not insist that the Empire has achieved the highest imaginable pinnacle of civilization; but then, one can imagine the Emperor presenting one with the Imperial Treasury, too, if one's imagination is active enough.

Yet even among the Seventeen Great Houses of the Empire, there are differences in what is considered proper behavior in various circumstances, and it is worth noting that, if you look hard enough, you will find that there are always very practical reasons for some phrase or action being considered polite or rude under certain circumstances. To pick an obvious example, among my own people, when arriving at the home of an acquaintance, one is expected to pound upon the door with one's fist, whereas among the Dragaerans, this is considered rude. I will not insult you by explaining why, in a culture rich in sorcery and steeped in paranoia, it is a bad idea to touch the door of someone's home. The practical has become a matter of courtesy.

In the Jhereg, the House to which I belong (and the criminal Organization for which I used to work), it is considered rude, when asking to meet with a superior or an equal, to arrive at the meeting first, whereas among the Dragons it is rude not to be first if you've done the inviting. The Dzur remain seated when greeting new arrivals to their tables at public or private houses; the Lyorn invariably rise. Except that the Dzur meeting the Lyorn might rise, knowing the Lyorn custom, whereas the Lyorn . . . well, you get the idea.

It is all very confusing.

As an Easterner, and, in several different ways, an outcast, I have had the opportunity to observe many of these customs and considerations of proper behavior, and so, on the assumption that you might one day have the chance to visit some of these fascinating and delightful people (okay, then, these irritating and obnoxious jerks), I herewith submit a small treatise on manners in the Dragaeran Empire. I hope you find it useful. But, in case I made an error somewhere, and you inadvertently commit a minor breach of etiquette, please, don't tell me about it; I have my own problems.

1

ADAPTING BEHAVIOR TO ENVIRONMENT

Just because they really are out to get you doesn't mean you aren't paranoid. If they've been after you long enough, paranoia can become a reflex.

Interesting things, reflexes: if you pay attention to them, you'll stand to learn some interesting things about yourself. This is one reason I avoid paying attention to my reflexes.

But sometimes I can't help it.

Let me pick an example at random:

I awoke almost instantly from a sound sleep to active stillness, and before reaching for a weapon, or dodging from a possible attack, or even opening my eyes, I reached out, mentally, psychically, for contact with my familiar. My mind to his, I said, *"What's going on, Loiosh?"* At that instant, all I knew was that something had happened to wake me up. I didn't even remember where I was, though one patch of ground in the wilderness is much like another, and that's where I'd been sleeping lately.

My first real clue that there might be a problem came when he didn't make any wisecracks. Instead there was a moment of mental silence, if you'll excuse the expression, and then Loiosh said, *"We may have been hunted down, Boss."*

"Well," I said. *"That wouldn't be good."*

Pretending to be calm to my familiar helps me to actually be calm. Loiosh accepts this as part of his job, and doesn't give me grief about it, much. In the meantime, without any conscious decision on my part, I was holding a neat, slim stiletto in my hand. Reflexes again.

I remained still, counting on Loiosh to tell me if and when I ought to move. While I waited, I contemplated my circumstances—in particular, the sharp, nasty stone that had insinuated itself onto the ground between my shoulder blades. I had a thick layer of darr skin between me and the ground, and a thin layer of chreotha fur between me and the sky.

"*Brigands, do you think, Loiosh?*"

"*Brigands come in bands, Boss. Whoever this is, there's only one of him.*"

"*So the Jhereg is more likely.*"

"*Or something else entirely.*"

I heard Rocza shift, caught the faint psychic whispers of Loiosh telling her to stay still. Just to fill you in on the basics, in case we haven't met before, Rocza is Loiosh's mate, which I'm sure must answer every question you have.

"*Coming closer, Boss.*"

"*Do I have a target, yet?*"

"*No.*"

"*Do you have any suggestions?*"

"*No. But I'm not worried, Boss. I'm sure you'll come up with a plan.*"

Reptiles are cold-blooded; a reptilian sense of humor will naturally display the same characteristics. This, in spite of being hunted and hounded by a massive and murderous criminal society that wants nothing less than the destruction of my soul, is probably the greatest burden I carry.

"*All right,*" I said, ignoring his remark. "*Fly as silently as you can away from whoever it is, and circle around. As soon as you see—*"

I was interrupted by the ostentatious clearing of a throat, followed by someone saying, "I beg your pardon for disturbing you at such an hour, Lord Taltos, but I'm certain you must be awake by now, and I'm afraid if I come any closer you might do something I'd regret."

I sat up, the knife poised for throwing. "You can't be who you sound like," I said.

"I am, though."

"It's not polite to lie."

She laughed. "Nor to accuse a friend of lying."

"You can't be—"

"It is, Boss."

"Well," I said after a long moment. "I'll be skinned for a norska."

"Probably," said Loiosh. *"But not by her."*

I heard her come a little closer; Loiosh could now see her, but I can't see as well at night as he can.

"Don't feel bad, Boss. We can't all have adequate vision."

"At least both of my eyes face forward, scavenger."

"Mind if I make a light?" I said.

"Please do."

I stood up slowly, put my knife away, and found my firekit close at hand. I lit a candle and held it up and away so we would both be illuminated. There was, fortunately, little wind. I saw her standing before me, looking very beautiful and incredibly out of place. She gave me a courtesy, and I bowed in response.

"Lord Taltos," she said.

"Lady Teldra," I replied. "Welcome to the wilderness."

She looked around. "Yes. Well, shall I start, or should it wait until morning?"

"If it is urgent enough to track me down in the middle of nowhere in the middle of the night, can it wait until morning?"

"It can, Lord Taltos. My urgency was to find you before you moved on, thus making the search more difficult. Again, I apologize for disturbing you."

"Not to worry. Did you bring any blankets?"

"I . . ."

"I know how difficult this must be for you, Lady Teldra, and I can't wait to hear about what brought it all about, but, believe me, we'll both be better off if you let me handle things for tonight. I'd prefer it that way. Please."

"Very well."

"Did you bring any blankets?"

"No."

"Is anyone following you?"

"No."

"Are you—forgive me—are you certain?"

"Yes."

I studied her face. Lady Teldra was worried about something. She was worried enough about something that she had allowed it to appear on her features, and something was wrong enough for her to have deliberately woken me up. This was almost more startling than her sudden appearance in the forest between Appertown and Ridge.

Startling. Yes.

When one knows an Issola, such as Lady Teldra, one gets so used to the grace, elegance, and manners of the House that one forgets its other side. The issola is a beautiful white bird. I'd seen several during my recent travels. One usually saw them standing, graceful and lovely in the early morning or late evening, in swamps or the shallow banks of rivers. They stand as if their only reason for being were to look lovely and graceful. And then the issola would be holding a fish in its beak, and you'd never see it strike. And then the fish would be gone in a single swallow, and the issola would be standing on one leg, looking lovely and graceful.

Lady Teldra looked lovely and graceful. I felt plain and clumsy. On the other hand, now that the adrenaline was no longer coursing through my system I realized that I was still pretty tired.

"Let's sleep," I said. "You can share my furs, as long as you don't get forward with me."

"My lord—"

"I'm kidding. Climb in."

I blew out the candle. It had been a long time since I'd slept curled up with a warm body—it brought back memories that I'd been trying to suppress, and the fact that she wasn't human did little to help me forget. There had been a time when, every night, I had gone to sleep next to a woman I loved, and, even better, woken up with her. Those days were over and beyond recall, and allowing myself to dwell on them could take from me the edge I needed to stay alert and alive.

It took a while, but eventually I fell asleep, and when I woke up it was dawn, and she had climbed out of the furs and had a fire going.

"Have you klava?" she said, when she saw I was awake.

"Not even coffee," I said. "But we're within a few miles of a town."

"Really? I'd have thought you'd stay at an inn, then."

"Loiosh works better out here, and these days I'm thinking more about survival than comfort."

"I'm sorry," she said, and seemed to mean it. But, of course, she was an Issola: she would always seem to mean it. In the light of dawn, I saw that she was dressed in white and green, in a gown suited less to the wilderness than to her duties at Castle Black, home of the Lord Morrolan, where she'd welcome you into his home, serve you wine, and convincingly seem delighted to see you. For almost the first time in the years that I'd known her, I wondered: Just exactly what *were* her duties for Morrolan?

She looked an inquiry at me, then held out her hand. I nodded and Loiosh flew over to her, landing delicately. Her hand was stiff and slightly tilted, her elbow sharply bent: she knew the technique, though as far as I knew she'd never held a jhereg before. This failed to startle me.

"A pleasure to see you," she told my familiar.

He gracefully lowered his head until it was below the level of her hand, then raised it again.

"I believe," said Lady Teldra in an amused tone, "that I am being mocked." I heard Loiosh giggle inside my head. He turned around on her hand, launched himself, and returned to my right shoulder. Rocza, by now on my left shoulder, shifted and wriggled, which she often did in the morning. It probably meant something. There are many interesting facets to the character of the wild jhereg—poisonous reptilian scavengers of the jungle—but for some reason I got stubborn and decided not to learn about them. I imagine Teldra knew a lot about the wild issola.

"I'll bet you know a lot about the wild issola," I said.

"I know a bit about them," she said. "But, your pardon Lord Taltos, I should imagine that isn't the question foremost on your mind."

"No, foremost on my mind is breakfast. There's bread, cheese, and the remains of a dried and salted wild boar in my pack, as well some dried gammon and jerky in my pouch. Help yourself while I vanish for a moment and get myself a little cleaned up. There's a stream about a hundred feet this way, just over that rise."

"Thank you, my lord. I found it earlier."

I went off and did what was necessary and filled my water flask. When I returned Teldra had broken off several chunks of bread and, while they toasted on the rocks next to the fire, she was cutting up strips of cheese to lay across them.

"No questions before you eat?" she said.

"Exactly."

"I can respect that."

The bread started smelling good. When she put the cheese over it, and the boar, my mouth started watering. The cheese was a smokey honin; I usually prefer something sharper, but it went well with boar. We ate, and I passed the water flask over. I almost apologized for the lack of wine, but Teldra would have been mortified to hear me apologize, so I didn't. The food was good. As I ate, I fed bits to Loiosh, some of which he passed on to Rocza.

When I was done eating, I wrapped my furs and few possessions in their leather cords so I could leave in a hurry if I had to. As I did so, I said, "Let's have it, then."

"Where should I start, Lord Ta—"

"Vlad," I said. "I'm sorry, Teldra, but titles just don't work with the surroundings."

"Very well, Vlad. What would you like to know first? How I found you, or why I wanted to?"

"Start with how you found me; it might be more urgent. If

you can find me, perhaps the Jhereg can find me."

"Not the way I did."

"Oh?"

She said, "Do you remember Morrolan's private tower, and the windows in it?"

I stared at her for some few moments, then said, "Oh. No, I don't suppose the Jhereg is very likely to find me that way. I don't think. Although the Left Hand—"

"Oh, that isn't the whole of it. By themselves, the windows could bring me here, but couldn't find you. I—"

"That's a relief."

"—had help."

"Of?"

"Well, Kiera the Thief, for one."

"Kiera. Yes." I did not believe Kiera would betray me, or do anything she knew would put me in danger without a very good reason.

"She knew more or less where you'd be—what part of the Empire, that is. She said you'd been nursing a sick boy back to health, and that he lived in this district, and that she expected you to be escorting him to his home by now."

"True enough."

"And then, once I knew the general area, I got more help. Sethra Lavode."

"Oh, her," I said. The most powerful sorceress and wizard in the world, yeah, well, I wasn't surprised she could find me. Especially because a year or so ago, when we had run into each other near Northport, she had said something about—"Loiosh?"

"Yes. She gave me a means of tracing him."

"Well, is my face red."

"Shut up."

"So," I said. "You had help from both Kiera and Sethra."

"Yes."

I watched her face, but if she knew anything, she betrayed nothing. Well, neither would I.

She said, "What happened to your hand?"

I looked at my maimed left hand, turned it over, and shrugged. "A sorcerer tried to eviscerate me from across a room, and either his aim was off, or I was too fast with Spellbreaker. Or not fast enough, depending on how you want to look at it."

"How did this come about, Vlad?"

I shook my head. "Later, Teldra. We're still hearing your story. For myself, I wouldn't care, but you know how curious Loiosh gets."

She flicked me her smile again; my familiar did not deign to make a rejoinder. Rocza, at that moment, flew off into the trees, probably thinking the breakfast scraps inadequate. Of the three of us, she seemed most happy to have spent the last few years away from cities.

"Shall I start now, or ought we to find Klava first?"

I'm not an Issola, but I can sometimes take a hint. "Sure," I said, standing up. "This way."

We hiked in silence at first; Teldra picking her way carefully, me just walking. I had, over the last few years, become something of a woodsman, albeit unwillingly. It seems that Teldra never had, and I allowed myself to enjoy a certain feeling of superiority.

"Kiera never explained what happened to the boy," said Teldra after a while.

"Not that much to tell," I said. "If I were just a bit more cynical, I'd say it was a debt of honor. He was hurt in my service, so I tried to help him."

"And you succeeded?"

"The Justicers are debating that one. I think so, at least in part."

"Where is he now?"

"Back with his family, not far from here." I recalled his family's reaction to his return, and then their reaction to me, and refrained from giving Teldra any additional information.

We reached Appertown, with its post office, dry goods store, and inn. The latter, which boasted a faded sign that had once been red and seemed to have a chicken's head painted on it, was almost deserted, but the three Teckla occupying a table in the back quickly looked away from Teldra while trying to glance at me covertly. If I had been wearing my Jhereg colors, instead of the nondescript leather I now affected, they wouldn't have dared to look at me, either.

The hostess, a Teckla who was too thin to give me much confidence in the food, seemed a bit wary as she asked what we wanted.

"Klava, if you have any," I said.

"Klava?" she repeated as if she'd never heard the word before.

"If not," said Teldra, "we should be glad of coffee."

"We have a klava press somewhere," she said. "But—"

"You must have eggshells," I said. "Have you any vanilla bean?"

"Oh, I'm certain we have that. But I don't know how to make the filter."

"I do," I said. "If you'll allow me into your kitchen—"

"Vlad," said Teldra softly. "I think coffee would do, wouldn't it? As long as there is honey and cream."

"Very well," I said. The hostess sent Teldra a look full of gratitude and scuttled off for coffee. She brought back two mugs, along with a pitcher of thick cream and a jar of honey. Teldra gave her a smile that our hostess probably valued more than the money we'd leave with her later. Along with the coffee, she brought us each a sample of the house bread—a small, round loaf with a hole in the middle, cut horizontally and lightly toasted. I tried it.

"Not bad," I said. "This would be good with smoked pinkfish and buttercheese."

"And a bit of onion," agreed Teldra.

As I mixed the proper proportions of my coffee, Teldra said, "How *do* you brew klava?"

"You don't know?"

She smiled. "I can serve it with the best, but I've never needed to learn how to brew it."

"You press coffee through a filter made of eggshells and wood chips with vanilla bean, then reheat it so it almost boils, then you pass it through a cloth to remove any oils brought out by the reheating."

"Wood chips?"

"Hickory works well, also fegra, cherrywood, and crocra. It's the wood, or combination of woods, that makes each version unique. Well, and how much vanilla you use. Also, some people add cinnamon, but I don't; cinnamon is just as good if you add it later. Everyone has his own recipe. Valabar's does it best, but they do everything best. I miss Valabar's."

"Is that all you miss, Lord Taltos?"

The expression on her face made it seem like light banter rather than an intrusive question, so I said, "Maybe one or two other things. And, even though we are enclosed by four walls, I still consider this the wilderness."

She smiled. "Very well, Vlad."

I took another sip of coffee and missed Valabar's. This inn was a single-story building, stretching back quite a ways from the road, and built of molded brick with what had once been very nice woodwork around the windows; but now the wood was old, scratched up, and showing signs of dry rot. There was no actual bar, such as Adrilankha's inns always had, but just various tables with glasses and bottles sitting on them. We sat near the front door; two doors led back, no doubt to various sleeping rooms, and another went back to the kitchen. I always notice the entrances and exits when I'm in a new place, although there haven't been many times in my life when noticing actually did me any good. It's just one of those things you do, like warming up your muscles before and after fencing practice. I once asked my grandfather, who taught me fencing, how, were I ever jumped by brigands, I could convince them to wait while I warmed up. He just rolled his eyes and gave me a flank strike, which I parried, causing the tip of his weapon to whip past my guard and leave a nasty welt on my forearm. After that I made my questions more serious.

"Would you like to share your thoughts, Vlad?"

"Have you ever had a practice saber whip around the bell of your weapon and leave a welt on your arm?"

"Why, no, I can't say I have."

"Then you wouldn't understand."

She laughed. You never know if an Issola is laughing to be polite. I resolved not to try to be funny around her.

"How long do you think that will last, Boss?"

We finished our coffee at about the same time and called for more, which was brought with a cheer and alacrity that showed the hostess had fallen under Teldra's spell. No surprise there.

I said, "So Kiera told you how to find me, Sethra did the locating, and Morrolan let you go into his tower and use one of his Magical Mystical Powerful Transcendental Wizard Windows to get here. What I'd like to know—"

"Not exactly," said Teldra.

"Oh?"

"Morrolan didn't exactly let me use the window."

"Go on."

"Morrolan . . . that is, I didn't ask him."

"You didn't ask him."

"I couldn't. I didn't—that is, I don't know where he is."

"I see. I begin to see. I think I begin to see."

"Perhaps I should begin at the beginning."

"Arbitrary. But still, not a bad choice."

"Almost a minute, Boss. Good work."

"Shut up, Loiosh."

"Well, to begin with, then, the world was made when the gods created a ball of amorphia to hang—"

"Maybe we should let Loiosh make the jokes."

"But you're the only one who can hear him."

"Believe me, Teldra, that's a blessing for you."

She smiled. She had dimples. I tried to remember how many Dragaerans I'd met who had dimples. Plenty of humans did, but I didn't recall seeing many on Dragaerans.

"Early in the morning, four days ago," she said, "I received a message from Her Majesty, the Empress, asking Morrolan to extend his hospitality to a certain Lady Marquana, House of the Athyra, who would be in the area on Imperial business."

"What sort of Imperial business?"

"Does it matter?"

"Probably not, but asking questions makes me feel smarter."

She dimpled again. "In point of fact, Vlad, I don't know."

I shrugged. She continued, "I went to find Morrolan, and he wasn't in the library. I attempted psychic contact, and failed to reach him."

"Is that unusual?"

"Unprecedented."

"Really? He's never been busy?"

"If so, he has told me in advance. The only time I have been unable to reach him is when he has been, well, off the world."

"Off the world?"

She studied me. "You know something of those windows."

"Ah. Yes. And this didn't happen often?"

"Twice before, and both times he told me ahead of time he would be out of touch, and left instructions about what to do in case of trouble."

"What were those instructions, Teldra?"

"To reach Sethra Lavode."

"Not Aliera?"

"This was before Aliera had, uh, re-emerged. I agree that, now, Aliera would be the obvious person to speak with first."

"And so did you speak with Aliera?"

Teldra tilted her head and smiled suddenly. "Why do you remind me so much of an Imperial Inquisitor?"

"Damn," I said. "I was aiming for Third Floor Relic."

"Who?"

"Ah ha."

"Ah ha?"

"I've just proven that you're not Sethra Lavode. *Did* you speak with Aliera?"

"She's gone too," said Teldra.

"My goodness," I suggested. "Four days, you say?"

"Yes."

"No message, no word, no communication?"

"No message, no word, no communication."

"I see." I tried to wrap my head around the idea that something might have happened to Morrolan and Aliera. It was hard. They'd always struck me as, for all practical purposes, indestructible. But Teldra had sought me out in the wilderness, and that meant, however unimaginable it might be, something serious had happened.

I forced my mind back to business. "So when did you make contact with Sethra?"

"As best I remember, Your Equitableness, it was—"

" 'Your Equitableness'? Are the Justicers really addressed that way, Teldra?"

"I thought you'd know."

"I never had an advocate, so I've never heard the forms used."

"Oh. I believe that's the term."

"It sounds silly, doesn't it? Want more coffee?"

"Yes, please, Your Equitableness. If you don't mind my asking, why didn't you hire an advocate?"

"Having an advocate makes one look guilty."

"But the Orb—"

"The Orb is an awfully literal-minded thing, Teldra. They asked their questions, and I answered, and they looked at the Orb, and then they let me go. And, speaking of questions, I think I'd just asked one."

"Very well, Your Equitableness."

I sighed. "Okay, I get the point. I'll just let you tell it."

"After we get more coffee. If I were a Justicer, I'd require you to find a place that served klava."

I signaled the hostess for coffee, which was supplied with oppressive good cheer.

Presently, Teldra said, "Morrolan and Aliera were gone, and with no message. I tried for psychic contact with each of them, and failed. After a day, I spoke with various people in the Castle—Fentor, whom you know—"

"Yes."

"And Surill, whom I believe you have not met."

"Correct. Who is he?"

"She. She currently leads Morrolan's circle of witches." I had heard that Morrolan had such a circle, though he rarely spoke of them and I never asked. "They were unable to help, though Surill said she had tried to reach Morrolan through her own means as well. So I sent a messenger to Dzur Mountain, to Sethra Lavode."

"A messenger? Why?"

"To get her a message."

"But—"

"I don't know her well enough for direct contact, Vlad. Not everyone does, you know."

"Oh," I said, feeling sheepish.

"She sent a message back asking me to visit her at Dzur Mountain, so I did."

"Oh, yeah? How's the old place holding up?"

Teldra gave me a look. "We had a long talk. Sethra explained to me about Phoenix Stone, gold and black, and the blocking of psychic contact. She also, in my opinion, seemed worried."

"To paraphrase Seapur," I put in, "if Sethra's scared, then I'm scared."

"Yes," said Teldra. "Your name came up."

"How did that happen?"

"In connection with gold and black Phoenix Stone."

I fingered the cords I wore around my neck, which had a

sample of each. "Yes," I said. Then, "What if they're already dead?"

"They aren't."

"Who told you that?"

"The Necromancer."

"Ah. Yes. Well. She'd know, wouldn't she?"

"Sethra believes you can help find them."

"Did she say how?"

"Not exactly. She mentioned something about Aliera's Great Weapon, Pathfinder, and some sort of link between it and some artifact you carry."

"Spellbreaker," I said.

"She didn't give it a name."

"That's the name," I said. "What does she want me to do?"

"Return with me to Dzur Mountain."

I drank some coffee.

"Boss, it isn't the same as returning to Adrilankha."

"I know that, Loiosh."

"If you'll be safe anywhere —"

"I know, Loiosh."

"And if there's anyone you owe —"

"I know, Loiosh."

"Sethra thinks I can help?"

"She does."

"And she thinks Morrolan and Aliera might be in trouble?"

"She thinks it probable."

I considered a little longer. Teldra was courteously silent. Exactly why I had to consider, I don't know; certainly the idea of returning to any of my old haunts, when the Jhereg had a large price on my head, was scary; but there was never any doubt about how I would decide. I guess I just needed a few minutes to work it through my viscera.

I had just about decided when Teldra said, "Vlad, it would be wrong of me to put unfair pressure on you, but—"

"Oh, go ahead, Teldra. What is it?"

"Do you remember Sethra's servant?"

"Tukko. Yes."

"He knows how to brew klava."

"He does? Verra! What are we hanging around here for?"

"I'll pay the shot," she offered politely.

2

Being a Good Listener

This is, I suppose, as good a time as any to tell you a little bit about myself. I was born human in a world of Dragaerans, an outcast in their Empire, so I learned how to get paid for killing them. Small, weak, and short-lived by their standards, I learned how to seem larger, stronger, and to stay alive. I became a part of a vast criminal domain within the Empire; got married, had my marriage fall apart, and so angered the Organization that, as I said earlier, they were now avidly hunting for me.

That's enough for now; it's too depressing to dwell on. Besides, I didn't have much time to think about it, because soon we had walked beyond the edge of Appertown, and Teldra said, "If you would remove the Phoenix Stone, can you be teleported? That is, if it is still on your person?"

"Yes," I said. "I keep a small box with me that I can put them in. It's made of—never mind. As long as the stones are in the box, they have no effect."

"Then, if you please, do so."

I swallowed. I had no reason not to trust Teldra—I *did* trust Teldra. But it still wasn't easy to bring myself to remove the artifacts that had protected and hidden me for the last few years. While I was hesitating, she was standing, motionless, with the air of one who expected to be waiting for a long time and had no trouble doing so.

I removed the cord from around my neck and secreted it away. The instant I closed the box, I felt horribly vulnerable. The hairs stood up on the back of my neck, and I kept slipping into Loiosh's mind to see, through him, if I smelled anything suspicious in the area.

"*Relax, Boss. Even if they detect you instantly, they can't—*"

"*I know.*"

"I apologize," said Teldra, "for the discomfort of the teleport."

I didn't say anything. In fact, thanks to an amulet I had of my grandfather, there would be no discomfort; were I an Issola, I'd have told her. But then, were I an Issola, I wouldn't be in this situation.

Teldra closed her eyes. Her lips began to move soundlessly, which is something some people do when in psychic contact; presumably she was in touch with Sethra, but I couldn't ask without interrupting her, and that, of course, would be rude. Presently her eyes opened. She nodded to me, accompanying the nod with a gracious smile, and beckoned. I took a step closer to her; there was a moment of disorientation, and I stood in a place I had thought never to see again: the Grand Hall of Sethra's Keep high in Dzur Mountain.

I've heard it said, "By his home shall you know him," and we all know that we must pay attention to anyone who reverses the subject and the auxiliary verb in his sentence, so let me tell you a bit about the home of Sethra Lavode. A bit is all I can tell you, because I don't know Dzur Mountain all that well. For example, I can't tell you how far down into the mountain her dwelling extends. I've been told that the mountain is riddled with natural caves, caverns, and tunnels, and that some of these connect to the areas she has carved out for herself.

One of these was where I had first appeared, long ago, in the company of Morrolan. It had seemed then that I was deep in the heart of the mountain and had to climb a long stone stairway to its peak; I have since learned that I was close to the top, and that when I emerged in Sethra's living area we were hardly closer: Dzur Mountain is very, very big.

She had a library, but somehow I had never gotten around to inspecting it, so I can't tell you what she reads. On one side of the library are a few well if plainly furnished guest rooms, some of which I have used from time to time; on the other is a wide spiral stairway that leads up to the kitchen, or down to a hallway from which one can reach one of three dining rooms of various sizes, two of which I'd eaten in, and the third of which, the Grand Hall, I stood in now; a sitting room where I'd once insulted Sethra (an insult stopping just smoke's weight short of mortal); and two doors that go I know not where. At the end of the corridor is another spiral stairway: I don't know where this one leads to going down, or how it goes up, because it seems to me that it should lead directly up into the middle of the library, but there isn't a stairway there.

There is little decoration. It is as if, over the millennia, she had lost patience for anything that attempted to brighten what was naturally dark, ornament what was naturally plain, enliven what was naturally severe. There were no bright colors in Dzur Mountain, yet nothing was rough; rather everything was subdued but smooth, as if her home were a monument to the effects of time. Her furnishings were all simple and comfortable, with cushions on hard stone chairs and light provided mostly by simple oil lamps or candles. There was little to show her history; or, indeed, that she had a history—that is, her home was noticeably lacking in those oddities one picks up over the years as gifts from friends, or objects acquired from traveling, or trophies won from enemies. The one thing of that kind was in the library, where there was a device covered in glass, with spinning metal inside. I had asked her about it, but Sethra denied knowing what it actually was and refused to say how she had acquired it or why she valued it. Other than that, as I say, there was nothing to which one could point and say, "Sethra Lavode has this object because it means something to her."

I admit that I have, from time to time, speculated on why she had arranged her home like that, but I kept coming up against the same question: Were I somehow to achieve her age, how would I want to surround myself? And to this question I could not know the answer, which would always end the speculation, leaving me only observations.

And that about concludes what I know about the home of Sethra Lavode—not much, considering how often I've been there. I've heard a great deal more, of course, running from the probable to the preposterous: labyrinths deep within the mountain where she conducts monstrous experiments; high towers in the very peak where she communes with the dead; hidden passageways to the Halls of Judgment; concealed rooms full of treasure; and so on. But I don't know anything about these (except I can pretty well deny the passageway to the Halls of Judgment: if that really exists, she owes me an apology for sending me the hard way). Little is known, more is suspected, and much is guessed at.

And there you have Sethra Lavode as well, which ought to prove the point about reversing the subject and the auxiliary verb.

I didn't see Sethra at once, so I turned around, and there she was: tall, pale, undead; she had forgotten more of sorcery, even the forbidden sorcery of the ancient world, than anyone else would ever learn. She was a vampire, but it didn't seem to bother her much; and to those who told stories of her it was almost superfluous, like hearing that the guy who is going to cut your heart out plans to kick you in the shin when he's done. Her origin was in prehistory, and some had come to believe that she was the living personification of the world itself, that it would end when she ended. I doubted this myself: I mislike the idea of a living personification being undead.

Her features were those of a Dragonlord, except that, if one looked for it (as I did), one could see hints of the Dzurlord in the shape of her ears and her eyes. She dressed in black, black, black—the only hints of color upon her today were a red stone about her neck, a yellow stone on a ring on her right hand, and the blue hilt of Iceflame at her hip. She wore enigma as if it had been created for her alone.

Teldra bowed to her very deeply—more deeply than I had ever seen her bow before. Sethra acknowledged it as if it were her due. I nodded, Sethra nodded back.

"Sethra Lavode," I said. "It has been some time." Now, there was an ambiguous remark for her to play with if she cared to.

She didn't. She held out her arm, and Loiosh flew to her, allowed his chin to be scratched, and then, just to show his high regard for her, he bent his head to allow her to scratch the scales that concealed his ears: a special mark of honor, because jhereg are very protective of their ears. I don't know if Sethra appreciated the honor. While she paid attention to Loiosh, I pulled the box from my pouch, opened it, and put the cord back around my neck. I felt better right away.

"Welcome to my home," said the Dark Lady of Dzur Mountain. "Please come with me."

"Always a pleasure," I said, and we followed her up to the sitting room, where she asked if we cared for wine.

"Klava," I said. "I was promised klava."

Sethra smiled. "And you?" she asked Teldra. "The same?"

"If you please."

Tukko emerged, shuffling, blinking, and twitching. "Klava," said Sethra Lavode.

Tukko did an imitation of a snake testing the air, gave a twitch that might have been a nod, and shuffled out again.

I watched him leave by a far door. "Just how old is he?" I asked.

"Younger than I am," said Sethra.

I nodded. "I just asked to give you another chance to be enigmatic."

"I know." She studied me. "You are looking well, Vlad."

"The outdoor life agrees with me," I said.

She went through the motions of smiling, and said, "And you, Lady Teldra. It is good of you to come, and I thank you for bringing our wandering Easterner with you."

"It was only my duty, Lady," said Teldra. "I must, in turn, thank you for your help, and your hospitality."

The mention of hospitality was Tukko's cue to emerge with a tray bearing two mugs of klava, a jar of honey, and a pot of thick cream. Teldra received hers with a smile of thanks; she took her klava as it came. I fiddled with mine until it looked right. It tasted right, too. I had missed it even more than I thought I had.

"The simple pleasures of civilization," I said. "I haven't tasted klava since Northport."

Sethra didn't bat an eye at the mention of Northport, even though—never mind. She said, "Perhaps we should turn our attention to business. Or would you rather wait until you've finished your drinks?"

"No, no," I said. "Drinking klava while talking business brings back all sorts of pleasant memories of happier days when I could sit around with like-minded fellows, contemplate my various affairs, and decide whose leg should be broken that morning."

Neither of them gave me the satisfaction of reacting, but Loiosh said, *"You're so sentimental, Boss, that I almost can't stand it,"* and flew back to my shoulder, evening up the weight. Rocza, by the way, had not moved the entire time. Presently, Tukko returned, this time with a tray full of some kind of raw dead thing, and set it down on the stone table in front of me. Loiosh and Rocza flew down and began nibbling. Neither Sethra nor Teldra jumped when they flew down. This is significant because pretty much anyone will be startled by a winged thing suddenly flying right in front of him.

I noticed for the first time that Tukko's hands always seemed to shake, but when he was carrying a tray, the tray never shook. I wondered if his various ills were an act, and, if so, why?

"I thank you on behalf of my familiar," I said.

"You and they are most welcome," said Sethra.

I sipped more klava. Damn, but I had missed that stuff.

"Morrolan and Aliera are both alive," said Sethra abruptly. "Or, at least, they were alive yesterday. They have, therefore, achieved a state where we cannot communicate with them. That means they are either surrounded by gold Phoenix Stone, or they have left the confines of our world. And, until we know otherwise, we must assume they are being held against their will, and that must involve someone with a great deal of power— perhaps even a god, though I consider that unlikely. No, I fear what we are facing is rather more powerful than a god."

"Good," I said. "I wouldn't want it to be too easy."

"No, Vlad. Wrong response. You should say, 'How can I help?' "

I snorted. "If I say that, you're liable to tell me."

"There's that danger," she admitted.

"What do you think happened?"

"I have no idea."

"Don't lie to me, Sethra."

"Vlad!" said Sethra and Teldra together, in entirely different tones.

"Oh, stop it. Sethra, my whole lifetime has been less than the flap of a wing to you, but to me, I've known you for a long time. You wouldn't have sent for me without knowing something, or at least having a strong suspicion."

"Vlad—"

"No, Sethra. Don't even. Morrolan used to pull that stuff on me. Go, do this, but I'm not going to tell you any of the reasons behind it. My bosses in the Jhereg were experts at it: Kill this guy, you don't need to know what he did. I'm done with that sort of rubbish. Where are Morrolan and Aliera, why are they missing, and what is all the other stuff you aren't telling me?"

Lady Teldra opened her mouth, but I cut her off. "No," I said. "I won't go into it like this. I want to know."

"Do you, then?" said Sethra, almost whispering. There was something in her voice I had never heard before: something chilling, and powerful, and very dark. I was in the presence of the Enchantress of Dzur Mountain, and I was daring to question her. For one of the few times since I'd known her, I felt the power of legend bearing down on me; I sat there, silent, and took it; I could say nothing, but I didn't crumble, either. She said, "Do you really want to know, Vladimir Taltos, Easterner, Jhereg, and renegade?"

"Yes," I said, though it took considerable effort; and even more effort to keep my voice level.

"And if I don't tell you, what then? You'll leave Morrolan e'Drien and Aliera e'Kieron to their fate? Is that what you're telling me?"

I looked into her eyes, which I discovered I had been avoiding. They were black and went on far past forever; the focus on me was terrible. I controlled my breathing as if I were fencing, or reaching the climax of a spell. "Are you going to make this a test of wills, Sethra? Is that it? You will threaten to leave them to their fate if I won't help, or I must threaten if you won't answer my questions? Is that how you want to play this game?"

"I don't want to make it a game, Vladimir Taltos."

Looking into her eyes, I saw again Aliera's face as I returned to life after the Sword and the Dagger of the Jhereg had taken me down; and I saw Morrolan in his Great Hall defending me from the Sorceress in Green, and, I recalled faces, incidents, and conversations that I didn't want to remember. Then I cursed. "All right," I said. "If you push it, you'll win. You're right. I owe them both too much. If one of us needs to back down, I will—I'll go run your Verra-be-damned errand for you, like a two-orb street Orca hired to bust heads. But—"

"Then I'll answer your questions," said Sethra, and I shut my mouth before I made things worse. "I'll answer you," said Sethra, "because you're right, you deserve to know. But I will speak of matters I have no wish to reveal so, damn you, be grateful."

"I'll be grateful," I said.

Teldra stood abruptly. "I shall be in the library," she said, "in case you—"

"Please," said Sethra. "I wish you to stay."

"I . . . very well," said Lady Teldra, and sat down again.

Tukko emerged, and I realized that my klava had gotten cold. He replaced it, freshened Teldra's, and left.

"Where should I begin?" she mused. I held my tongue in check and waited.

"Perhaps," she said, "I should ask: Who are the gods? No, I've already taken a false step. That is not the question: Ask, rather, *What* are the gods? What freaks of chance, what hidden talents, what cataclysmic events combined to produce those whom your people worship, and mine strive to emulate? What are they, why are they, what do they do? Is their power acquired only because there are those who worship them? Is their power, in fact, imaginary? There are no simple answers to the question you have asked, because everything is tied to everything else."

I drank klava, and listened.

"Part of the answer to the question I have posed is this: The gods are beings who are able to manifest in at least two places at once, and yet who are not subject to the forcible control of any other being; this latter marking the difference between a god and a demon." That much, actually, I knew already, but I let her continue. "An interesting ability, and one that implies many others. The Jenoine, for all their talents and skills, cannot be in two places at once. Many of the gods, of course, can be in many, many places at once. I don't understand entirely how it works; I am neither god nor demon."

"I don't think I've ever met a demon," I said. "Unless a certain Jhereg who goes by that name means it more literally than I think he does."

"You have," said Sethra. "The Necromancer."

I stared. "She's a demon?"

"Yes. But I suggest you don't try to control her; she is liable to take it wrong."

"I'll take that advice to heart."

She nodded and continued. "As I say, this one skill implies many others. How did they acquire this skill? Some of the younger ones have been taught by some of the older ones; I was once offered godhood. But this still begs the question: Whence came the oldest of the gods, and how did they acquire their abilities?

"We must go back a long way, Vlad. A long way even to me. Before the Empire, and even before the thirty-one tribes that became the Empire."

"Wait. Thirty-one?"

"Yes."

"Uh . . . why thirty-one? I mean, is the number significant of anything?"

"Not as far as I know. It's just the number of tribes there happened to be then. And please don't interrupt; this is difficult enough."

"I'll try."

She nodded. "Your people came first, my good Easterner. I imagine that doesn't startle you, perhaps you guessed it, or were told something of the kind by Aliera, who indulges in much enlightened speculation. Well, I tell you now what is no guess: Your people predate mine. How they came here, I do not know, but I know they arrived, they were not produced by Nature, as were the dragon, the dzur, the jhereg, and the Serioli. Yet even these were changed by—but no, all things in their proper time.

"Your people were here, though in what state I cannot say, and the animals, and were found here by others, by those we call the Jenoine. I don't know what they call themselves, and I don't know where they're from, except that it isn't here. They came here, as your people came here, only later."

Yes, I had known some of this before, too.

"There is so much we don't know, Vlad; that we can't know. I have said nothing of what I saw, what I later learned, what I have since deduced, because of all that I don't know. Were those who came here representative of all Jenoine? Were their actions typical? What were their motives when they arrived, and how did these motives change? Is the word 'motive,' as we understand it, even meaningful when discussing them?"

That was a rhetorical question if I'd ever heard one, so I didn't answer it.

"You have met Verra, her you call the Demon Goddess. That name—but never mind that now. She is of yet another species, and was brought to this world as a servant of the Jenoine. She was there when they began their experiments with the plants and the trees, and then with the animals, and then with the people who came to be called Easterners: changing some of them a little, some of them a great deal, some of them not at all. Improving, in certain cases, upon them: extending their lifespans and the abilities of their minds, and making into them the people who came to be called Human. Yes, Vlad, our beings and even our languages come from your people, and you can take whatever pride in that you care to. Aliera, of course, refuses to believe it, but it is true."

I had a pleasant moment imagining taunting Aliera about that, but Sethra was still speaking.

"From what Verra has said, I would guess that they were, in their own minds, benevolent; but one must sift her words to discover this, for she hates them. She was their servant, and they were not kind to her. For that matter, she was not kind to them, either. Of this, I know only what hints she has dropped, and a few words from Barlen, her consort, but it is clear that it was Verra, and a few others, who sabotaged their work, who created the Great Sea of Amorphia, who unleashed upon the world that which we call sorcery, who themselves became the first of those we know as gods, and who destroyed all of the Jenoine who then lived on this world.

"I have lived through Adron's Disaster, in which those same powers were unleashed a second time upon the world, and the Lesser Sea was created. The Great Sea, in area, is seven times that of the Lesser Sea; I cannot, in my own mind, imagine the cataclysm of the moment when it came into being, that instant when for the first time the Unknowable took form."

This was something I didn't care to imagine.

"But," continued Sethra before I had to mentally go there, "the Unknowable is, by definition, formlessness: the totality of content, with nonexistence of form. What happens when the Unknowable takes form? One answer is, it ceases to be unknowable. As soon as there was a Sea of Amorphia, there had, sooner or later, to be a Goddess named Verra to codify and define the Elder Sorcery that could manipulate it; and a Serioli named Cly!ng Fr'ngtha that made the Elder Sorcery tangible by embodying it in objects blurring the distinction between animate and inanimate; and a Human"—she meant a Dragaeran—"named Zerika to craft an Orb that would make this power subject to any mind that could discipline itself to learn the patterns and codes by which the Orb translated the raw power of amorphia into the fingers that shape reality. Now the Unknowable is knowable again, and it is a power such as exists, so far as I know and so far as the Necromancer has been able to discover, nowhere else in the universe—in any universe, for there is more than one, as the Necromancer has demonstrated."

I had some trouble with this, but just sort of mentally stored it away for future consideration, and kept listening.

"So in our world, thanks to the gods, there exists this power, and, somewhere, are the Jenoine, filled with lust for the power, and hatred for those who destroyed their brethren—or so I believe we might think of their feelings and not be too far from the truth.

"Who is it, Vlad, who might protect us from this jealous and angry species, who see us all as the rebellious objects of science—as test subjects placed in a maze who not only escaped it, but killed the observers and now in their arrogance operate the maze as they please and will not let those who built it so much as observe? Who might protect us from the Jenoine?"

I guessed what the answer was going to be, and I was right, but I didn't interrupt.

"The gods," said Sethra. "Above all else, that is their task.

"The place we call the Paths of the Dead sits, as I think you know better than most, both in and out of our world, and at its heart is the place we call the Halls of Judgment, because our legends tell us that this is where we go upon death to have our lives judged. And, as far as it goes, this is the truth. I know how your mind works by now, Vlad, and I see the glimmer of understanding in your eyes; I suspect that you begin to glimpse the true purpose of the Halls of Judgment."

I swallowed. She was right, I was getting a glimmering.

"Yes," she said. "It is there that the gods sift souls as a Serioli sifts for gold in a mountain stream. The gods search for those who can be useful to them in their long war. It is in the Halls of Judgment that they sometimes glimpse pieces of what to us is the future, and try to interpret these glimpses, and prepare to meet each threat as it develops. And as they sit those who are considered worthy are brought to them, upon death, for this reason. It is a way of building the forces to protect their world."

"Their world?" I said, catching significance in that.

She nodded. "Yes. Their world, not ours."

"I see."

"Yes. As they review the dead, some they have no use for; these are allowed to reincarnate, or are taken to be servants in the Paths of the Dead—those who wear the Purple Robes. Others have skills that might someday be useful, and those are held in the Paths of the Dead against that use, or reincarnated into circumstances where their skills can develop. A few study for the Godhood themselves, and a tiny number are sent out once more, as Undead, because their usefulness in the world has not expired with their lives. I became one of these latter some years ago."

I nodded. "Okay, I think I'm starting to get it."

"Yes? But here is where it starts becoming complicated."

I rolled my eyes.

"Stop it," she said. "That expression is not your most endearing. Listen and try to understand."

I sighed. "All right."

She nodded. "I have told you about the gods and the Jenoine, but there are other factors, and chief of these are the Serioli. You have never met one, but—You have? I didn't know or have forgotten. But I am sure you know little about them. I know little about them, though I have had more to do with them than any other human being in the world.

"The Serioli are native to the world, which neither your people nor mine are. In some measure, perhaps they resent us both, though most of them recognize that we are not responsible for what has been done to us. But above all, they resent the gods, because the gods, in a very real way, rule the world. The Serioli did not evolve as a people to be ruled—who would so evolve?

"It was the gods who sent the dreams that inspired Kieron the Conqueror to gather the tribes and move east, and the visions that led Zerika to create the Orb; thus it was the gods who created the Empire that drove the Serioli from their homes, that destroyed much of their culture, killed many of them in battles.

They—and while it is hard to speak of a whole people as if they had a single voice, here I think I am not too wrong—they hate the gods. This does not always make them friends of the Jenoine, but it does make them the enemies of the gods. Do you see?"

"I think so," I said slowly.

"And some of the Serioli believe that an enemy of their enemy must be their friend."

I nodded.

"The gods," she continued, "are forever seeking ways to seal our world, so the Jenoine cannot reach us. And factions among the Serioli keep searching for ways to allow the Jenoine access. And into this conflict come those Serioli who, years ago, crafted those half-living, half-inanimate artifacts called the Great Weapons, each of which is, in one way or another, obviously or not, directed against the gods."

I blinked. "The Great Weapons are—but that doesn't make any sense. Why—? Okay, never mind. Keep going."

"I never said it would be simple."

"Yeah."

"Where was I? Ah, yes: the Great Weapons. Jenoine are very hard to kill, Vlad. We know of no poison that works on them, their internal organs are duplicated; they have no spine to sever, and they have an almost perfect natural immunity to the disruptive effects of amorphia. They regenerate when injured, and I have seen them, on more than one occasion, resist even powerful Morganti weapons, as if their very souls are hidden away from their bodies. But this cannot be, because the Great Weapons can kill Jenoine. The Great Weapons are the only reliable way to kill Jenoine—if you can survive long enough to find a way to strike, and if you don't miss and if they fail to defend against it.

"Do you see the contradiction, Vlad? Do you see the irony?"

"Yeah, I'm always good with irony."

"I know. You always have been, even in the days before the Empire I remember that about you."

"I . . . okay."

"Do you see it?"

I nodded. "The Great Weapons were created to destroy the gods, but now they're being used to defend the gods. Cute."

"Yes. We who carry the Great Weapons are the appointed of the gods—even those of us who, like Zungaron—"

"Who?"

"Never mind. Even those of us who have one only by accident and have not the least clue what it is for, or what to do with it. If we defy the gods, by intention or accident, we are likely to find life difficult. And yet, we are the only humans whom the gods have reason to fear, and to hate."

I blinked. "I've never envied you, Sethra. Now I envy you even less."

She smiled. "The result," she said, "is that we must look out for each other—the reasons for that should be obvious."

I nodded.

"The gods hate our weapons and need us who wield them; the Jenoine fear our weapons and hate the gods. Do you understand?"

I nodded again.

"Think back to your own past, Vlad: I know what Aliera told you about your past lives, so consider her words now. Millennia ago, back in the days when we were creating an Empire, though only Zerika knew that we were doing so, the seeds of all of this were planted. Consider those you know of who were once your family, and those who mattered to you in a time too faded in the mist for you to imagine, much less remember. Kieron is gone now, and remains in the Paths of the Dead awaiting his moment. I, who had some importance in the tribe, am here, watching the Great Weapons, observing the Jenoine, listening to the gods, and trying to see that nothing upsets the balance.

"I think we were all, even then, marked out by the gods. I can't say I like it much, or that you should, but there it is. Now Aliera has been taken, and Morrolan as well. Who could and would take them both?

"A human agency? I wonder if there is anyone who could take two such as Aliera and Morrolan, and hide them from me.

But, even if such a person exists, he could not hide them from the Necromancer. If there was a human involvement, then, it was in the service of someone more powerful.

"The gods? An unlikely possibility, but one that cannot be overlooked. I did not overlook it; I have ways of finding out such things, I used them, and I believe the gods have nothing to do with this; indeed, some of them are rather concerned by it. Perhaps a rogue god, and this could still be true, but such a one would have trouble hiding from Trout, who knows the motives of the gods. No, I do not believe it was any of the gods.

"A demon? No, the demons have their own lives, and no concern for our world, except when they are summoned; and that only begs the question of who did the summoning and why?

"The Serioli? I doubt it, because I have never heard of their doing anything of the kind, but I hope it is the Serioli, because if it is not them, then it is the Jenoine. The Jenoine, who wish the weapons to be used against the gods—which, after all, is what they were designed for.

"I know you, Vlad: you are uncomfortable with things like causes and reasons, however much you ask for them. And however much you protest, you are and always have been happiest when you had a single task you could accomplish, without worrying about the whys and the consequences. Well, but you asked, and so I answer. Our friends are in danger. And it may be that much else is in danger as well; until we know more, it is impossible to say for certain if this is part of a move against the Empire, but we certainly must be aware of the possibility. You may be able to help ward off a threat to the Empire, you may have the means of helping those who are your friends and mine; it seems to me that you certainly have a duty to try, and I would have told you nothing except that, but you wanted the whole story. The whole story would have taken longer to tell than you expect to live, Easterner, but at least I gave you a piece of it. I hope you're happy."

3

DROPPING IN UNEXPECTEDLY

Once again I had allowed my klava to get cold; once again Tukko appeared and brought me more.

All right, so the Jenoine had taken short, cocky Aliera, and tall, arrogant Morrolan, her cousin. I confess that a little part of me was pleased that someone had shown them they weren't as ultimately tough as they acted. But other parts of me couldn't forget that, well, that we'd all saved each other's lives more than once, and that they had both been kind to me when they had no good reason to, and that, however irritating I might find them, we had a lot of history among the three of us, and, though it hurt to admit it, even some affection.

I spent a moment reliving memories that I won't share with you. Preparing and drinking the klava brought me back, at least to the point where I was able to speak. "Of course I'll do what I can, but saving the world just isn't my style, Sethra. I specialize in smaller things: breaking legs, collecting debts, knocking off the occasional squealer. You know, small stuff."

Neither she nor Teldra replied. At length I said, "Okay. What do you need me to do?"

"There is a procedure," she said, "that I believe might work. You must be the one to do it, however."

"Uh . . . if I ask why me, will I get an answer lasting less than an hour?"

"Because you have the chain you call Spellbreaker."

"I see. Well, actually, I don't."

"Use Spellbreaker to make contact with Blackwand, then

follow the link through one of Morrolan's windows."

"That's it?" I said.

"That's it. Your artifact should be able to connect to the Great Weapon, even across necromantic boundaries, because Blackwand should always be able to sense, at some level, what is happening in those windows. Or so I think. It will either work, or it won't."

"Yeah, I imagine those are the options. The question is, what then? I mean, if it works, what do I do?"

"Improvise."

"Improvise?"

"How can I say what to do, when I don't know where you are going, or what you will find there?"

"You know I don't care much for improvising."

"I know. But you are good at it."

"Thank you so much."

"And you don't rely on sorcery; you have other abilities."

"Great. Once I open up the way, if it works, and I get there, if I do, will I have any help?"

"What about me, Boss?"

"Shut up, Loiosh."

"No," said Sethra. "There will be none to give you."

"I see. I just go in, and improvise. While I'm improvising, what will you be doing?"

"Waiting."

"Can you, I don't know, keep an eye on me? Maybe yank me back if I get in over my head?"

"I don't know how. If I can't reach them where they are, I don't know how I'd be able to watch you there."

"Uh . . . magic?"

"If sorcery worked there, I don't think we'd be having this problem, and I can't think what other magic we might use. Un-like you, I'm not a witch."

"If you'd asked, I could have taught you. But you're saying that witchcraft will still function?"

"It should; that's one reason I wanted you for this."

"Witchcraft is not usually useful—"

"Have you forgotten the Paths of the Dead, Vlad?"

"I've tried to." I had visited the place where the dead hang around like old Dragonlords with no battles to fight except the ones they've already lost, and, even though I was living at the time, I just didn't enjoy the experience enough to dwell on the memory.

She didn't answer. I said, "How about the Necromancer?"

She cocked her head to the side. "That *is* a thought, Vlad. And not a bad one at that."

"See what a good vacation will do for the creative powers?"

"I'll speak to her."

I ran it through my mind. "Sethra, do you understand what you're asking me to do?"

"Yes."

Yes, of course she did. She was, to begin with, a Dragon; moreover she had led armies. She had no problem ordering people off to get killed—it was a way of life for her.

"Before I go jumping into this, tell me one thing: Do you have any reason to believe I might get out of this alive?"

"Oh, yes, certainly," she said. "I have a high regard for your skills."

"Ah. My skills. Well, that's reassuring."

"Don't underestimate yourself, Vlad."

Anything else I said would sound self-pitying, so I shut up; but Teldra said, "I will go along."

Sethra and I looked at her. She had said it as if she were announcing the wine she intended to serve with dinner.

"Teldra," said Sethra at last. "I am not certain you are qualified for this mission."

"Perhaps I am not," she said. "But I am not quite as helpless as you, perhaps, believe I am."

"Nevertheless," said Sethra. "This is the kind of activity that Vlad is trained for"—this, by the way, was news to me—"and you are not."

"Are you certain of that, Lady?" said Teldra. "I speak not of

Vlad's training, but perhaps with what lies before us, my talents would not be useless."

"I see," said Sethra slowly, considering her words. Sethra had obviously picked up some meaning that had escaped me entirely. "Yes, you may be right after all."

I said, "Sethra, would you mind explaining this to me? I think I'm missing something."

"Yes, I believe you are," said Sethra.

"It is difficult to explain," said Teldra. "But, if you wish—"

"I'm changing my mind about explanations," I said. "Just tell me if I need to know."

"You don't need to know," said Sethra.

Teldra said, "And then?"

"Yes, you ought to go along."

"Then let us begin at once," she said.

"No," I said.

"Is there a reason to wait, Vlad, or is it that you need time to gather your nerve."

"No, my nerve is far too scattered for mere time to gather it. But if I'm going to go off and get killed I'm going to finish my Verra-be-damned klava first. Now please give me some peace to enjoy it."

Sethra smiled. "Do you know, Vlad, whatever happens to you, you do certainly remain yourself."

"That's good. I haven't had as much practice being me as you have being you. But does that mean I get to finish my klava?"

"By all means," said Sethra. "While you do so, I'll attempt to reach the Necromancer."

Sethra's face went blank and I stopped watching her, because it is rude to watch the face of someone having a psychic conversation with another, and it was hard for me to be rude while Lady Teldra was sitting there. I drank klava. It really was very good.

"The Necromancer," said Sethra presently, "will be there,

and will attempt to monitor the proceedings, but she cannot guarantee her success."

I grunted and drank the rest of my klava. I enjoyed it. I remain grateful that they permitted it. Sethra still seemed to be amused. I could not, of course, guess what Teldra was thinking.

"Okay," I said at last. "I'm done. Let's go get killed. Is everybody ready?"

Sethra shrugged. "For now, I have nothing to do."

"The teleport," I said. "I'm a little out of practice."

"Very well, I think I can manage that."

I hid the two specimens of Phoenix Stone, one gold and one black, in their box, and once more I felt naked, but I was too frightened by the idea of the Jenoine to let a little thing like the Jhereg worry me unduly. Isn't it funny how the tiniest change in circumstances can alter all of your priorities?

"Ready, Loiosh?"

"Oh, sure, Boss. Couldn't be better."

"Ready," I told Sethra. Teldra stood next to me, and Sethra, without, so far as I could tell, so much as furrowing her brow, caused the sitting to room to vanish, and the courtyard of Castle Black to appear around me.

I felt like saying hello to it; I had a lot of memories tied up in that place, and not all of them were even bad. It was big, and it was a castle, and it was made all of black marble shot through with veins of silver, and it floated a mile or so in the air, and no one except me thought there was anything strange about that.

I guess you could say similar things about Morrolan, if you wanted to return to an earlier theme. I replaced the cord about my neck.

"I propose," I said, "that we head straight up the Tower and do this, or at least attempt it, because I don't want to give myself time to think about it."

"Very well," said Teldra.

The familiar doors opened to us as we approached them. I said, "Are you not frightened at all?"

"Would you rather I were, Vlad?"

"Good question. I'm not sure."

In and up and around and about; and add a few more prepositions to the mix, and eventually we were climbing the narrow metal staircase up to Morrolan's Tower. I'd been there before. It was not one of the places I missed.

"There ought to be a guardian here," I said.

"Pardon?"

"We shouldn't be able to just walk up and do this. We ought to have to fight our way past some sort of legendary half-man half-monster that has guarded this place since the beginning of time, and cannot be harmed by any weapon, nor moved by any words, nor evaded by any motion."

"I see," said Teldra. "Why?"

"I don't know. A warm-up for the rough stuff."

"Do irony and grey laughter help ease your fears?"

"Yes."

She nodded. "Was that a rude question on my part?"

"I'm not sure. I'll get back to you on that."

I pushed open the door over my head. It fell over with a boom and I caught the faint odor of formaldehyde, which I hadn't remembered from before. I climbed up and looked around. From my previous experience, I knew better than to count the number of windows; besides, all of them except one were covered up. The view out the open one was of a deep purple with pinpoints of light dotting it here and there; it reminded me a bit of the sky in the East. It actually took me a moment to realize that the Necromancer was already there, standing very still against the curtain between two of the windows. Teldra came up behind me and carefully shut the trapdoor.

"Vlad," said the Necromancer. "It is a pleasure to see you again."

I didn't know how to respond to her; I have never known how to respond to her. In some ways, she was more enigmatic even than Sethra Lavode. She looked creepy; I imagine on purpose. She was thin, even for a Dragaeran, and dressed entirely in dull black, without even silver buttons, and she was very, very pale, and she was an expert in what I think of as death, but, from what I've picked up of her conversation, she sees as something entirely different; to her "place" doesn't mean the same thing as it means to me, nor does "life" or "the soul." What to the Athyra are issues of epistemology and ontology are to her matters of engineering. I made a fervent wish that I would never arrive in a circumstance where "place" and "life" and "the soul" became matters of engineering.

It is wishes like that that get you in trouble.

How in blazes had I gotten myself mixed up with weirdos like this in the first place?

"Your natural charm, Boss."

"Shut up, Loiosh."

Once again, I removed the cord from around my neck, and put away the Phoenix Stones. This time, I remember feeling nothing in particular as I did so. I allowed Spellbreaker, a gold chain of small links, just less than two feet in length, to fall into my left hand from where it was coiled around my wrist. I looked at it. It was made of the same substance as the gold Phoenix Stone I had just put away, but it was different. Things had been done to it. Someone, some Serioli smith, I believe, had worked it, shaped it, and made it into something very special—exactly what, I had only gotten hints of over the years, like the Serioli who, when I asked if it was a Great Weapon, said, "Not yet." Heh.

This time, the links of the chain were very small; perhaps a quarter of an inch long, which meant that there were more of them than on other occasions, when the chain had been, say, fourteen inches long and each link had measured an inch and a half. For some reason, I found the idea that the number of links changed to be more disconcerting than that the overall length of the chain would vary.

I turned my eyes to the window, then back to the chain. In my mind, I drew a picture of Blackwand, Morrolan's weapon.

Or, rather, I tried to draw a picture of Blackwand; but it kept sliding away from me.

"*Help, Loiosh.*"

"*I'm there, Boss.*"

I pictured it in its sheath, though I had seen the damned thing naked. About five feet in length, it was: a longsword, as some called it, the hilt smooth and black, the guard a simple crosspiece, gleaming like silver; on top of the hilt a piece of smooth, glistening black stone, that stone called Verra's Tears, which was obsidian that had been smoothed away by Black Water. The scabbard I had seen Morrolan use most recently—he had several—was very plain, and seemed to be leather, although there had to be more to it than that. It was an old sheath, and there were a few threads coming loose at the seams, and a slight tear in the leather near the very top.

With Loiosh's help, the picture became clear, then very clear, then clear enough that I became frightened, then Lady Teldra was next to me in response to something I said, then there was a motion from around my shoulder, then I sent Spellbreaker out into the window in front of me.

And it all worked, just like Sethra Lavode had said it would.

Shame about that.

The window blurred and shifted, filled with lights, and darkness, and indistinct shapes. Herds of animals I didn't recognize grazed upon green fields beneath a sky that was a peculiar grey; strange appendages like fingers worked upon a small metallic object, striking it with a tool; a mountain peak appeared below me, stark against a sky that was black, black, black; there was an ocean of green, waves that seemed huge and that crashed against the window but didn't pass through; a young girl who may have been human or Dragaeran and who I might or might not have recognized made impossible eye contact with me; an athyra-like bird screeched horribly and fell along a wooded path, then vanished into nothing as it landed; violet sparks came from a wheel that spun at incredible speeds, though to no purpose I could imagine; a man with a pen made odd scratches on a long roll of parchment; deep under water, a strange creature with scales all of green and yellow worked upon a piece of red fabric, embroidering it with a thin silver needle and blue thread. And all of this with no trace of sound—that, perhaps, the most peculiar thing of all.

Now the window shows darkness pierced by flickerings of light as of a storm, the source of the light beyond the scope of my vision, but in those flickerings I see Blackwand, itself, only barely more real than in my vision, until suddenly I realize that, though it is concealed in its sheath, and that sheath attached to a familiar figure, I *feel* Blackwand; and that tiny portion of my brain which remains free to have opinions and feelings regrets that we have been successful.

Teldra and I, in perfect unison, following Spellbreaker, took one step forward through the window. There was no sense of disorientation, the way there is when teleporting, nor was there the delay. In a way, I think this made it worse—the changes were sharper than any I had known before, and it was lucky that I didn't have to defend myself at once. The first thing I noticed was that I felt heavier—perhaps the result of a general protection spell against anyone who doesn't belong, or it might also be some natural property of the place. The air smelled funny, sort of sweet, with a queer kind of tang in it. There were no sounds; what had seemed to be a flickering light was some sort of dim lamp, forty or fifty feet away, that was hanging from the ceiling and swaying back and forth, and it was in this light that I saw Morrolan and Aliera, which was the second thing that struck me; but the first demanded my immediate attention.

"*Loiosh, where is Rocza?*" I was, to be honest, surprised at the sinking fear I felt in the pit of my stomach.

"*I had her stay behind. I didn't want to worry about her.*"

I was equally surprised by the relief that flooded through me. "*You could have told me.*"

"*It was a last-minute decision.*"

I turned my attention to the Dragonlords we had come to rescue. They were both sitting on the floor against a stone wall, with what seemed to be iron manacles on their wrists, and they were both awake. Both had their weapons with them.

Morrolan cleared his throat and said, "Welcome. I find myself filled with the desire to say something like, 'What took you so long, Vlad,' but I fear that you, Lady Teldra, might take it wrong, so I will refrain."

"Damned decent of you," I said.

"Hello, Vlad," said Aliera. "I wondered who she would send into this trap."

"It's a trap?" I said. "Why, now, that's hard to believe."

Morrolan snorted.

I said, "How did they come to leave you your weapons?"

"Do you imagine," said Aliera, "that they would be willing to touch them, or even come near them?"

"I see. So you have your weapons, but are unable to move."

"Well, you probably noticed that you have no link to the Orb."

"Uh," I said, because, in fact, in all the disorientation, that little fact had escaped me. "Let's see if we can get you out of those things."

"Good luck," said Aliera.

"Oh?"

I inspected them. There was a fair bit of slack—enough to reach the plain, white ceramic chamber pots a few paces from the wall (the contents of which I didn't bother to inspect), but not much more. The chain was thick, and seemingly of some material a lot like iron, but smoother, and—

"There's no lock. They don't open."

"Noticed that right away, did you?" said Aliera.

"Bugger," I suggested. "How did they get them on you in the first place?"

"I don't know," said Morrolan.

I looked at them. "Well, so here you are, unable to move, to escape, or to act in any way. Good. There are a number of things I've wanted to say to you both over the years."

"Funny, Vlad," said Morrolan.

"I thought it was funny, Boss."

Teldra said, "Do you think our arrival here has been detected?"

"I have no way of knowing," said Morrolan.

"I'd have to assume so," said Aliera.

"Well," I said. "That ought to make things more interesting. Does anyone have a suggestion for getting you two out of those manacles?"

"You should have brought Kiera," said Aliera.

"Yeah," I said. "Right. What could I have been thinking of to have forgotten to have a Kiera in my pocket?"

I knelt down next to Morrolan and studied the manacles. They were completely smooth, as if they had been created, fully formed, around his wrists out of some material I had never encountered before; something very hard, dull grey, and at least as strong as iron.

"How did you get here?" said Aliera.

"The windows in my tower," said Morrolan. "He used Spellbreaker to find Pathfinder."

"Blackwand, actually, but yes."

"So is the window still open?"

I said, "No," at the same time Morrolan said, "Yes."

I said, "Uh, I defer to your expertise."

"Yes it is," said Morrolan, "but I know of no way to reach it without using powers to which I have no access from here, so it may as well not be."

Aliera said, "Have the Jenoine access to such powers?"

"Excuse me?" said Morrolan.

"Can they use your window to reach our world?"

Very softly, under his breath, Morrolan cursed. "I hadn't thought of that," he said.

"I should imagine," I said, "that Sethra didn't, either."

Morrolan and Aliera were cousins, both of the House of the Dragon. Morrolan was the sort of fellow who would restyle his hair every week or so, and take great care of his nails; and in his youth, had put entire villages to the sword when the mood took him. Aliera was short for a Dragaeran (still taller than me, of course), compact, brilliant, and more fond of a good duel than of any other entertainment you cared to name. They were both better sorcerers than I'll ever live to be, though a bit over-shadowed by their association with Sethra Lavode; but that only meant they were often underestimated.

They both carried Great Weapons; these were rarely under-estimated.

Morrolan didn't hate Easterners as much as you'd expect; Aliera didn't hate me as much as you'd expect. Exactly how I got mixed up with these two is a long story, and probably not worth repeating, but, over the years, it is possible my association with them had done me more good than harm—at least up until now.

I studied where the chains from Morrolan's manacles joined the wall, and there was nothing there to work on—it was as if the chains were built in when the wall was first constructed. The wall itself seemed to be made of stone, except there were no stones in it, just one solid piece, as if someone had carved it out of a mountain. Well, why not? Sethra did something like that. Of course, her walls weren't so smooth as this.

"They don't seem to be in a hurry," I said.

"We can assume," said Aliera, "until proven otherwise, that they are watching and listening, and, since they know they have us all trapped, they have no need to be in a hurry, and by listening might get useful information from us."

"Such as the fact that they can use the window to reach our world," said Morrolan, "which we were just kind enough to tell them."

"And you are even now repeating, in case they missed it before."

"As if—"

"Oh, cut it out," I said.

I flipped two fingers to the world in general, just in case they were watching and the gesture was universal, then noticed for the first time that there didn't seem to be any doors in the room.

I took some time to look around the room a little more, feeling all eyes on me, but seeing no need to explain myself. The room was about two hundred feet by a hundred and fifty feet, and empty save for several tall metal objects that looked a bit like bookshelves, but were devoid of books. Most likely, this was some sort of storage room. And, as far as I could see, there was no way into or out of it. A good way to keep your property from being stolen. I'd have to remember that, in case I ever again had property to protect and the opportunity to protect it.

"There aren't any doors," I remarked.

Aliera and Morrolan gave me a look as if I'd just announced that knives were sometimes sharp. Teldra nodded solemnly, but I think she'd already noticed.

I thought about communicating with them psychically, but without the Orb it's damned difficult, not to mention exhausting.

Morrolan closed his eyes for a moment, then touched the hilt of Blackwand. "No one is listening to us," he said aloud.

Aliera's head whipped around, and she stared at him. "How can you know that?"

"Blackwand is not without power, cousin. Nor, for that matter, am I."

Aliera looked dubious, but didn't say anything more.

"*Hey, Boss, do you think the Necromancer has been able to maintain contact?*"

"*I'd give whole worlds to know, Loiosh.*"

Aloud I said, "Why don't you guys tell me what happened?"

They both started speaking at once, which I ought to have predicted; then they glared at each other. Finally, Aliera nodded toward Morrolan, who shrugged and said, "I don't know. I was in the library, and then I was here, being used to ornament this wall."

"I," said Aliera, "was in my bedchamber." She said this as if being snatched from the library ought to give Morrolan no cause for complaint.

"You have no idea how it happened?"

"None," said Aliera. "I was there, then I was here, manacled. I had no sensation of time passing, or that I had lost consciousness, although that proves nothing. On the other hand, Pathfinder has no sensation of time passing, and that, I believe, does prove something."

"Blackwand and I had the same experience," he said. "Which I hope means that they have the ability to transport us, instantly, off our world and into manacles chained to a wall; because if not, it means they have the ability to interfere with a Great Weapon, and then I should be worried."

I chewed that over, then asked Morrolan, "You had no indication that, I don't know, your security system had been breached?"

"No," he said.

"Is this something they've been able to do any time, and just decided to now? Or do they have something new?"

"I've been wondering the same thing," said Morrolan.

"This doesn't give us much to work with," I suggested. "And I don't suppose either of you have any suggestions about getting out of here?"

They didn't.

I studied the chains that held them, and was wondering what it would take to break them, and what to do once they were broken, when Aliera said, "If we could reach Sethra—" which is as far as she got before our hosts finally decided to grace us with their presence.

4

MAKING ACQUAINTANCES

I was looking at Morrolan and Aliera, and saw their eyes suddenly focus on something over my shoulder, so I turned just as Loiosh gave a sort of agitated, undefined psychic squeal. I don't actually *know* that they appeared through the floor, but it seemed like it at the time; as if they sort of formed from the floor up. There were two of them.

I said, "Are those—?"

"Yes," said Morrolan. "That's what they look like."

"Heh. They're ugly enough, anyway."

It is hard to say what my first impression of them was. I saw them emerge, and my memory supplies their image; I don't know exactly what I noticed first. They were big—bigger than Dragaerans, I'd say more than nine feet tall, which I ought to have guessed from the size of the ceilings, but that's the sort of thing I always figure out after the fact. But whereas Dragaerans are thin, at least compared to humans, the Jenoine were broad, heavy, strong-looking, with thick arms, ending in hands with some reasonable number of fingers and one thumb per hand, but from where I stood they didn't seem to have any wrists. Nor hair of any kind. It was hard to see their faces, either, but there seemed to be two large, round eyes, both facing forward, and a mouth of some sort. They were naked, and, as far I could tell, sexless.

And I'll mention again, because it impressed me so much, that they were very big.

I hated the idea of trying to fight them. I felt Loiosh draw

himself up and do the jhereg dance—which is what I call it
when he tries to make himself look bigger. It is one of the things
I don't make fun of him for, because I've caught myself doing
the same thing in my own way, although just at the moment
I'd have liked to make myself look smaller. Vanishing would
have been even better.

"Don't draw a weapon," whispered someone, and it took me
a moment to realize it was Teldra. I wasn't certain what good a
weapon would do me, so I saw no reason to argue with her.
Besides, if she had some inkling of an idea about what to do,
she was a long way ahead of me. The thought did flash through
my mind, in light of what Sethra had told me, to grab, say,
Pathfinder from Aliera's side; but laying hands on another's
Great Weapon is as close to certain death as you can come
without having Mario after you.

But the thought did make me realize that neither of the
Jenoine appeared to be armed. It didn't take a genius to realize
that if they didn't carry weapons, it was because they didn't
think they'd need any. This was not a comforting thought either.

At some point in there, it hit me that I was now in the
presence of the Jenoine, of those half-mythological creatures
that were spoken of in whispers, and the subject of as much
ignorant speculation as Sethra herself. I had never truly believed
in them, and now, here they were, and here was I, and typically,
I had to worry about what to do about it, and I didn't have a
clue.

Evidently, Lady Teldra did.

She took a step toward them, holding both hands in front
of her, palms out, and emitted a series of sounds midway between
a cat screeching and a hyena with hiccups.

"Be damned," murmured Morrolan.

I could see that, whatever else was happening, she had their
attention. One of them moved a step closer to her, and, in a
deep, rasping voice, spoke in the same language. If I could read
the expression on that one's face, I'd guess it was mildly star-

tled—its eyes, at any rate, had widened a little. Do facial expressions translate among species? There was another question for later contemplation. I was getting quite a collection of them. Evidently, I had thought it a good idea at some point to put Spellbreaker away; it was once more wrapped snugly around my left wrist. Amazing how light it felt that way, and how much heavier it got once I let it drop into my hand.

"Loiosh, why does my mind wander whenever I'm terrified?"

"It doesn't, Boss; your mind wanders whenever you're frustrated because you can't do anything."

"Oh."

"Or maybe it just always wanders and I don't notice it the rest of the time."

Teldra spoke again, the Jenoine responded. I waited patiently, like a prisoner whose fate was being settled by a magistrate while he stood helpless. It was enough to bring on the headache. I feel very fortunate not to be subject to the headache. There were many questions I should have liked to ask Morrolan and Aliera, but I was afraid it wouldn't be polite to carry on a conversation while Teldra was involved in screeching and coughing with the Jenoine, so I remained patient and tried to look tough and imperturbable—not for the Jenoine, who probably couldn't tell the difference, but for Morrolan and Aliera, who probably wouldn't care.

The conversation continued. I couldn't tell if Teldra was negotiating for our lives, laying down conditions to the Jenoine under which she wouldn't lay waste to their world, or asking if they knew any good recipes for klava.

I was just wondering if I'd be willing to try their version of klava, when the two Jenoine and Lady Teldra abruptly vanished. No fading, as of a teleport, and none of the shimmering and twisting of form that accompanied necromantic transportation, so this was something else entirely, and what should be surprising about that? Whatever it was, it was fast and neat—there wasn't even the rush of displaced air that I'm used to, which indicates to me that natural laws were being suspended, and that didn't surprise me, either.

"They're gone," said Morrolan, which was too obvious even for me to make a crack about how obvious it was.

"Now," said Aliera, "might be a good time to get us out of these."

"Good idea," I said. "How do we do that?"

Morrolan ignored me. "If Teldra is involved in negotiations," he said to Aliera, "we may jeopardize them by—"

"If Teldra is involved in negotiations," said Aliera, "it is in order to give us time to get out of here."

"What makes you think so?"

"Don't be a fool."

"*Here we go,*" said Loiosh.

"Lady Teldra," I cut in, "did not leave our presence willingly."

That stopped them, at least for a moment. "How do you know that?" snapped Aliera.

"She vanished suddenly, without saying a word about it. It was rude."

"Good point," said Morrolan.

Okay, Vlad, I told myself. Teldra has just been taken away by all-powerful, legendary demigods; Sethra and the Necromancer are so far away that the term "distance" is meaningless; and Morrolan and Aliera are chained to a wall by some no doubt magical substance impervious to everything. That leaves you. Do something.

Morrolan and Aliera were looking at me, as if they expected the same thing. Well, fine. I tried to figure out what I needed to know, before I could even start formulating a plan. There were so many things. I didn't know what powers and abilities the Jenoine had, or, except in the most general terms, what their goals might be. Of course, I knew a bit about what Morrolan and Aliera could do, and Teldra—now, Teldra was a nice little mystery herself. I should have insisted on an answer from Sethra about why she was along. What is it she knew, or what skill did she have that . . .

Hmmmmmm.

"Morrolan, would you mind telling me, just because I'm curious, exactly what Lady Teldra does for you?"

"I don't understand, Vlad. You've seen her. She greets guests, she sees that they get where they are going within the Castle, and that I am informed about arrivals and departures. I thought you knew that."

"I did. I do. What else does she do?"

"Isn't that enough?"

"No."

He shrugged. "Well, that's what she does, enough or not."

I shook my head. "I'm missing something."

"He's an Easterner, Morrolan," said Aliera.

I bit back a smart remark, because Aliera's observation seemed to elicit an "Oh" expression from Morrolan. He said, "That's true."

"Okay," I said. "What is obvious to you that isn't to me?"

"The gods," said Aliera.

"What about them?"

"We consider them guests as well," said Morrolan. "Permanent guests of our homes, at all times; I had forgotten that you don't think of them that way."

"I don't see the point."

"Teldra," said Aliera, "is, in your terms, Morrolan's High Priestess."

"Ah ha."

"Ah ha?" said Morrolan.

"That's what I was looking for."

"Why?" said Morrolan and Aliera together, and I felt Loiosh asking the same thing.

"I don't know exactly. But I knew there had to be some connection there, and some reason Sethra agreed to send her, and because I need to understand all of these connections if I'm going to do anything useful."

Morrolan shrugged again. "Okay," he said. "Now you understand the profound truth that someone who knows how to be polite to a Dragonlord, a Teckla, or an Emperor might know how to be polite to a god as well."

"Not to mention a Jenoine," I remarked.

"Yes, a Jenoine, too."

"And she speaks their language."

"Obviously."

"What has that to do with her duties as High Priestess, or whatever?"

"Nothing," he said. "But she knows many languages. Many Issola do. It's a custom, such as Dragons knowing how to fight, and Jhereg knowing how to offer a bribe." I let that go. He said, "Is any of this important?"

"I don't know."

"Then, perhaps, you might turn your attention to doing something useful."

"Two problems, Morrolan. First, I'm stumped. Second, as Aliera said, if Teldra is talking to them, we may not want to irritate them during her negotiations."

"But as *you* said, Vlad, she didn't leave willingly."

"I know. But are you certain she can't talk them around? She's evidently used to dealing with beings who are far more powerful than she is; can you think of a better negotiator?"

He thought about that.

Loiosh said, *"I don't know if we ever want to cross them, Boss. I'm scared of those things."*

"They're worth being scared of," I said. *"They'd kill without a second thought."*

"I hate to say this, Boss, but so would you."

"Yeah, but I'm a nice guy."

"Try Spellbreaker," said Morrolan. I looked at him. "On the chains," he said. "Try Spellbreaker."

I looked at Aliera, who shrugged.

"Can't hurt," I said.

"What are you worried about, Boss?"

"Looking ridiculous."

"It was his idea."

I let Spellbreaker fall into my hand. It was only about a foot and a half long and the links were nearly an inch long. I took a step forward, and struck the length of chain connecting Morrolan's right wrist to the wall. The ringing sound was loud, though hearing the sound made me realize the room didn't echo as much as I would have thought it should. Nothing else happened. I felt ridiculous. I wrapped Spellbreaker up again. Morrolan shrugged; evidently he didn't feel ridiculous.

"If Spellbreaker is still changing, Loiosh, there's something that is still happening, I mean, something magical, even though we're no longer at home."

"Seems reasonable, Boss."

"And why am I so heavy? It's like I have to work to lift my arms."

"Yeah. Don't expect me to fly anywhere."

"So, okay, Sethra was wrong. There's sorcery here. Or, if not sorcery, something else; something that can make us feel heavy, and that makes it so hard to breathe. I'd really like to avoid having to fight here."

"Okay, Boss. But just for the record, where is it you haven't wanted to avoid fighting?"

That didn't deserve an answer, so I didn't give one. About then, I noticed something else, and cursed.

"What is it, Vlad?"

"I'm starting to get light-headed."

"Oh, that."

"What does 'oh, that' mean?"

Aliera said, "Try to take shallow breaths."

"Uh . . ."

"Try it. If you don't, you'll get dizzy."

"If you say so."

I tried to make my breaths shallow. At least it didn't make things any worse. I said, "Are they poisoning the air?"

"Not on purpose," said Morrolan.

"What does 'not on purpose' mean?"

"It seems to be the nature of the world. Just make your breaths shallow and you'll be fine. Soon you'll stop needing to think about it."

"Oh, good."

I took Aliera's hand and weighed the manacle in it. It was heavy, and seemed not too dissimilar to cast iron, maybe three-quarters of an inch thick. The chain seemed to have been made as one piece of it, and I saw no way to break it, or separate the chain. I studied where the chain joined the wall again, and still saw nothing. I probably would have started to get frustrated at that point, but before I had the chance Loiosh said, *"Boss, they're back,"* which gave me other things to think about.

"They're back" wasn't entirely accurate; only one of the Jenoine was back, but Teldra was with him, looking none the worse for wear, and holding something small and black in the palm of her hand. I permitted myself to hope it was a key to the manacles.

I held my tongue as she walked up to us; there's something about courtesy that's contagious. She said, "I have negotiated with the Jenoine."

I studied her face at that moment, I suppose feeling something momentous about to occur, and I couldn't get anything from her expression.

"They will release you, Morrolan and Aliera, if Vlad agrees to perform a task for them."

"I can hardly wait," I muttered, but either no one heard me, or they all ignored me.

"They want Vlad to perform a killing, a murder."

"Did you explain that I'm no longer in that line of work?"

"I made no agreement of any kind," she said. "I merely spoke to them, and they stated the conditions."

"And otherwise we'll be killed, I assume," said Aliera, as if she were being threatened with not being allowed to dinner.

"That wasn't specified."

"That's why we were taken," said Aliera, giving me a look.

"In order to coerce Vlad into doing what they want."

"You'd think," said Morrolan, "that if that was true, they'd have taken Cawti, or better yet—" He broke off abruptly and scowled.

"They're separated," said Aliera.

"So?" said Morrolan. "Who knows how the Jenoine think, and what they know? They may not know much more of our customs, not to mention emotions, than we know of theirs."

"They know enough to have us here, bait for Vlad. You'll notice he's here."

"Makes me wonder what they would have done if you hadn't been along, Lady Teldra."

"Some of them speak our language," she said.

I cleared my throat. "I notice none of you are asking the obvious question."

"You mean," said Morrolan, "who is it she wants killed? It is obviously either Sethra, or a god, and you certainly aren't going to do it, so what difference does it make?"

"I should think a god," said Aliera judiciously. "Probably Verra."

Teldra bowed to her.

"Verra?" I said. "They want me to kill Verra?"

"Yes," said Teldra.

"Well, I have been annoyed with her now and then. I mean, I can't say I haven't thought about it."

"It isn't a joking matter, Vlad," said Morrolan.

"I think it is, Boss."

"That's two of us, if it comes to a vote."

"Did they have any suggestions as to how I was to accomplish this task?"

She held out the object in her palm. It was a small, black cube, perhaps an inch on a side. It didn't seem to reflect any light. "I am told," she said, "that this will bring you to the presence of the Goddess." With her other hand, she took from her belt a sheathed knife I hadn't noticed before. "This is a very powerful Morganti dagger; it will be sufficient to, as they put it, prevent the Goddess from manifesting on our world."

"That means kill her," said Morrolan.

"Not exactly," said Aliera.

"Close enough.

I made some sort of grunting sound; I'm not sure what it meant, because I'm not sure what I was thinking. Teldra set the two objects down at my feet, then stepped back. There was something of ritual about how she did it; as if she were saying, "Here, now my work is done, and I say nothing about your work, what it is, or if you ought to do it."

I stared at the black cube and at the Morganti dagger. I could feel its emanations even from its sheath.

I said, "Teldra, do you trust them?"

"Vlad!" said Aliera. "You aren't considering doing it!"

"Yes," said Teldra. "I think they were telling the truth."

I grunted again.

"Look on the bright side, Boss: you've done a king, now you'll be able to say you've—"

"That's not the bright side. The bright side is the pleasure of rescuing Morrolan and Aliera. They'll never live it down."

Morrolan was staring at me. "Vlad, you can't be thinking about it. Think! Verra, the Demon Goddess. Your ancestors have worshiped her—"

"Leave it alone, Morrolan."

"Leave it alone? She is my goddess, too. How can I let you destroy her to save me?"

I laughed. "How can you stop me?"

"Vlad—"

"Oh, be still, dammit. I don't want to hear anything from anyone for a while, okay? Except you, Teldra, I want you to answer a question or two: Did they say anything about how long I had to make up my mind?"

"It wasn't mentioned," she said.

"Did they say anything about feeding us?"

"No."

Aliera opened her mouth to make another passionate and

irritating plea, so I turned and walked away to the far side of the room. What I needed was time to think; usually needing time to think only happens when you haven't got any, but this time I at least had the chance to work a few things through in my head: Aliera and Morrolan wouldn't subject themselves to the indignity of yelling across the room, Teldra was too polite to say anything, and, for a miracle, even Loiosh gave me some peace.

So I ran a lot of stuff around my brain, for whatever that would do. The fact is, I don't think all that well when I'm just standing and thinking; I need to be talking, or doing something active, then the thoughts flow. But I did my best, and eventually sorted the matter out into several categories of things that I didn't understand. This was progress.

Categories, if you'll excuse a brief digression, are a useful way to get a handle on things you don't understand, as long as you don't get too attached to them and forget that things like to pop out of one category and into another, and that sometimes the whole category turns itself inside out and becomes something different. It's useful, for example, to categorize your target as a sorcerer, if he is one; but if you get too attached to your category it'll leave you embarrassed when he suddenly pulls a knife on you.

Just thought I'd share my reflections on categories.

In this case, I broke the unknowns down into: the abilities of the Jenoine, the plans of the Jenoine, and the nature of this world we were in.

I decided to start with the latter. I walked back.

"You have no link to the Orb, correct?"

Morrolan and Aliera nodded.

"Your Great Weapons seem to be behaving normally?"

They nodded again.

"What about time?"

"Excuse me?" said Aliera.

"I know time works differently in different places. I've been to the Paths of the Dead. Exactly how differently does it work here?"

"As far as I know," said Morrolan, "an hour here is an hour at home."

I shook my head. "No, I know that isn't true. How long have you been here?"

"I don't know," said Aliera. "Several hours."

"Several days," I told her. "Five, to be exact."

They look properly startled. Before they could respond, I said, "What about Verra's Halls? How does time work there?"

"What difference does that make?" asked Aliera.

"I'm just curious."

Morrolan looked suspicious, and like he didn't want to answer. I glanced at Teldra, who said, "I don't know. I assume time flows the same there as it does at home, but I don't actually know."

"Okay," I said.

The reason that assassins make so much money is that, first of all, there aren't many who have what it takes to dispassionately murder someone; and, of those, there aren't many who can get away with it. I used to be one of them. Whatever there is in me that made me able to shove the knife, I still had. What made me able to get away with it so many times—sixty-three, to be exact—was that I understood the key ingredient: knowledge. You have to know things. You have to know everything there is to know about your target, about the environment, about your weapons, about your own abilities. Then you can make a plan. A plan built on ignorance can be worse than charging in with no plan at all; if you have no plan, you might get lucky.

I gestured toward the cube on the floor. "How do you use that thing?"

"All you need to do is hold it," said Teldra.

"Vlad—" said Aliera.

"Oh, stuff it," I said. "Morrolan, if I get you two out of those things, will you be able to get us out of here? Back home?"

He hesitated, then looked disgusted and shook his head. "Maybe," he said, "but probably not."

Aliera said, "Can you get us out, Vlad?"

"I'm still thinking about that," I said. "But even if I can I don't know how much good it will do."

"I would rather," she said, "be free to act, no matter what happens after."

"I understand that," I told her.

Either way was a gamble—picking up the cube, or attempting to free Morrolan and Aliera. I don't like gambling, especially when I don't know the odds; or at least the stakes. When possible, I'd rather be running the game than playing it. But now the Jenoine were running it, and I didn't even know the rules. I didn't know how to free them, and I didn't know if I could kill Verra. Freeing them might accomplish nothing; killing my Demon Goddess was not high on my list of ways to spend an afternoon.

I reached down and picked up the Morganti dagger; stuffed it into my belt. It wasn't easy to do—I'd never liked those things, and I could tell instantly that this was a particularly nasty one. Well, I suppose it would have to be, if they expected me to kill the Goddess with it.

Morrolan snapped, "What are you doing, Vlad?"

"Can always use a good Morganti dagger, right?"

"Boss, you're not going to—"

"I've got to do something. I'm bored."

"Oh. You're bored. Well, that's a good reason—"

"Drop it."

So I didn't have a plan. I did, as I stood there, start to get the seeds of what might, sometime, become a vague step generally in the direction of an intention. I may be stating that too strongly.

I took a good look around the room, noting the tall, thin metal shelves; the flat grey look of the walls; the height of the ceiling. I tried to fix it in my mind. I could not imagine what circumstances might lead me to try teleporting here, but that is the sort of thinking that goes with paying attention to details, in case you're curious about how my mind works.

My chest hurt. I tried to keep my breathing shallow, and to forget about how heavy I felt. It would be impossible to exert myself without taking deep breaths. I felt Aliera and Morrolan watching me. One step, and I was committed, and I still just didn't have enough information. But the only other option was standing around doing nothing, and that would only be effective for so long.

No, if I was going to do something, I had to have information, and there was no one here who could give it to me, which left only one option.

I reached into my pouch and pulled out two pieces of gammon. I handed one to Aliera and one to Morrolan. "If you're going to be helpless and miserable," I said, "at least you can eat a little."

They both accepted it, and they both looked like they were trying to decide if they should thank me, but neither said anything. I flexed my fingers.

All right.

"Lady Teldra," I said, "would you come here, please? Take my hand, if you would."

She did so, asking no questions but looking curious. Her hand was dry and cool. I reached down with my other hand, not letting her go, and picked up the small black cube.

Aliera said, "Vlad, what are you doing?"

The cube was very heavy for its size, but didn't seem to do anything except make the walls of the room turn a dull, ugly white. Or, at any rate, that was my first reaction; it took a moment to realize that Teldra, Loiosh, and I now stood in the Halls of Verra, the Demon Goddess.

5

PLEASANTRIES WITH DEITIES

Everything was too big and too white. The ceiling too high, the walls too far apart, the pillars spaced along the walls too big around, and everything the same uniform, ugly, chalky, pasty color. It was huge. It was only a hallway.

The next thing I noticed was that it was easier to breathe, and I didn't feel as heavy and sluggish as I had a second ago. It was only then that I realized that the little black cube had, after doing its job, neatly vanished.

"I got to get me one of those," I remarked. My voice sounded funny; it took me a second to realize it was because there was no echo—it was as if the corridor was absorbing the sound.

"I'll pass one along next time we get a shipment," said Teldra. Her voice sounded odd, too.

I had to look at her before I knew she was kidding. It was a very un-Teldra-like remark; I guess she was rattled too.

She said, "Where are we?"

"Where we're supposed to be. Or where we're not supposed to be, depending on how you look at it. But this is the home of Verra. I've been here before. Straight up ahead there, through those doors, is where I've seen her."

"You've been in her presence, then?"

"Yes, a couple of times. Once here, once elsewhere. Or maybe more often than that, if you use 'presence' loosely enough."

"We are surrounded by the color of illness; not very encouraging."

"I think it means something else to her."

"I suspected as much. But what?"

"I don't know, exactly. Is it important?"

"It is something I ought to have known."

"As Morrolan's High Priestess, you mean?"

She nodded. "Something like that can be important. And just in general, the more I know of the gods, the better."

"You must already know a great deal; maybe there are things you ought to tell me about Verra, before we go through those doors."

"Perhaps there are," she said. "But one thing I know, my dear Easterner, is that to you she is the Demon Goddess, and to me she is Verra, and we know her differently. Whatever I know might not be useful; indeed, it might mislead you."

I grunted. "Are the walls white?"

"Yes."

"I see them that way, too."

"Point taken."

"Then let's hear it."

"On the other hand," she said, smiling a little, "it may be that I can't tell you anything useful, and you're just procrastinating, because you aren't in a hurry to go through those doors."

"Point taken," I said, and started walking toward the doors.

"Wait," she said.

I waited.

"A god," said Lady Teldra, "is the living, sentient embodiment of a symbol."

"Oh," I said. "Well, that clears up everything."

"Your people, Easterners, might speak of a god of life, a god of death, a god of mountains, and so on. Isn't that true?"

"Sometimes," I said. "I think so. My education was a bit spotty."

"Those are all symbols."

"Death is a symbol?"

"Certainly. Very much so. Death, in fact, is a very powerful symbol because it defines life."

There were many things I could say to that, but I settled for, "All right, go on."

She looked around, gesturing to the walls. "We stand in the halls of a very powerful being; one with skills and abilities that surpass those of any mortal. By tradition, she represents the random arbitrariness of life."

"That's the rumor."

"Well, look around. Does her home appear random and arbitrary?"

I grunted, because I don't like giving obvious answers to pointed questions. "What are you getting at?"

"That she isn't just a symbol, she's also a person."

"Uh . . ."

"The tradition isn't wrong," said Teldra, "it is merely imprecise. She—" Teldra stopped and frowned, as if looking for the right words. "Your goddess," she said at last, "is capricious. At any rate, that is her reputation. It may be only that we expect a being with her power to behave with a certain consistency and decorum, whereas she follows her whims as much as any of us do. But don't depend on her."

"I shan't," I said. "I never have." That wasn't strictly true. At one time I did, but I had learned.

"Then that is all I can tell you," said Teldra.

"All right," I said. "Thanks. Let's go."

And we went, for several paces, until we reached doors that made Morrolan's look diminutive, and there we stopped, because, unlike Morrolan's, these didn't open as we stood before them.

"Maybe we're supposed to say something," I suggested.

"Maybe we aren't supposed to go in," said Teldra.

I studied the massive doors, and the corridor behind me. "Last time I was here," I told her, "there was a sort of fog in the hallway. Now there isn't. Do you suppose it means something?"

She shook her head; the sort of head shake that comes in answer to a question one doesn't know the answer to. I cursed under my breath, and, just because I couldn't think of anything else to do, clapped at the door.

Nothing happened.

"Too bad, Boss. She's not home. Guess we'd better —"

"Shut up, Loiosh."

I then pushed at the door, because I'd have felt stupid if they opened inward and weren't secured. It didn't work, leaving me feeling stupid. The doors were filled with designs, all white-on-white, abstract designs reminiscent of embroidery from my ancestral homeland. All very nice. There were no handles on the doors. The space between the doors was wide enough to admit a pry-bar, or a knife blade, but I didn't have a pry-bar, or a blade with me that wouldn't snap from the weight of those doors. On the other hand, I had some spare knives. I pulled a stiletto from my boot, and was about to insert it between the doors when Teldra said, "Vlad."

I turned my head without moving the knife. "Yes?"

"Are you quite certain that breaking in is a good idea?"

"You're afraid I'll offend her?"

"Well, yes."

"You don't think killing her will offend her?"

She showed me a smile. "Vlad, we both know you have no intention of killing her."

"Do we know that, Boss?"

"Well, Teldra does, at any rate."

I turned back to the door, slipped the knife in, put some pressure on it, and promptly snapped the blade. The sound was dull and, like our voices, didn't echo. I stared at the hilt and the inch and a half of of blade left in my hand, shrugged, and discarded it. It made more of a thump than a clatter as it fell to the floor.

"Okay," I said. "Next idea."

"You could pray to her," she said.

"Yeah," I said. "But what if she answered?"

"Do the gods answer, when you pray?"

"Sometimes. I've had her answer once, at any rate, and

maybe twice. Or there may be other occasions I'm forgetting about. That's the sort of thing I'd like to forget. How do we get in here?"

"I don't know," she said. "You'd know better than me; you've had personal contact with her."

"Yeah. From which I know nothing except—" I put my face up against the door and yelled, "Verra! It's me, Vlad! You've had your joke, now open the bloody damn door."

The door began to swing inward. The last time I'd been here, the doors had opened outward. At least, I think they did. But this time they opened inward, and mists and fogs rolled out; the mist that had been in the corridor last time was now in the room.

"You can get the same effect with dry ice," I told Teldra.

"What's dry ice, Vlad?"

"It is an Eastern secret for keeping things cold. I learned of it from Valabar's."

"Witchcraft?"

"I guess so."

She nodded. "Shall we go in? I believe we've been invited."

"Yeah, sure, all right," I said, and stepped into the fog.

I walked forward with more confidence than I felt. I walked a long time, reminding myself that distances seem greater when you can't see, and the room was plenty big without help.

"Wall, Boss."

I stopped and cursed under my breath. Then I said, "Verra—"

There was a chuckle that seemed to come from all around me, and the fog cleared away and vanished—not going anywhere, just thinning out until it was gone, a process that took about five seconds. I was standing at the far end of the room; Verra sat on her chair, or throne, or dais, about twenty yards to my left and behind me. I made my way to the front of it and, while Teldra made some sort obeisance, I said, "What was that all about?"

She gave me an ironic indulgent look, if you can imagine

such a thing. On the throne on the dais (all of white), she looked even taller than she was. She wore a hoodless robe that was mostly pale red with black embroidery. Her fingers were long and had an extra joint to them. Her hair, this time, was shoulder-length and wavy: a subdued brown with red highlights, and very thick, so it seemed to have an iridescent quality. Her eyes didn't glow, but it seemed like they ought to have.

She was my God—insofar, at least, as I had one. When I was a child, my grandfather had spoken of her, but given few details of the sort that might be useful, and my father never mentioned her at all, but it had been impressed upon my young mind that one made the proper observances at the proper times of the year. More than that, her power and presence were so deeply ingrained in me that all through life my thoughts would flash to her briefly at times of danger, or in moments of despair; and even in moments of great joy or triumph I would think of her, sending her my gratitude and the hopes that I would not be punished for enjoying my happiness.

When I had first met her in person, so many years ago, the shock had been so great that I couldn't assimilate it. At other times, I had felt her presence, but didn't know how often this feeling was only supplied by my imagination, and how often she had truly been with me. There were occasions, such as my one experience as a soldier of the line, when I could not imagine how I had survived without her having some hand in the matter, but she had never told me she actually did. Of course, I hadn't asked, either.

To know her as real—that is, a flesh-and-blood individual with whom I had spoken—was something I could never reconcile with the idea of a presence watching over me; perhaps watching me at times I didn't want to be watched. I had buried my own reactions, only to have them emerge as hatred some time later when she had visited misfortune upon my head, or maybe allowed misfortune to visit me, whichever. Since then I had tried not to even think of her, but in this I had failed, and now here she was, and to rescue my friends, I had to destroy her.

"Well?" I said. "Why the games?"

"An odd question," she said. I had forgotten the peculiar sound her voice had: not exactly an echo, but more as if there were two of her speaking, mostly in unison, but sometimes they'd fall a bit out of synchronization. She continued, "How can you complain of my treatment of you, when you are only here to assassinate me?"

"There is that," I agreed. "Goddess, may I be permitted to put a question?"

"Very well, assassin," said the Demon Goddess.

"Was this all your doing?" And, for a second, I actually had made Verra look astonished. Then the expression was gone. I continued, "The last time, if you recall—"

"Yes, Taltos Vladimir, I remember. But no, this was none of my doing. I did not arrange this, nor expect it. I did not expect you to arrive here; I did not think you would be able to do so without my assistance. Tell me, how *did* you manage that? I can't believe the Issola standing next to you accomplished it for you."

I wanted to say something like, "It's a trade secret," but even I have limits beyond which I won't go.

Teldra said, "Goddess, it was the Jenoine."

Verra nodded, slowly. "Yes," she said. "It had to be. Do you know who? Or which faction?"

"I was unable to learn, Goddess. I can tell you that one addressed the other by the honorific 'ker.' "

"Well done, Issola. It is a term used by what among the Jenoine is the equivalent of the military. It is useful information."

"I am only too happy to be of service," she said.

The Demon Goddess narrowed her eyes a little at this pronouncement, and said to me, "And you, little Easterner. Are you, also, only too happy to be of service?"

"I haven't decided yet," I said. "How many places can you be at once?"

"Well," she said. "You've been studying. Sethra Lavode, I take it?"

I grunted. "Yes, but I knew that much, at least, from a long time ago."

"Many," said the Goddess, in answer to my question. "But there is one place I cannot be, and your countrymen are responsible for that."

"An ancestor?"

"No. It was a blood prince, and you are of peasant stock."

That stung. "All right," I said. "Thanks for the compliment. I still want to know."

"I cannot appear among the Jenoine, Vlad, which is what you're really asking, isn't it?"

"Supernatural powers, immortality, and clever, too."

"Don't try my patience, Fenarian. I mean that."

I swallowed and nodded.

"Goddess," said Teldra, presumably breaking in to take me off the hook, "our friends are being held captive. Can you and will you help us?"

"Sit down here at my feet," she said, "and we'll talk."

Teldra sat on the dais as if there was nothing distasteful about doing so; I did my best to emulate her but I don't think I managed to keep the scowl entirely off my face.

"Speak," said Verra, and Teldra did so. I occasionally filled in a detail or speculation. Verra remained silent the entire time. She must have known some of what was going on, to judge from her comment about my being there to assassinate her, but she just listened and gave no hint about what she had known.

"There is more to this," said the Goddess when we were finished, "than you are aware of."

"No shit?" I said.

She gave me an indulgent smile, which did nothing to improve my mood. I felt Teldra's hand on my arm; if it had been anyone else, I'd probably have bit it.

Verra said, "I do not, however, intend to explain everything to you."

"Well, there's a new experience for me."

"Little Easterner," said Verra, "you seem determined to express your displeasure to me in more and more obvious ways until I take notice. Very well, I take notice. You are wroth with me because I have used you; because I have offended against your innate right to be a useless cyst on the hindquarters of life. Yes, well, you may continue to be wroth with me, because I intend to continue making you useful. You may attempt to kill me, in which case I will destroy you; or may continue to annoy me; in which case I will cause you sufficient pain to make you stop; or you may shut up and accept the inevitable."

I opened my mouth, Teldra squeezed my arm, I shut my mouth.

"Say, 'Thank you, Teldra,' " said Verra.

"Thank you Teldra," I said.

"Boss, where did this self-destructive streak come from?"

"Shut up, Loiosh."

Verra said, "I have been waiting for some time, and so has Sethra, for the Jenoine to put their plans in motion, without knowing exactly what form they would take, or, indeed, what those plans were. But we knew they were preparing something. Now they have begun, and we are only able to respond and react until we know more about their intentions."

I said, "Sethra once tried to explain to me about offensive-defensive strat—"

"Keep still," she said, and I suddenly felt like someone was driving a spike into my head. I gasped, and the pain went away.

"Very convincing," I said, when I could speak again.

"They have made the first move," said Verra, as if nothing had happened. "We don't yet know what it means. The Jenoine are, in some ways, not unlike the Yendi; they will have anticipated our response, and worked it into their plans. They will have secondary and tertiary responses to our moves. Their objective will be concealed under layers of illusion and misdirection."

I bit back a suggestion that she let me know when she had

the problem wrapped up; I was learning. She continued, "There are some things, however, that we can be certain of: one is that they must find a way to neutralize Sethra, Morrolan, and Aliera, among others whose names you don't know."

"They have two of them; why haven't they killed them?"

"You know how hard it is to kill the wielder of a Great Weapon."

"I remember a Jhereg who managed it, once."

"So Morrolan told me. Yes, it can be done, by a judicious combination of sorcery, surprise, and more sorcery. But even then, had Morrolan not been returned to life, Blackwand would have continued to guard his soul. And it might have done far more than that; the Jhereg assassin was a fool. By now, Vlad, you should begin to understand something about the Great Weapons."

That shut me up. I remembered some of the tricks those things can do. Once I had seen Aliera—but never mind.

"But can they continue to hold Morrolan and Aliera captive?"

"It seems they can. I hadn't thought so, and I still don't know how."

"Probably with help from the Serioli," I suggested.

She actually looked startled. At least, she sat back in her chair and stared at me. That was twice in the same conversation; I felt smug.

"Well, well," she said after a moment. "You know more than I should have thought."

I shrugged.

"Yes, it may be the Serioli," she agreed. She frowned, and seemed lost in thought. It flashed through my mind that I had never before seen her lost in thought, and the idea of that powerful mind bending its energies in some direction made me feel more puny and pathetic than all the pyrotechnics she had displayed before. What was I doing here, anyway?

"*Don't you remember, Boss? You're going to kill her.*"

"*Oh, right. That.*"

Verra finished her thought. "It is complex," she announced. "They are playing a deep game, and there is no way to understand all of it at this stage."

I stared at the ceiling, which was white, and very high over my head. I said, "Isn't it a pain when you have to come up with a plan based on incomplete information?" No one responded. I said, "Goddess, do you have a guess about what killing you has to do with it? I mean did they think I actually could, and would, or was it just a complex piece of subterfuge?"

She said, "Oh, anything they can do to make me uncomfortable is all to the good, as far as they're concerned; it may be nothing more than that. If it is part of something deeper, then I don't know what. Yes, it is very possible that they expected you to march in here and kill me. Or perhaps they hope merely to confuse me, and hinder my efficiency."

" 'The ways of the gods are mysterious,' " I quoted.

"Yes."

"Also annoying, capricious—"

Teldra gave my arm a squeeze, and I shut up.

"Goddess," said Teldra. "Can you tell us what we are to do?"

"What to do?" she said. "In order to accomplish what? In order to serve whom? Me? Aliera? Morrolan? Sethra?"

"I was thinking of the Serioli," I said. "At least, no Serioli has ever annoyed me. That makes them unique on the list."

Verra snapped her head toward me, and I couldn't keep myself from flinching. She noticed it and smiled, and I felt myself flushing.

"If you please, Goddess," said Teldra, "you were telling us what we ought to do."

"Yes," she said. "I was. The problem is not only that we do not know everything; it is also that we do not all have the same interests. This makes the problem complicated."

"Simple things are never problems," I told her. "Unfortunate, maybe, but if it isn't complicated, it isn't really a problem."

The Goddess nodded. "Very good, Vlad; I didn't expect such wisdom from you."

I grunted and didn't tell her I was quoting my grandfather; I'd rather she stayed impressed.

"The Jenoine," said the Goddess, "have achieved access to your world on several occasions, most recently just a few years ago. We have beat off attacks on the Great Sea of Chaos, on the Halls of Judgment, on the Imperial Palace, and, lately, on Dzur Mountain. Their efforts have not been successful. I will share with you some of my thoughts."

I almost said, "Thank you so much," but caught myself.

She continued, "I cannot think why they are making this effort so recently after their last failure. Two possibilities come to mind: the attack on Dzur Mountain was part of something larger, and this is another piece of it; or they have had a sudden and unexpected opportunity."

"If they were looking for an opportunity, why didn't they make their move during the Interregnum?"

"What makes you think they didn't?" said Verra.

"Oh," I said.

We fell silent, then, in the Halls of Verra; and for the first time I wondered where we were. Up in a mountain? Beneath the ground? Floating in the air like Castle Black? On another world?

"First of all," said the Goddess suddenly, "you must free Morrolan and Aliera."

"No," I said. "That's just what they're expecting us to do."

"You are jesting," she said. "But are nevertheless correct."

I shrugged. "All right. How?"

She frowned. "Describe for me how they are held."

I did so, and she said, "Very well. I am familiar with the substance. Here is what you must do," and she told me.

"Oh," I said. "And that will work?"

"I believe so."

"You believe so? What if you're wrong?"

"Then perhaps the Jenoine won't kill you for trying."

"Great. All right. Say it works. What then?"

"If Morrolan cannot reach through to his portal, then it is

because the Jenoine are preventing him from doing so. You must force them to stop."

"Force them?"

"Yes."

"And just how do I go about doing that, or are you going to express confidence that I'll come up with something?"

"Come, my little Easterner. Have all your years in the Jhereg been wasted? Do you not even know how to threaten and intimidate?"

Just then, I felt about as intimidating as a norska. I said, "Usually, Goddess, in order to make a threat, one requires the power to carry it out. At least, one requires this in cases where the threat won't be believed."

"Very good, little one. You search for the general law that applies to the specific case. You have become a philosopher."

I hadn't known it was that easy.

She said, "Once Morrolan and Aliera are free, Pathfinder and Blackwand ought to prove a sufficiently intimidating threat, don't you think?"

"Okay," I said. "I mean, they intimidate me."

"Well, there you have it," said the Goddess.

"But don't tell them I said so. What do we do then? I mean, after I've released Morrolan and Aliera, threatened the Jenoine into letting us go, and let Morrolan bring us home. I mean, that's just enough to get us warmed up; you must have a whole plan after that."

"You will then return to Castle Black and await my orders."

I opened my mouth to object, and then shut it. Yes, if there was one place I'd be safe, it was Castle Black—there are reasons for that going back to ancient history, but I won't go into them now.

"All right," I said. "Sure. No problem. Except that the Jenoine will have anticipated this, won't they? And they'll have made plans for it."

"Yes," said the Goddess.

"So you're saying that this will all be a trap."

"Probably."

"But we're not worried about the trap, because we'll have a secret weapon prepared for them."

"What secret weapon is that, little one?"

"I was hoping you'd tell me."

"Your courage, wits, and skill at improvisation, little one. That is our secret weapon."

"Oh, good."

"And, my dear Easterner, do not make the mistake of thinking that I jest; I am quite serious."

"Oh, better."

"There is no question in my mind that you can do it."

"Oh, best."

"Do you doubt me, Taltos Vladimir?"

"Perpetually, Demon Goddess."

She gave a short barking laugh. "Go now. Make trouble for the Jenoine instead of for me, and I, I will do as I have been doing: watching over your family."

That was a low blow—there just wasn't anything I could say to it. I wanted to ask how my grandfather was doing, but I wouldn't give her the satisfaction.

"All right," I said.

"Lady Teldra," said the Goddess. "You may stay here, if you wish."

"Thank you, Goddess, but I will accompany my friend."

There was something so matter-of-fact about the way she called me her friend that it caught me up short.

"As you wish," said Verra. Then she frowned. "Of course, I'm not entirely certain how to get back to Morrolan and Aliera."

I sighed. "I suppose you could return us to Castle Black, and we could do it all over again."

"What exactly did you do, little one?"

So I told her that, and her eyes narrowed. "Let me see this chain," she said, so I let it fall into my hand and held it out to her, but instead of just lying there like it was supposed to, it twisted and curled in my hand until it was hanging in midair, my hand providing a base, coiled like a snake about to strike—in particular, about to strike Verra, who drew back with a sharp intake of breath. I almost let go of the chain, but didn't quite. It had never done that before.

"Goddess," I said. "I didn't—"

"I know," she said.

She gritted her teeth and said, "You have no idea, do you?"

"I—"

"Never mind."

She reached out and made motions in the air with her forefinger, and where her finger had been there was a dark line in the air, roughly the size and shape of a sword. It quickly filled in, and I was staring at the image of Pathfinder, hanging in the air in front of me.

"Go ahead," said the Goddess. "Do it."

I hated to sound like an idiot, but, "Do what?" I said.

"Make contact between your toy and Aliera's."

I swallowed. I wasn't entirely happy with the way my "toy" was behaving, but I couldn't think of any good way to get out of doing what she wanted. I started to take a step forward to bring the chain into contact with the image, but it was ahead of me—it reached out on its own, and seemed to grow longer. No, dammit, it did grow longer. The end of it wrapped around the image of Pathfinder's hilt. I braced myself for something to happen when they made contact, but I felt nothing. I concentrated most of my energy on trying to look as if I wasn't at all disturbed by any of this.

"All right," said the Demon Goddess. "I've found them."

Teldra came up next to me and put her hand on my right arm.

The Goddess gave an aimless gesture with her right hand, and a rectangular shape appeared to my left—like the frame of a door, glowing a sort of dull red, and just sitting in the middle of the room. The other side of it looked exactly like this side of it, just showing more of Verra's pasty-white hall.

"Step through," said the Goddess. "And good luck."

"Thank you so much," I said, and, Loiosh on my shoulder and Teldra at my side, walked through the doorway into nothing.

6

TRADING AT THE MARKET

The worst part of that means of transportation was that nothing happened. When I teleport, even without the waves of nausea, there is still the time-delay, and the twisting sense of movement in some inexplicable direction. And then there's Morrolan's window—however that works: you may not feel anything, but you at least see that you are stepping through something, from one place to another, and if there is no reason for those places to be near each other, well, you can use the window to fool your mind. But with this there wasn't even that: one instant I was standing before the Demon Goddess, in her Halls, wherever they were, and then everything was different—I weighed more, the air smelled funny, and the walls were different—that much I approved of. It's damned lucky I didn't have to do anything as I arrived, because I was in no condition to defend myself from a playful kitten.

And, on top of it, I had an instant of terror before I realized that I was, in fact, back in the same place I'd left Morrolan and Aliera, just in a different part of the room and facing a different direction; but turning around, I saw them, across the room and still attached to their wall. My heart rate returned to normal, leaving only the lingering question of what I'd have done if Verra had misplaced me.

Some questions demand answers; others one prefers to just put away and not think about.

Aliera and Morrolan were looking at me. I gave them a jaunty salute from across the room, and walked up to them.

Aliera said, "Well?"

"Well, what?"

"Vlad—"

"Oh. The Demon Goddess? I killed her, of course."

They both immediately glanced over my shoulder at Teldra, who must have given some sign, because Aliera gave me a disgusted look, while Morrolan said, "Your sense of humor, Vlad, leaves something—"

"Yeah, yeah," I said. "Save it. Have our hosts been back?"

"Not yet."

"Well, we should expect them any time."

Aliera gave Morrolan a glance that I interpreted as, "Look who's the strategist now?"

"And then we'll do what?" asked Morrolan.

"What happened with Verra?" asked Aliera.

I answered the second question. "The Goddess and I discussed politics," I said. "And, in fact, I failed to so much as draw this . . . thing."

It hung at my hip, that thing. I had avoided studying it, or really looking at it, but I did so now. It had a shiny black polished hilt, with a simple silver crosspiece, knobbed on the ends. The pommel was also silver: a round ball that would hurt like a bitch if I cracked it on someone's head. The hilt was a bit smaller than usual with Dragaeran weapons, but that was okay, because my hands are small, too. It was very smooth and cool to the touch, I remembered. The blade, which I hadn't yet seen, would be of that ugly, dull, grey-black metal that Morganti blades always have, and might have a blood-groove in it; I didn't take it out to look. It was long for a knife and short for a sword. Impractical in every way, and was probably not even balanced all that well, most likely being a bit blade-heavy. This, of course, was useful for chopping away in battle—military-issue swords are often blade-heavy—but chopping away in battle was not something I did much of.

And it was very strong. I could feel it, even through the sheath—a sort of presence in the back of my mind, whispering its hunger. It wanted to kill, and couldn't care a copper penny who or what it killed; as vicious as a Dragon in the heat of rage, as heartless as a Dzur on a spree; as cold as an Orca closing a deal.

I hated it.

I had used Morganti weapons before, but I had never liked them, never had any interest in being near them. Once, I had had to stand in a room with more of them than I could count; I still sometimes have bad dreams that I can trace to that experience. And this one really was damned powerful. I had taken it along only because I feared the Jenoine might be observing me, and if I didn't have it along, they might have stopped me from traveling to Verra. I no longer wanted it, but didn't feel comfortable just throwing it into a corner of the room, either. I mentally cursed it, and wished that it and all its siblings would get lost somewhere.

I turned my eyes and my mind away from the weapon at my hip, and back to Morrolan and Aliera, who shared some traits with the thing, but at least had a few redeeming virtues. I stood over them, and, in an effort to think about something else, returned to studying, yet again, the manacles, the chains, the spot where they joined the wall, and all the rest. The slightly sweet, slightly bitter taste of the air reminded me that I had to keep my breathing shallow.

"You're scowling," said Morrolan.

"Yeah," I said. "You do it better, but you've had longer to practice."

I knelt down for yet another, closer look, convinced that if I kept staring I'd see something. Years ago I wore an assassin's cloak with all sorts of goodies in it, including a bit of oil which might have allowed me to slide the manacles off. But I didn't carry those things anymore.

"It probably wouldn't have worked anyway without breaking her hand."

"Aliera," I said, "do you mind if I break your hand?"

"If that is the only way to get me out of these," she said, "no, I don't."

I hadn't expected that answer, although I should have.

"That goes for us both," said Morrolan.

Of course it does, I thought but didn't say.

I had killed people without examining them this closely. The manacles were fairly tight, but there was a bit of room between iron and skin.

"What are you thinking, Vlad?" said Morrolan.

"I'm meditating on helplessness as a way of life, and captivity as an expression of artistic fulfillment."

"What are you thinking, Vlad?" he repeated patiently.

I shrugged. "I'm wondering how much time we have. I assume the Jenoine know I've returned. But they never seem to be in much of a hurry. They don't behave the way I expect captors to behave. That confuses me."

Morrolan shrugged. "Have you ever been held captive?"

"Yes."

"I mean, have you ever been held captive by someone other than the Empire?"

"Yes," I said, and didn't elaborate. To avoid dwelling on a memory that wasn't entirely pleasant, featuring, as it did, far too much potato soup, I considered what the Goddess had told me. She had said I'd be able to . . . Okay, maybe. It's hard to argue with one's Goddess.

During this interval, I had continued to study wall, chains, manacles, and wrists; and, I suppose, I had continued to scowl.

"You have an idea, don't you?" said Aliera.

I grunted. "I don't know how much fun it will be for you."

"Do it," she said.

"It might be painful."

"Do it," said Morrolan.

"It might be dangerous."

"Do it," said Aliera.

"You may not survive."

"Do it," said Morrolan.

"It might mean the end of civilization as we know it."

Aliera gave me a disgusted look.

I shrugged. "Just wondering how far you'd go."

"Do it," he repeated.

I was convinced. I couldn't remember the last time I'd heard Morrolan and Aliera agree on anything; how could I fail to go along?

"If they agree, Boss, it must mean it's a bad idea."

"Probably true."

I pulled off my jerkin. The room was suddenly chilly. Morrolan and Aliera looked away from my bare chest, which seemed a bit funny. I took a knife from my belt, and began cutting strips of leather from what had been a shirt only seconds before, but was now merely a supply of fabric. Funny how quickly things can change, isn't it?

"What are you doing, Vlad?" asked Aliera.

I didn't answer. Not answering Aliera when she asks questions like that is one of the pleasures that I had missed since I'd been away.

When I had four strips cut off, I worked them around Aliera's and Morrolan's wrists, between manacle and skin. Aliera was easy; Morrolan had thicker wrists and it took me a while, but I managed. I probably hurt him a little while I was doing it, but, of course, he wouldn't give me the satisfaction of letting me know if I had.

When I was done, there turned out to be enough of a jerkin left to do some good, so I put the remainder back on; it made my stomach seem even colder than it had been.

I sat down cross-legged in front of and between Morrolan and Aliera. I really wanted this to work. Not only was it necessary to accomplish my mission and save the world or whatever the hell I was trying to save, and very possibly the only way for me to get out of this alive, but, more important, if I managed to rescue Aliera and Morrolan it would be something I would never let them forget; the pleasure would be almost too sweet. On the other hand, if I accidentally amputated both of their

hands, I'd feel bad. And that was, in fact, a possibility, even
though the Goddess hadn't seemed to doubt that I could pull it
off; hence the addition of the strips of leather; for one thing,
they were symbolically important as barriers, and symbols are
very important in witchcraft. And for another, well, maybe, if
all else failed, the leather would give their wrists some protection
from what I was about to do to them.

"Morrolan," I said, "give me your right hand. Aliera, your
left." They did so, clanking. Crazily, it entered my head to wonder what my friend Aibynn, who was a musician, would have
said about the note the chains gave off—I mention this as an
example of how one's mind works at such moments. Or maybe
as an example of how whacked my friend Aibynn is, I don't
know.

Teldra said, "Is there anything useful I can do?"

"No, but thanks for asking. Just stay out of my line of vision
so you don't distract me." She obligingly backed up a couple of
steps.

"*Okay, Loiosh. Help me out.*"

"*Sure you know what you're doing, Boss?*"

"*Of course not. Now help me out.*"

"*Okay.*"

I started to get light-headed again, and reminded myself to
take shallow breaths; that actually had seemed to help, now that
I thought about it. Getting dizzy in the middle of this spell
would not be in any of our best interest.

"*I'll keep track of your breathing, Boss.*"

"*Good. Let's start, then.*"

Connecting to them came easily; I knew them well by now.

"Energy" is a term that I can't define, at least as I'm using
it now: it is uncomfortably vague, and can be twisted into all
sorts of bizarre meanings. I've heard it used by sorcerers in a very
precise, no-nonsense way, as something they could measure and
portion out in precise increments; they even have a word for an
increment, though I can't recall it at the moment. I've also
heard "energy" used in casual conversation as a way of making

something vague and meaningless sound precise and full of significance: "I knew she was mine when I felt the energy pass between us." I've heard natural philosophers use the word much the way sorcerers do, and fools of various flavors use it the way lovers do.

But, whatever it means, energy lies at the heart of witchcraft.

When you have understood the piece of the world you want to change, and aligned your will with the world as it actually is, then and only then can you begin to change it; not to hit the point too hard, but I suppose this is true even in what one does with one's more mundane abilities. The difference is that, when practicing the art of the witch, one can actually *feel* the alignment, *feel* the changes taking place. I call this feeling energy, because I can't think of a better term for it; inside of myself, it comes with a quickening of the heartbeat, a sense of being, for a while, a little more alive, and a sureness of one's convictions. Outside of myself, well, stuff starts happening.

So, yes, connecting to Morrolan and Aliera came easily, and the energy began to build.

Every skill—certainly every physical skill—really consists of learning which muscles ought to be tense, and which relaxed, and when. Increased skill comes with strengthening certain muscles, and, even more, with achieving finer control of the particular muscles used. In the Eastern science of defense, for example, one must learn to keep the proper amount of tension in the thumb, fingers, and wrist, so that the point of the weapon stays in line: too little tension and the weapon can be knocked out of your hand, which is embarrassing; too much and one responds too slowly, which is equally embarrassing. In fact, to show you how picky it can be, your first step in actually mastering the art is when you get control of your ring finger. Later, one learns the proper amount of tension for the forward knee and the rear foot, and so on. It is a training of mind and of muscle, which in the novice are constantly at odds with each other, and in the expert are so strongly united that it is impossible to separate conscious decisions from those made by trained muscles. This state is what we talk about when we refer to "reflexes," which can tell you a lot about yourself.

I say this to make the obvious point that the art of the witch is very similar, except that the "muscles" in question all exist within the mind of the witch. With the simplest spells, all that is needed is the concentration of power; with the more complex spells, a subtlety and flexibility of mind is required. Typically, a witch will use all sort of tools, herbs, and amulets, because these help to focus the mind onto the required path; but when necessary, the swordsman forgets about proper form and technique, and takes the opening that desperation requires and opportunity presents.

Now that I think about it, most of my life has consisted of taking the opening that desperation required and opportunity presented.

I did without tools, herbs, and amulets; instead I built them as metaphors in my mind. I imagined the manacles as four burning pyres, with visible heat patterns emerging from them that I then turned into strips of cloth—not to be confused with the actual strips of leather, which were metaphorically walls keeping the heat from their arms, which were, oh, never mind. I took hold of the metaphorical cloth, not the real leather, and I pulled, throwing it carelessly to my metaphorical side. Fortunately, there was no one in the metaphorical way.

"*Loiosh, look to their wrists; make sure I don't hurt them.*"

"*Got it, Boss.*"

I pulled, and pulled, and it seemed as if I were pulling fabric from an endless spool. Somewhere far, far away, there was conversation; I imagine Morrolan or Aliera or both were making comments or asking questions, but none of it registered—fortunately for all of us. Morrolan, at least, ought to have understood that conversation was a bad idea; that I needed to concentrate or Bad Things would happen. This was a thought I had later; at the time, I was, well, concentrating.

Eventually it became harder to pull, and the flames from the

pyres were almost extinguished. I continued because I didn't
know just how far I'd have to go.

"*Boss, I can't keep it all away from them.*"

"*Are they being hurt?*"

"*A little.*"

"A little more, then," I said, and kept going, though it was
now pretty tough, and slow, and I realized I was becoming exhausted. It was what they call the point of diminishing returns
when they want to sound all fancy and technical; to me it was
a signal that I was about done.

"*Boss —*"

"*Okay,*" I said. "*That will have to do,*" and I pulled out of
my metaphors and symbols and use of energy as a precise vague-
ness, and came back to the world; whatever world it was, at any
rate.

". . . very cold," Aliera was saying. She and Morrolan looked
to be all right, so I just grunted at her, thought about using
Spellbreaker, but didn't know if it might have some additional
effects, and I didn't want any additional effects just then. I
pulled from behind my back a knife with a particularly strong,
heavy hilt. I flipped the knife, caught the blade, and raised it
over my head, then got a good hold on Aliera's left arm.

"What are you doing, Vlad?" asked Aliera as I brought the
knife down as hard as I could on the manacle, being careful not
to touch the bitter cold metal with my hand. It shattered with
a sound like broken pottery, rather than iron, and her wrist was
free. I repeated the process on her other arm and broke the hilt
of the knife as well as the manacle, leaving me staring at a blade
and a tang, with a bit of bone hilt still clinging to it. Oh, well.
I had more knives.

I pulled another and used it on Morrolan's right arm, breaking the knife's hilt and doing nothing to the manacle. I scowled
and pulled yet another, wishing I carried as many as I used to,
but this one turned out to do the job: there were now four
lengths of chain hanging from the wall. Morrolan and Aliera
stood up.

Hot damn.

"Good work, Vlad," said Morrolan, alternately rubbing each wrist with the opposite hand. "I'll take over now."

Figured.

I couldn't really object; I didn't have any energy to object with. It wasn't the sort of exhaustion you get when you've just run half a mile; my breathing was easy, and I was even remembering, with occasional nudges from Loiosh, to make my breaths shallow. And it wasn't sleepiness: I wanted to lie down, but I was nowhere near sleep. No, it was its own thing, the aftermath of a spell. A lethargy that I can only compare to the aftermath of sex, and that is too obvious an analogy, and has been used too often in books on witchcraft, for me to want to push it, so let's just say I was too tired to object.

Morrolan rubbed each wrist in turn, as if to warm them up, or to assure himself that they were still there. Then did something quickly with his hands, and he was suddenly holding a thin, black, polished stick in his right hand. It was about five feet long, had rounded ends, a few silver tracings on it, and I'd never seen it before.

"What is that?" I managed to say.

"My wizard's staff," said Morrolan. "I am a wizard. We have staves, you know. They go with the office."

"And I've never seen you use it before because . . . ?"

"In my own world, Blackwand has pretty much replaced it, but here, there are limits to what Blackwand can do, so I revert to my earlier skills and implements."

"I suppose it is immensely powerful and you can do all sorts of amazing things with it."

"Naturally."

"And you've had it with you all along?"

"I always have it with me."

"Then please explain to me why, by Verra's skinny ass, couldn't you have—?"

"While I was fettered," he said, "its power was nullified. The Jenoine are rather skilled in counterspells. Now I am unfettered, and, if there are no objections, I propose to use it. You don't mind, do you, Vlad? Or have you other questions?"

"If that means you intend to get us out of here," I said, "then I'm all for it. If you have some other plan, we'll have to negotiate."

"That's my plan," said Morrolan.

"Not, however, theirs," said Aliera, sweetly. I followed the direction of her gaze, and saw that the two Jenoine were back.

"So," I said to no one in particular. "I guess it comes down to negotiation after all."

I looked at the Jenoine, then glanced back, and saw, heard, and felt Pathfinder and Blackwand being drawn from their sheaths, Morrolan first transferring the staff to his left hand. Then he set the staff spinning; it seemed very light in his hand. I hoped he was doing more than showing off how good he was at making a stick spin.

The wizard's staff was spinning at his side, he held Blackwand in his other hand, and next to him stood Aliera, holding Pathfinder, with its point at the Jenoine's face. In the Jhereg, we call this "negotiating from a position of strength." I suspect the Dragons have a similar term.

I didn't have a position of strength. I didn't draw a weapon, because I wasn't sure what to draw, and because I was in no condition to wield a flyswatter.

Teldra barked, coughed, grumbled, and chattered at them; one of them replied similarly. I strained to guess the tone of the conversation, then gave it up as hopeless.

"*Any idea, Loiosh?*"

"*Sorry, Boss. Not a clue.*"

"*I hate sitting around while other people decide what's going to happen to me.*"

"*Well, you can always do something stupid.*"

"*No, I think I'm over that, for the moment.*"

"*Note down the date.*"

"*Oh, shut up.*"

Morrolan and Aliera took a step toward the Jenoine; Teldra kept talking.

The big, ugly thing just stood there, not appearing to notice the Great Weapons, much less the wizard's staff, or the cold-blooded, highly skilled Easterner assassin who was bravely cowering next to the Dragonlords.

"Do that thing's eyes remind you of something, Boss?"

"Yes, Loiosh. Fish eyes. Is it important?"

"Probably not."

From my position, I couldn't see Morrolan's face, but I had a partial view of Aliera's: there was a gleam in her eye, and a sort of twisted grin on her lip. Morrolan, I was sure, was scowling. He scowled well. Aliera grinned, Morrolan scowled, and I sneered. There you have it.

They closed with the Jenoine, and I suddenly thought of the Morganti dagger in my belt. Well, I could join them. I mean, it wasn't a Great Weapon, but it was a Pretty Good Weapon. I might do some good. I might be able to help. I might prefer to cower as far back in a corner as I could.

"Good plan, Boss. Let's go with it."

"Sold," I told him. I managed to stand up, then took a step backward, stopped, drew the Morganti dagger, and went up to stand next to Morrolan.

"Boss—"

This had happened to me before—going forward into danger that wasn't at all my type of danger, when I knew I ought to go back, and I hadn't then understood why I did it, and I didn't know this time. Bugger. The Morganti dagger seemed alive in my hand. Yes, it was a dull, grey color. Yes, it did have a blood-groove. It was a narrow blade, very light and useful-feeling in my hand, about eighteen inches long, and not nearly as blade-heavy as I'd suspected it would be. It was also hungry, and, as I'd suspected, it was very powerful; I felt it and hated it.

And worried about it, as well. The Jenoine had given it to me, and now I was going to use it against them. Wouldn't they have thought of that? Was that what they wanted me to do?

Could it hurt them, in any case? According to Verra, no it couldn't. But if not, then I didn't have anything that could.

The Jenoine took a step forward, and extended its left hand; I felt the sick tumble in my stomach that accompanies the realization that action, and a sort of action I hate, is now inevitable: The *maybes* had dissolved into the dust, the *I hopes* had taken wing, the alternatives had narrowed to one, which was the same as vanishing to none at all—I've never understood the arithmetic of that.

All right, then. If Morrolan could fight with two weapons at once, so could I; I let Spellbreaker fall into my left hand.

"Tell it," said Morrolan, still spinning his staff, "that it will permit us to leave at once, or we shall destroy it."

Teldra said, "Lord, that's what I've been telling her, though I have perhaps phrased it differently."

"And?"

"She is considering her options."

"How rational," said Aliera.

"Was Aliera being ironic, Boss? Or was that an insult?"

"We'll probably never know, Loiosh."

"Vlad," said Morrolan. "I can feel the gate. Are you ready to go through it?"

"Sure," I said. "But now, what's the plan. Are we trying to escape, or do we want to kill this thing?"

The thing we were talking about kept looking at us; I had the impression it was holding itself ready for action, and that it didn't seem terribly worried.

"Kill it," said Aliera, and, at the same time, Morrolan said, "If we can get out cleanly, we should."

"I'm with you, Morrolan."

Aliera sniffed disdainfully.

Then things happened too fast for me to follow—it was one of those. I can't tell you who attacked first, or what form the attack took. I can't tell if the Jenoine's response was physical, magical, or some combination. I only know that, suddenly, everyone was moving, and I was lost in the combinations of limb, steel, and spell. I know that I was looking for an opening to use the Morganti dagger I held, and I know that I was trying to keep Spellbreaker in between me and anything nasty that it might send at me, and I know that I failed miserably at both efforts.

I can't tell you what Morrolan, Aliera, and Teldra were up to, but my part in the affair was mercifully brief—I lost consciousness within a matter of seconds. And, while I couldn't be sure what their situation was after it was over, at least mine was easily and readily understood when I awoke: I was manacled to the wall in almost exactly the same spot Aliera had occupied before. Teldra was next to me, unconscious, blood trailing down from the corner of her dainty mouth.

Well, Morrolan and Aliera were now free, in exchange for an Issola seneschal and an Easterner ex-assassin. A neat two-for-two swap. I wondered who had come out ahead on the trade. I was pretty sure it wasn't me.

7

Asking for and Receiving Assistance

"*Think you can wake her up, Boss?*"

"Don't know, Loiosh. Any reason why I should?"

"*Uh . . . I'll get back to you on that. Think you can break these manacles the way you broke the other ones?*"

I hefted them . . . they were lighter than they seemed.

"I hate repeating a trick," I told him. "But I'm willing to make an exception this time."

"*That's big of you, Boss.*"

"But I'm going to wait, if you don't mind; I don't think I could manage a sleep spell right now."

While I waited and recovered, I did a quick check, and found to my surprise that the Jenoine had left me all my weapons. Why would they do that? The Morganti weapon was lying on the floor, no doubt right where it had fallen; they hadn't even taken it. Why would they capture me, but leave me all my weapons? They weren't supposed to do that. Maybe I should get them a copy of the rules.

Teldra stirred next to me.

"Good morning," I told her.

She squeezed her eyes shut without ever opening them, then did so again, and again. I waited.

"Any idea what that thing did to me, Loiosh? Why I lost consciousness?"

"*No, Boss. It happened too fast. I didn't notice it even looking at you—you just went down.*"

I looked at Teldra again; she was working on becoming conscious, but it was taking a while.

"Okay, let's make a note not to underestimate the Jenoine."

"Right, Boss."

I leaned my head back, started to take a deep breath, and caught myself. I hate it when I need to take a deep breath but I can't—I'd have to find a different psychological crutch.

I caught an echo of my familiar's psychic snicker.

"You aren't helping any."

"What happened?" said Teldra.

"To begin with," I said, "the world was created from the seeds of amorphia spread from the droppings of a giant . . . no, I guess you aren't awake enough to appreciate my wit. I don't know what happened, Teldra. We're right where Morrolan and Aliera were, but I'm assuming our friends got away. Well, I don't know; maybe I shouldn't assume that. I hope they got away. I don't know. Tough bastards, those guys."

She chuckled. "Morrolan and Aliera, or the Jenoine?"

"Well, yeah."

Teldra nodded.

"How do you feel?" I asked her.

She stared at me. I recognized the look; I'd been on the other side of it often enough.

"Sorry," I said. "Stupid question."

She flashed me a Lady Teldra smile.

"It seems she's all right, Boss."

"Guess so."

Teldra seemed about to speak, but I closed my eyes and rested my head against the wall behind me, and she held her peace. The wall was smoother than it looked. I relaxed, prepared myself, and considered what I was about to do. After several minutes, Teldra said, "You're going to do something, aren't you?"

"Eventually."

"Can I help?"

I stirred, opened my eyes, looked at her. "Any training in witchcraft?"

She shook her head.

"Then I'm afraid not," I said.

I closed my eyes again and muttered, "Trágya."

"Legalább," she agreed.

My head snapped around. "You speak Fenarian?"

"Why yes," she said.

I grunted, wondering why I was surprised. "How many languages do you speak, Teldra?"

"Several," she said. "And you, Vlad?"

I shook my head. "None well. A bit of Fenarian. A smattering of a few other Eastern languages. But not enough to actually think in any of them—I always have to translate in my head."

"I see."

"How do you do that? How do you learn to think in another language?"

"Hmmm. It isn't an all or nothing thing, Vlad. You say you don't think in Fenarian, but what would you say if I said, Köszönöm?"

"Szivesen."

"Well?"

"Well, what?"

"Why did you say that?"

"You said, 'Thank you'; I said, 'You're welcome.'"

"But did you make that translation in your head, or was it automatic?"

"Ah. I see." I thought about that. "Okay, you're right. It was automatic."

"That's the beginning of thinking in the language."

"Like whenever I make a comment, Boss, and you say—"

"Shut up, Loiosh."

"Okay," I said. "You make a good point. But if I've got the basics, the rest is awful slow to follow."

"But it will get there if you keep speaking it. It starts with rote responses, such as thank you and you're welcome."

"Basic courtesy," I said. "Maybe all languages have rote responses for those: hello, how are you, that sort of thing. I wonder."

"They do," said Teldra.

"Are you sure?"

"The languages without courtesy built into them didn't survive long enough for us to remember them. Because, of course—"

"Yes," I said. "I see."

I pondered this linguistic profundity for a moment.

I considered what I had just done, and was soon going to do again. "Is witchcraft a language?"

"Hmmm. I don't know. I should imagine it is. I know that sorcery is."

"Witchcraft," I said, "does not have courtesy built into it."

She laughed. "All right. If we're counting, you've scored a point. If we are going to call those languages, and we might as well, they don't have built-in courtesy." She frowned suddenly. "Unless we consider . . . no, that's too far-fetched."

I didn't want to encourage her to go wherever she had been about to go, so I said, "How did you and Morrolan meet, anyway? If you don't mind my asking."

"It was out East," said Teldra. "During the Interregnum, in a village whose name translated to 'Blackchapel.' This was before he knew who he was, and—"

"Before he knew who he was?"

"Before he knew he was human."

I blinked. "I think you're going to have to explain that."

"I didn't realize you didn't know," said Teldra. "Certainly, it is no secret."

"All right."

"The Lord Morrolan was brought to the East, beyond his ancestral homelands, as an infant, just around the time of Adron's Disaster. His parents didn't survive, and so he was raised by Easterners. He grew up thinking he was simply an extraordinarily tall Easterner."

"You're kidding!"

"No, my lord."

"Well I'll be—really? He thought he was human? I mean, Easterner?"

She nodded.

I shook my head. "Amazing."

"Yes."

"Most extraordinarily tall," I reflected. "How did he find out?"

"It couldn't be concealed forever," she said. "In any case, I was also in the East, and of much the same age. We met at about the time he was completing his pact with Verra, in which I was able to be of some service to him, and I was also of some help when he was gathering his Circle of Witches."

I nodded. I knew this circle existed—they occupied the East Tower, but I had never had occasion to go there, and still didn't know exactly what he used them for. But, no doubt, I would never know all there was to know about Morrolan.

I shook my head, trying to get used to the idea of Morrolan being raised as an Easterner.

"Where in the East was he?"

"There are—or, rather, were—a series of small kingdoms near Lake Nivaper, just south of the Hookjaw Mountains."

"Yes, I know them. They speak Fenarian in some of them."

She nodded. "His name at the time was Fenarian: Sötétcsil-leg. 'Morrolan' is just the same thing, rendered into the ancient tongue of the Dragon."

"Amazing," I said. "All right, so you helped him sacrifice villages of Easterners to the Demon Goddess. Then what?"

She smiled. "That was later, and they were Dragaeran villages. Eventually, he returned to reclaim his ancestral homeland, and he was gracious enough to give me residence. I was poor, of course, and had nowhere else to go. I remain very grateful to him."

I nodded, wondering what she was leaving out. Most likely, anything that was to her credit or Morrolan's discredit. She was like that. It sometimes made me a little uncomfortable to never know exactly what she was thinking, but, on the other hand, it was nice to know that there was at least one being in the world who wouldn't say anything nasty about me.

"You're awful sensitive for an assassin, Boss."

"You've said that before, Loiosh."

We returned to silence; I waited to recover and hoped I'd have time to do so; in the meantime my mind wandered, starting with the rather remarkable revelations about Morrolan and proceeding from there. I don't remember most of what I thought about—the sort of flitting, random thoughts that can only just barely be called thinking. But then I did eventually have a real, true thought, and it brought me up so sharply that it burst out of my mouth before my brain had entirely finished processing it: "Aw nuts. If Morrolan and Aliera did escape, I'll bet they're going to want to rescue us."

"Of course," said Teldra.

"Ready to start, Loiosh?"

"Boss—"

"I'll be fine."

"Boss—"

"If I'm still chained to this wall when Morrolan and Aliera show up, I'll almost certainly die of shame. The chances of messing up the spell are much less."

I got the impression Loiosh wasn't convinced. I wasn't either.

"Teldra," I said. "I've changed my mind. You can help."

"Yes?"

"You saw what I did with the knives?"

"Yes."

"Good," I said, and reached to hand her some—and only then realized that the Spellbreaker was back around my wrist. I stopped, hand in midair, and looked at Teldra.

"What is it, Vlad?"

"Loiosh," I said, *"how did it get back there? Last I remember, it was in my hand, and I was waving it around like an idiot. I can't*

believe the Jenoine not only let me keep it, but were kind enough to put it back around my wrist for me."

"They didn't, Boss."

"Talk."

"It sort of slithered over to you, and, uh, it kind of crawled up your arm."

"On its own?"

" 'Fraid so, Boss."

Well. Wasn't *that* interesting?

I handed Teldra my last three daggers, pulling them out of various places. I hoped they would be enough—I used to carry a lot more.

"You know what to do?"

"I know what to do, but not when to do it."

"I'll try to say something. If I seem to lose consciousness, that would be a good time. Oh, give me one back for a second, I need to expose some more skin first."

She didn't ask, and I didn't explain; I just cut away four more strips from my jerkin. The air was even colder with still more of my belly exposed. I handed two of the strips to Teldra, asking her if she knew what to do with them. She nodded. She didn't appear at all nervous, which I attribute to acting ability, probably inherited; stupidity would be the only other possible explanation, and I didn't think she was stupid.

When we had managed to get the leather between the manacles and our wrists, she nodded at me, as if signaling that she was ready. I gave her back the last knife. I was now as close to unarmed as I'd been in some time. My rapier—

"Where is my rapier?" I said.

"Across the room, I think."

"How did that happen?"

"I don't know."

I considered the matter further, saying aloud, "If they know how we got out the last time, they might have done something to prevent this from working."

"I know," said Teldra.

"But they keep not behaving the way captors are supposed to."

"They probably weren't raised on the right sorts of bedtime stories and songs."

"And bad theater," I agreed. "But I'm starting to think they have a whole other plan in mind."

"What sort of plan?"

"I'm not sure," I said, which was not an outright lie, at any rate. "All right, then. Let's try it."

She said, "Vlad, do you think we're doing what they want us to?"

I paused, then sighed. "I wish I knew. Are you willing to go through with it anyway?"

She smiled. "Of course. It would be rude not to," proving that even Issolas are capable of self-directed irony. This, while maybe not an important discovery, was, somehow, a pleasing one.

"Let's do it, then."

She nodded. I held out my hand, and she took it; her hand was dry and cool.

I began.

You don't need to hear about it again, do you? I knew better than to let my fear interfere with what I had to do. Loiosh was his usual steady self, and, to make a long story short, I turned out to be sufficiently rested not to destroy myself.

The big difference between doing it on someone else and doing it on myself was that the coldness from my wrists became more and more insistent, and there was an awareness somewhere deep inside me that I could be seriously hurting myself. I had to trust Loiosh.

I was used to trusting Loiosh; over the years, I've gotten pretty good at it.

I concentrated, and pulled at imaginary skeins of fabric until it rolled over me, covered me, and I felt like I was going to drown in it; the chill on my wrists beginning to feel like heat, and insisting more and more on my attention; but I still had a

bit left in me when the whole thing was shattered—quite literally—and I was pulled back to a hazy sort of half consciousness, vaguely pleased that my wrists were now free, noting that
Teldra's were as well, and hoping that I wouldn't have to do
anything strenuous like moving for at least a year or so.

She said something, but I didn't quite catch it. I tried to
ask her to repeat it, but that, too, was beyond me.

In case you've missed it, I was more than a little exhausted.
I closed my eyes, leaned against the wall, and concentrated on
keeping my breathing even and shallow.

"I imagine," I said after a while, "they ought to be showing
up any second."

"The Jenoine?" asked Teldra. "Or our friends?"

"Both, I should imagine. At the same time, presumably.
That's how it ought to work out."

*"You're just saying that, Boss, because you know if you say it
it won't happen that way."*

"I'm an Easterner, chum. I can be superstitious if I want to."

I rested, and recovered, and felt hungry. I found some more
dried gammon in my pouch and offered some to Teldra, who
gratefully accepted; then I watched her attempt to eat it daintily.
She succeeded. I'd have been more astonished if I could have
spared the energy for astonishment.

"Well," I said, "the longer it takes them—any of them—to
show up, the better for us."

She nodded, and continued being dainty with dried gammon.

I wondered why she didn't make me feel rude and uncouth,
but I suppose that was part of her talent. Or magic. You can
always say it's magic if you don't understand it; and, who knows,
you might be right.

While we stayed there—free of the chains but unable to
move (in my case, unable to move for a number of reasons)—
my imagination took flight. I wondered what Morrolan and Aliera were doing. They must be with Sethra, talking things over,
making plans. Had they made contact with Verra? Was she go-

ing to take an active role in this? How about the Necromancer?

I pictured the lot of them, sitting in the library at Castle Black, or in one of the sitting rooms at Dzur Mountain, or in Verra's Hall; planning, scheming, debating.

Or maybe they'd all just gone and decided to take a nap, figuring, hey, what's one Issola and one Easterner? Maybe they'd just leave us here.

Or maybe they were eating, the bastards.

Meanwhile, in this structure, or near it, perhaps the Jenoine were coming up with their own schemes, or chuckling about how well this one had worked (did Jenoine chuckle? I couldn't imagine it). Perhaps they, too, had forgotten us. Perhaps, in the grand scheme of things, we didn't matter. Verra had as much as told me that I mattered because she was going to make me matter. I had mixed feelings about this.

Eventually, various needs brought me to my feet; I carried one of the chamber pots into a corner of the place and relieved myself, feeling like a drunk who's just staggered out of Coriaton's Public House. Then I made it back, drank some water, and waited.

Time dragged, and my imagination soared, and I considered my Fate. Teldra remained silent, perhaps aware of my thoughts and not wishing to disturb them, or perhaps she was busy with her own thoughts. Even Loiosh remained still.

But I considered who I was, and whether, when all was said and done, I would make a difference in the world. I had rarely had such thoughts—lately I hadn't had time for them, and before that they had never occurred to me.

But had Fate included me in its plans?

Did I even believe in Fate?

"Teldra, do you believe in Fate?"

My words shattered the stillness, like a sorcerous explosion, but she hardly blinked.

She said, "In a sense."

"Yes?"

"I believe in paths and choices. I don't believe in an inescapable fate, but I believe we are each given several possible directions, and sometimes we choose one without being aware of having made the choice."

I nodded. "I think I understand."

"But at other times, we know. Sometimes you realize you cannot stand still, and to move forward, or move back, or move to the side will set you on a new path."

"Does it matter to you if you make a difference in the world?"

"I do make a difference, Lord Taltos."

"Vlad."

"Very well. Vlad. I make a difference whether I wish to or not. I hope to make a good difference, if only in a small way."

"I wonder," I said. "I wonder whether a small way is enough for me. And I wonder if a big way is too much."

"Hmmm. What brought this up, if I may ask, Vlad?"

"I don't know. Too much time on my hands, boredom, and remembering my conversation with Verra."

"What about your conversation with Verra?"

"What she said about me being a tool."

"Oh," said Lady Teldra. "There is another thing about the Goddess."

"Yes?"

"Sometimes, when she speaks to us, we do not hear the same thing."

"I don't understand."

"It has been said that she speaks in words we can each understand, and that we will each understand her in our own way."

"Isn't that true of everyone?"

"Perhaps. But I didn't hear anything about you being a tool; I heard . . . well, it doesn't matter what I heard."

"Hmmmm," I said wisely, and didn't press the matter, though I wanted to badly. "I think," I said, "that I may be approaching one of those decision points you were talking about."

"Maybe," she said. "But I suspect, my lord, that you made

your decision some time ago, and are just now beginning to understand its significance."

I let that one float around for a bit, then felt myself snarling. "All right, there's only so much of this I can take. I need to be doing something."

"You're feeling better, then?"

I considered, then said, "Yes, in fact, I am."

"Well then," said Teldra, "I am ready. But I don't know what we ought to be doing."

"It's not like I have a plan or anything," I said. "But it seems to me that, if we aren't going to just wait for our friends or our enemies, we should see if we can get out of this room."

"But then, will they be able to find us? Our friends, I mean."

"I hope so." I shrugged. "One would think that they could reach us psychically, if they were close enough."

I stood up, moving slowly and carefully, and walked across the room to where my rapier lay, all unnoticed and neglected. I checked it—it was fine. I returned it to my sheath. Then I walked over to the Morganti dagger. I thought for a while, made a decision, then hesitated because I didn't want to, then made myself pick it up and put it into its sheath.

"I don't see any doors," said Teldra.

"Of course not," I told her. "That would make everything too easy."

I stretched a bit—pleased to be up and around and walking. Teldra walked next to me, Loiosh on my shoulder, a rapier at my hip, a very strong Morganti dagger in a sheath next to it, Spellbreaker around my wrist, and my remaining couple of daggers concealed about my person. I felt ready for anything, as long as it wasn't too threatening.

We walked around the big, almost empty room, looking at walls, floor, and ceiling. It took a fair bit of time, but I didn't mind; I was pretty much recovered—though I felt generally sore and rather tired, and Loiosh had to keep reminding me to take shallow breaths. Except for the empty shelves placed here and there, seemingly at random, there wasn't much to see. Everything was very plain, flat, featureless—depressing.

Eventually we made it back to the place where we had been shackled. I said, "There's no way out."

Teldra nodded.

"Which answers the question about whether the Jenoine have sorcery, I imagine."

"Sorcery," agreed Teldra, "or, at any rate, something very much like it. But I thought that had been answered when they first appeared."

"Yeah. Or when they knocked me out. Okay. So, now what?"

"I don't know."

She didn't say, "Coming up with plans is your job," but I had the feeling she was thinking it. I didn't scowl, but she probably had the feeling I wanted to.

I said, "If I felt able to perform a spell, I might test the solidity of the wall." I pushed against the nearest wall, demonstrating, then said, "Hmmmm."

"What?" She pushed against it too. "What is it, Vlad? It feels like a wall."

"Yes, but what if it isn't everywhere?"

"Illusory walls?"

"Maybe," I said. "But I was thinking real walls, but a doorway made to look like a section of wall."

"Oh. Yes, that would be possible."

"You go that way, I'll go this way."

She nodded agreement, and we went around the room, pushing at the walls everywhere. If they were illusion, the illusion included the tactile, and didn't give when pushed.

"So much for that," I said, when we were back to where we had started.

She nodded. "Next idea?"

"You sure it isn't your turn?"

Her smile flicked on and off.

"You know, Boss, they don't actually have to have a doorway at all."

"I know, I know. But that's what they say about the keep of an Athyra wizard. And we know better."

"Just because it wasn't true—"

"I know, Loiosh. Now shut up and let me think."

He refrained from any cracks about that. I have come to appreciate the small blessings in life.

I considered matters for a bit, then said, "All right—if we're going to test it, we're going to test it."

Teldra gave me a look of inquiry. I let Spellbreaker fall into my hand. I could see Teldra wanting to ask what I was up to, but she didn't, and I didn't volunteer the information—if I was going to look ridiculous, at least I didn't have to explain why.

I struck Spellbreaker against the wall above where we had been chained up. It gave off a dull ringing sound.

"Vlad?"

"Get used to that sound, Teldra."

"Very well," she said.

I took a step to the right, and struck the wall again. It sounded just the same. I took another step, and another, and so on.

It was a big room, and it took a while, but I just told myself I was killing time until either the Jenoine reappeared, or Morrolan and Aliera showed up to rescue us, or something else happened.

Move a step—whap. Move a step—whap. Move a step—and then, when I found it, I almost missed it anyway. I was about a third of the way from where I started when I struck the wall, and started to move past it, but noticed that Spellbreaker had changed again. It was shorter, the links smaller. I stopped, looked at it, then at the spot of blank wall I was facing.

I struck the wall again, and a light tingle went up my arm, and I was looking at a doorway. Not even a door: rather a large stonework arch, maybe twelve feet high at its top, and big enough for four of me to walk past arm in arm. It was just there, as if to say, "What took you so long?"

I glanced back at Lady Teldra, who had been walking beside me to keep me company.

"Yes," she said. "I see it, too."

I not only saw it, but I felt the wind through it. Through it, mostly what we could see was darkness, except for the points of light in the sky.

"Stars," said Lady Teldra.

"I know them," I said. "They have them in the East, too."

"I know," she said. "I remember."

"I don't know exactly what they are; some say the homes of the gods."

"Some say each is a world," said Teldra. "That when we go through a necromantic gate, we are stepping onto one of those points of light, from which we could look back and see our own world as a point of light. I like that notion."

"I'm not entirely certain that I do," I said. "I've never liked stepping into the unknown."

She refrained from any of the obvious observations she could have made to that, merely falling silent and waiting with me. Even as I watched, I realized that it was becoming brighter; it was dawn wherever we were, and I started to be able to make out features of the landscape.

It took several long moments before I was able to bring myself to step through the archway, toward the strange world, the emptiness, and the stars of the heavens.

8

FISHING ETIQUETTE

Here's a quick story for you, before we go any further:

In the earliest days of the World, Darkness mated with Chaos and produced three daughters. The first was Night, the second was Pain, and the third was Magic. Now Chaos went on and mated with the Sky, producing a son who was Evil. One day, Evil, being jealous of his stepsisters, captured Magic and took her away to his secret fortress beyond the World. But Magic called upon her Mother, Darkness, who heard her cries, and, seeing everything, saw what Evil had done.

Darkness then summoned Chaos and said, "Look what your son has done! He has taken Magic from the World."

Chaos then turned on his son, Evil, and cast him out, and rescued Magic, restoring her to the World. Then Evil cried out, saying that he repented his act, and praying that his father not abandon him. Chaos could not turn his heart from his only son, so he relented and permitted Evil into the world as well, but from that moment on, Magic has mistrusted Evil, though Evil still pursues Magic; and Darkness watches over them both, so that wherever you find Evil, you will find Darkness there, watching; and Chaos will sometimes be found in the aid of Magic, and sometimes in the aid of Evil.

Do you like it? It is an old story of my people, and there are some who believe it literally. I myself think there are elements of truth in it, because another name for Magic is Verra, the Demon Goddess, and, who knows, perhaps the Jenoine really are Evil. Beyond that, I don't care to venture; if there is a personification of Darkness, not to mention Chaos, then I don't want to know about it.

So here we were, maybe in the power of Evil; at least on their world, and maybe Magic would help us, and I was very much afraid that, if the Jenoine didn't get me, I'd trip over my own metaphors and break my neck.

These were my thoughts, then, as we stepped out of the door, and I don't know how it was for Teldra, but for me there was a shock: the sudden realization that the entire world was not that one room of that one building.

"Anything or anyone, Loiosh?"

"Not as far as I can tell, Boss."

We walked twenty-five or thirty feet away from it, and looked back; I was half expecting it to have vanished, but it was still there, the outside looking quite a bit like the inside, except that the surface was rougher—it seemed to be just chunks of rock stuck together. A closer look indicated an odd shape to the structure—it was hard to tell from this close, but it seemed that it had an angle to it; that it wasn't quite straight up, and there were bits of projections sticking out. Was this significant of anything? Stupid question. What was significant and what wasn't with these beings?

I turned my attention to the landscape, and eventually thought of Dzur Mountain.

There was nothing there that actually looked like Dzur Mountain, mind you, but—

Okay. A stream, maybe fifty or sixty feet wide, cut across and dominated the landscape, flowing diagonally toward me from my right to my left, about a hundred yards away at its nearest point; a few spindly trees with stubby branches and massive leaves all along their lengths dotted the banks on both sides, and what seemed to be a stonework bridge appeared not far away. To my right were a couple of low hills, all brown and rocky, and to my left the ground was flat but sloping gently down, maybe dipping to meet the stream, maybe not. And above it all (quite literally) was this terrible, bright object burning

down on everything. I'm not trying to be mysterious—I had
been to the East, and I knew damned well that it was a Furnace,
just as we had in the Empire, only here, as out East (and a few
places in the far West), it wasn't hidden by a constant overcast.
But I had forgotten how painfully bright it was, and how dark
were the shadows it caused when it met anything else. It was
low in the sky, a little to my left as I stepped out of the door,
and, among other things, it highlighted everything else, including the few white puffy bits of overcast in a sky that was otherwise as blue as the sky above Fenario, giving me a very strange
feeling of homesickness that juxtaposed with the harsh certainty
that I was in a world that, perhaps, no other human had ever
set foot on before.

So Teldra and I studied all of this, and that's when I thought
of Dzur Mountain. It was a very nice mix of natural elements,
here, and I'd swear someone had crafted it. I don't know why—
I'm not sure what the indications were; but it looked for all the
world like someone had sat down and said, "Okay, the river runs
this way, straight, then we'll put a curve in here. How 'bout a
couple of hills?" and like that.

"You're right," said Teldra.

I looked at her. "I beg your pardon?"

"Dzur Mountain," she said.

"Oh. I hadn't realized I'd spoken out loud."

"You muttered it under your breath."

"Hmmm." I wondered where I'd developed the habit of doing that? Probably from being alone so much of the time. I was
going to have to watch out for that; it wasn't a good habit.

"Nothing lives," murmured Teldra.

I started to ask what she meant—I mean, there was grass,
and there were trees and such. Then realized: I saw no birds in
the air, no small animals hopping around, much less big ones;
looking at my feet, I didn't even see any insects. "You're right,"
I said. "We seem to be the only living things here."

"Oh," she said, smiling. "That time I did it."

My hand strayed to my rapier, and I suddenly had the feeling that this entire world—everything that had happened since walking through Morrolan's window—was a massive illusion; was one of those elaborate living dreams, such as I had encountered in the Paths of the Dead.

"It's real enough, Boss."

"Are you sure?"

"I'm sure. If there is a glamour, it's to conceal something, not to alter the appearance of what we're seeing."

"That's sort of a fine distinction, chum."

"I know," he told me.

Well, that was part of Loiosh's job, so I had to trust him. Besides: if he was wrong, and it was all an elaborate dream like the ones in the Paths, well, there had been no way out of those except to treat them as real and work through them.

But the lack of critters was hard to get used to.

"What do you think, Teldra? Was this whole area fabricated?"

"Maybe, Vlad. Maybe the whole world."

"No," I said. "I know it wasn't the whole world."

"Oh?" she said. "How can you tell?"

"Because if they can do that, we don't have a chance against them."

She laughed. "Ah. I see. I'm not familiar with that logic."

I shrugged. "Actually, I'm not kidding. That's one thing I learned in the course of my long and checkered career. If your only chance of living through something is if your enemy isn't a sorcerer, or doesn't have a spare dagger, or can't jump an eleven-foot crevasse, then you assume your enemy isn't a sorcerer, or doesn't have a spare dagger, or can't jump an eleven-foot crevasse."

"Hmmmm," said Teldra. "I see. It makes a very practical sort of sense."

"Yes," I said, involuntarily remembering the guy who could jump an eleven-foot crevasse, much to my disgust—but I survived that one anyway, because he turned out to be wearing the wrong kind of boots. Long story; never mind.

There was a bit of a breeze coming from my left; not too strong, just enough to tickle the back of the neck. It brought no smells except the sort of sweet scent that seemed to be part of the air here. This reminded me, again, to keep my breathing even and shallow.

"Well," I said, "Teldra, you must have studied all the old songs and stories, and you must be better read in history than I am, and since I almost never attend the theater, you must attend more often than I do."

"Perhaps," she said.

"Well then? What does one typically do in a situation like this?"

Teldra looked at me.

"I mean, usually when one finds oneself on an entirely different world, barely able to breathe, surrounded by a bizarre environment, beset with enemies with the strength of gods, and with no way home—what are the usual steps?"

She barely cracked a smile.

"Usually," she said, "one calls for help of one's patron god, who then assigns one an impossible task in exchange for minimal aid, which aid turns out to be ironically fatal. Or else one discovers a powerful artifact of unknown properties, which, upon use, proves to take over one's soul, so that, after the rescue, one kills one's beloved."

"I see. Well, now you know why I almost never attend the theater."

Teldra supplied the obligatory chuckle and I looked out once more at the world around us—suddenly taken by the fear that Morrolan and Aliera would not come, and the Jenoine would not come, and we would find no way out; that we would remain here for the rest of our days. Which days, now that I thought of it, wouldn't be long if we didn't figure out how we were going to eat. But I knew this fear was groundless. Whatever Morrolan had done in the past, I knew that he would never stop trying to rescue us as long as he was alive. And, of course, things being as they were, death might not manage to stop him either.

I sighed.

"*You know, Loiosh, if anyone had told me yesterday at this time that thirty hours later I would have rescued Morrolan and Aliera, nearly killed the Demon Goddess, and found myself trapped in a prison the size of the world, unable to decide if I was hoping to be saved or was hoping not to be saved, I'd have said, 'Yeah, sounds about right.' *"

"*You probably would have, Boss.*"

"*I think this says something about my life choices.*"

"*Uh huh.*"

I looked around at the world, noticing the perfection of the stream, the hills, the mountains—the general sense that everything had been planned and crafted. I had the sudden irrational (and, I'm sure, wrong) notion that this little part of the world was all there was—that everywhere out of sight was just sort of grey and unfinished; and I was also again reminded of the Paths of the Dead, though I'm not sure why.

Teldra and I began walking. The ground was soft and springy, and we soon reached the banks of the stream, which were only two or three feet above the flow. I leaned over and stared into it, watching it. It hardly seemed to be moving, yet occasionally the crests would break into diminutive whitecaps. It was neither blue nor green nor red, as is most of the water I've seen, but sort of an olive; I could not imagine what accounted for this. I couldn't see the bottom, but it seemed neither shallow nor dirty.

"*What is it, Boss?*"

"This water."

"*What about it?*"

"I don't know. It's no more natural than the rest of this place, but . . . it isn't perfect."

He said nothing; I continued studying it. Teldra remained a foot or two behind me, silent, the soul of patience. I stooped, then knelt. I reached out toward the water, then changed my mind, holding my hand motionless. Then I—how shall I put this—extended my senses. It's hard to describe; it's sort of like the difference between hearing something and intensive listening; or between resting your hand on velvet, and closing your eyes and luxuriating in the feel of it; only with a sense that . . . oh, forget it. It's a witch thing.

In any case, I reached out, for the water, and—

"Yes," I said aloud.

"Yes?" echoed Lady Teldra.

"Yes," I agreed.

She waited.

I turned to her. "The water," I said. "It isn't water."

She waited.

"*Boss —*"

"*I don't know, Loiosh; I'm working on it.*"

Aloud I said, "The water isn't like the rest of the place. Well, it is and it isn't. It's—I don't know. I want to follow it."

"*All right, Vlad. Upstream or down?*"

"Uh . . . you ask good questions."

The source or the result; the theoretical or the practical; find out what it all means, or go straight for where something can be done about it. A moment of sublime indecision, with a chance to learn something deep and important about myself. Or perhaps not; I know that by inclination I'm a source man; I like to understand things as completely as possible, but if I was to do something before things were done to me, I couldn't take the time.

"Downstream," I said. "Let's see where this goes."

She nodded, Loiosh mumbled an agreement into my mind, and we set off. The stream meandered gently, the ground underfoot was soft and springy if uneven; the air still had that sweetness. I was getting used to taking shallow breaths. The scenery didn't change much, and the water was quieter than the forest streams I'd become used to finding by sound and smell.

After most of a mile, I realized that I was hearing something—a low sort of rumble. It was oddly difficult to localize, but seemed to come from ahead of us.

"*Loiosh, you said you couldn't fly, but —*"

"No, I can do it, I think."

"Then —"

"I'm on my way, Boss."

He left my shoulder and flew off ahead of me, his flight strong and smooth, mostly gliding, wings flapping now and then, smoothly; quite graceful, actually.

"Gee, thanks, Boss."

"Oh, shut up. Are you all right?"

"Yeah, I can manage. I just have to glide a lot, and I won't be able to keep this up very long."

"You won't have to. What do you see?"

"I'd say water, only you claim it isn't water, so . . . wait a minute. It's getting louder. It's —"

"Yes?"

"Well, it's safe enough. Come ahead."

"All right."

The ground rose a little, leaving the water—or whatever it was—about twenty feet below us in a sort of cleft, like a scale model of a river valley, all green and stuff. Loiosh returned to my shoulder as I took the last few steps. The roaring became louder—like, each step noticeably increased the volume; soon we'd have had to shout to be heard, and at about that time we came over a rise and saw it—a waterfall, or it would have been a waterfall if whatever was falling had been water. Certainly, it behaved like water as it went over the lip and struck the bottom, about a hundred or a hundred and twenty feet below; complete with what seemed to be mist springing up from it. The lip was narrower than the stream, I'd say about thirty-five feet. The "water," for lack of a better word, rushed over it in a tremendous hurry to reach the bottom. I watched, fascinated the way one sometimes is by nature, though I hesitate to call it "nature"—I didn't believe this was any more natural than anything else I'd seen since I got here.

It fell majestically. It foamed and swirled in the pool at the bottom, before heading off downstream; I picked out particles and watched them plummet; I watched the mist rise and curl. I wondered what it was.

On my arm, I felt Spellbreaker stir. Just a little; a sort of twitch that could almost have been my imagination, but no, it wasn't.

And then I knew.

Of course, you—who have heard all of my story to this point, and are now sitting back drinking your favorite wine and listening to my voice pour out—you had it figured a long time ago. And, I suppose, I ought to have too. But it is one thing to hear about it, and quite another to be there with it, watching it, hearing it, and not really wanting to believe that you're looking at what you think you're looking at.

"Amorphia," I said aloud, naming it, making it real. According to some of the beliefs surrounding the practice of witchcraft, to name it was to give it power; according to others, to name it was to give myself power over it. This felt like the former.

"What?" shouted Teldra.

I leaned over until I was talking into her ear. "Amorphia," I repeated, making my voice calm, as if I were announcing nothing of any importance. "The stuff of chaos."

She stared at it, then nodded slowly, leaned over, and spoke into my ear. "Yes," she said. "You're right. It is amorphia. Only controlled. Going where the Jenoine wish it to go, and doing what they wish it to do."

I nodded, and led us back from the brink, just a score or so of paces over the hill so we could speak in normal tones. I said, "I didn't think amorphia occurred anywhere except at home."

"Neither did I," she said.

I grunted. "So, which is scarier—that they have created a river of amorphia, or that they are able to create a river of amorphia? Or, for that matter, the fact that the Jenoine have permitted us to see all of this?"

"I begin to believe," she said, "that the reason we haven't

been molested is that, quite simply, we are too insignificant to worry about."

"Insulting," I said, "but it could be true. It would explain why we've been permitted to see this, too—we just don't matter."

Teldra exhaled briefly through her nose and watched the scene. I watched with her. She said, "And we were wondering if there was any magic here."

I listened to chaos splash over the cliff. From where we stood, we could see the rush of the gathered amorphia about to plunge over the falls. Now that I knew—or, perhaps, now that I had admitted to myself what it was—it looked even less like water; the color changed as you tried to focus on it, but now appeared mostly to fluctuate between steely grey and a dark, unhealthy green. And while it almost behaved as water should, it didn't quite do that, either.

"Well, we've certainly learned something," I remarked into the air.

Amorphia. The stuff of chaos. According to some, the stuff of life; according to others, the basic building block of all matter and energy. I didn't know; I wasn't a magical philosopher, and I'd certainly never studied the ancient, illegal, and frightening branch of sorcery devoted to such things.

I'd used amorphia once, and since then had skimmed a couple of Morrolan's books to pick up useful-looking spells, but I'd never studied it.

I *had* used it once.

A long time ago, in the heart of the city, trying to save the life of Morrolan (who was dead at the time; don't ask), faced by several sorceresses of the Bitch Patrol—the Left Hand of the Jhereg—I had called upon abilities I didn't know I had, I had hurled something at them they could not have anticipated any more than they could counter it.

Yes, I had done it once.

I let that memory play around in my head, remembering the feel of a tavern floor against my face, and a sense of desperation;

a desire to do something, anything, and the explosive release of a power I had inherited because, once, my soul had been close kin to the soul of some idiots who played around with that power. That day, I had been an idiot, too, and had been rescued by Aliera before I dissolved myself and a section of Adrilankha into the basic component of all matter and energy, or whatever it was.

I remembered that day, years ago, and separated from me by so many experiences that it might as well have happened to a different person.

Only I wasn't, really, a different person. And, try as I might, I couldn't shy away from the implications of that.

"Boss —"

"Not now, Loiosh. Let me work it through on my own; there are too many angles to this thing."

"All right."

If anyone asked me if I knew the Elder Sorcery, I could say no with a clear conscience. I *didn't* know it, in any meaningful way.

But—

The Elder Sorcery is, perhaps, the most difficult branch of magic, at least until you try to throw them all together and tie them up in some object where you also keep your soul so you get to call yourself a "wizard" for whatever satisfaction that will bring you. I had once harbored illusions about learning sorcery as it was practiced before the Empire, before the Orb, before what I'd call civilization. I had a sort of start, owing to an accidental relationship in my past life. I abandoned the study early on, because not only was it difficult, and scary, but I just had too damned much else going on in my life at the time.

But I did have a pretty good memory of step one—that is, the first and easiest spell, the one necessary to continue on to the more difficult spells. And this spell, if I could pull it off, just might prove useful.

My brain raced, and worked at a few of the angles until it ran down, by which time I had already opened up my small pouch of witchcraft supplies, and dug around for a bit. I didn't have a lot of stuff with me, and everything I did have was valuable, but what can you do? I picked out the ceramic bottle of dira juice because it wasn't too hard to come by, and the main use it had was treating a particular jungle fever that I'd so far managed to avoid. I poured the contents on the ground. I noticed Teldra looking a question at me. I shook my head.

I found a loop of leather and hung it around the neck of the bottle; then I walked over to the bank where the amorphia flowed like water.

Teldra cleared her throat. "I was just wondering," she said, "how you're going to keep the bottle from dissolving in the amorphia you're trying to capture."

"Oh," I said. "You've known Morrolan a great deal longer than I have; haven't you read any of his books?"

"Not on the Elder Sorcery. Have you?"

"Yes," I said.

"Oh." She considered. "And you learned how to do whatever it is you're doing?"

The questions were a bit intrusive for Teldra, but I couldn't blame her; hanging around while an incompetent plays around with amorphia is worth at least a couple of innocent questions.

"More or less," I told her.

She bit her lip and didn't ask anything else, for which she ought to have received whatever sorts of medals her House gives out.

I started the bottle spinning in a wide, slow loop, directly in front of me, about a foot over the stream. "It really isn't that difficult," I said, "if all you want to do is capture some of it. It's just a question of speed." As I spoke, I started spinning the bottle a little faster—not much. "Amorphia will take, uh, some measurable fraction of a second before it begins to operate on matter that comes in contact with it. The trick is just to get it before it destroys or alters whatever vessel you're using to capture it." I glanced at her. "Move a couple of steps to the right, please."

She did so, silent.

The other trick is the little matter of the spell.

There isn't a lot to say about it. It's a pretty simple spell, really—well described by the book. You just draw the power through your link to the Orb. . . .

Yeah.

There's the catch. The whole "link to the Orb" problem. I was currently missing one of those.

To the left, however, there were alternatives, if you were willing to risk interaction with unfettered, raw amorphia. I happened to have a supply of that near to hand.

I stared at the stream.

Do you know how hard it is to look at water? To see it, when it's flowing past you? You see foam, or swirls, or crests, or whitewaters, or maybe the streambed, or maybe the reflection off the surface, but it is very hard to actually see the water. It is even harder when it isn't actually water, but amorphia, the quintessence of formlessness; it is hard to see formlessness, because what we see is form. Try it sometime, if you have any raw chaos lying about; it is simultaneously too much and too little to grasp.

But I kept trying, staring at and then past the subtle color shifts, rigorously refusing to believe in the shapes my mind tried to impose on the shapelessness. And at length—I don't know how long it was—I began to seep into it. Those sorcerers who spend a lot of time working with amorphia say that every such experience is a step closer to madness. Judging from Aliera and Morrolan, I think that is probably true. But fortunately, I didn't have to go too far, just enough contact for one little spell.

I felt a response within me; something like and yet unlike the first feelings that a spell is working. To the right, I felt as if I were secure and comfortable and relaxed, and to the left I felt as if I were on the edge of a precipice and one small step, or the loss of my balance, would send me hurtling over into insanity.

The balance issue was a good metaphor, and also quite real, because, as I readied the spell, I leaned over the stream. Should

I slip in, it would be a quicker death than many that I've come near, but it isn't how I choose to spend my last measurable fraction of a second.

I changed the angle, so instead of spinning parallel to the stream, it was almost perpendicular. I timed the spin—it was just over a second for a full loop. I wished I remembered just what the measurement on that measurable fraction of a second was; at the time, that hadn't been the sort of detail I was interested in, not being able to imagine being in this situation. Was it around half a second? A little less? I sped up the spin just a trifle, then let my breath out slowly.

"Here we go," I said aloud. "Keep your eye on this thing; there should be something flying out onto the shore behind me." I executed, or perhaps I should say *released* the spell as I lowered my arm so the bottle splashed into the stream.

The first good news was that I didn't fall in; but I hadn't really expected to.

The second good news was that the stream didn't splash on me; I'd been afraid of that, but couldn't think of a good way to avoid it.

The third good news was that the leather suddenly felt lighter in my hand, and a glance told me that there was nothing hanging on the end.

But the real good news was that Teldra cried out, "I saw it! Something flashed. It went off that way."

I followed her pointing finger, dropping the leather just in case there were unpleasant things clinging to the end of it.

The grass here wasn't terribly long; it only took five minutes or so before I found it. I reached down and picked it up, just as if doing so didn't scare me.

It took the form of a small stone, perfectly round and about an inch in diameter; it was very heavy for its size, and had a sort of milky hue somewhere in between blue and purple.

"Got it," I said, holding it up.

She came over and inspected it, Loiosh doing the same from my shoulder.

"Pure amorphia," I said, "but in a form that can be worked with."

"If you say so," said Teldra.

"I say so."

I slipped it into my pouch as if it were no big deal.

Teldra nodded as if it were no big deal, and said, "All right, then, Vlad, what next?"

That was a good question. But I now had Spellbreaker, a powerful Morganti dagger, a chunk of amorphia, my training as a witch, and my native wit. Might as well use them for something.

I said aloud, "Patience my ass; I'm going to go out and kill something."

9

Teldra frowned. "Excuse me?"

"Never mind; an old Jhereg joke. Let's go back."

"Back, Vlad?"

"To our prison."

I watched her face, and decided she was struggling between courteously agreeing and rudely asking if I had lost my mind. I politely cut in before she had to choose.

"This place"—I gestured aimlessly—"gives me the creeps. I don't mean just here, I mean this whole area. The Jenoine will be able to find us anywhere on their world, if they want to, so being out here will only make it harder for Morrolan and Aliera to find us."

"Ah," she said. "You've resigned yourself to being rescued, then?"

"Heh. I'm still thinking about it."

"And you have another idea, don't you?"

"Hmmm. Sort of a plan."

She smiled. "That's good enough for me," she said, and we headed back for the building that had been our prison. I should, perhaps, have been surprised that it hadn't vanished while we were out of sight, but it hadn't, and the door was still where we'd left it. We went back inside. The door vanished as we stepped through, but I wouldn't give it the satisfaction of being startled by that.

"What's the plan this time, Boss?"

"If I told you, you'd just laugh."

"*Probably.*"

"*You could learn a lot from Teldra.*"

"*The ocean says the river is wet. The snow says the ice is cold.*"

"*Is that like, the jhereg says the yendi is a reptile?*"

"*Shut up, Boss.*"

I studied the big, empty room on the big empty world, considered my predicament, thought over my idea, and tried to be optimistic. I glanced over to where the shackles still hung on the wall. The Jenoine could put us back in them easier than I'd gotten out of them. But why should they? After all, the whole reason—

"Teldra, do you think I'm paranoid?"

She blinked. "Lord Taltos?"

"I keep seeing devious plots everywhere, and thinking that everyone must have two or three layers of subterfuge behind every action."

"I recall, my lord, your affair with the Sorceress in Green. It seems to me you were correct on that occasion."

"She's a Yendi."

"And these are Jenoine. Much more worrisome. With a Yendi, one at least *knows* everything is subterfuge and misdirection. With the Jenoine, we don't understand them, and we don't know if they understand us."

I nodded. "Okay, a point."

She continued, "I think it reasonable to wonder if we are doing what they want us to—if they have everything planned, and each step we have taken is in accordance with their wishes. Didn't Sethra say as much? Yet it is uncertain, because we behave unpredictably, and we don't yet know to what extent they can anticipate and understand us. I'm working on that," she added.

"You're working on that?"

"Yes."

I wanted to ask her in exactly what way was she working on it, but if she had wanted me to know, she'd have told me. All right, then. I'd go ahead and assume I was right in my surmises until I found out I was wrong—by which time it would probably be too late, and I wouldn't have to worry about it. There are advantages to fatalism.

"Hungry, Teldra?"

"No, thank you."

I grunted and shared a bit of jerky with Loiosh. Teldra went over to the wall and sat down, her knees up, arms around her knees—she managed to make the position look dignified and graceful.

I said, "Teldra, what, exactly, is the soul?"

"I hope you're asking rhetorically, Vlad. I've never studied magical philosophy. I only know the mundane answer—that which is left after the death the physical body—the life essence—the personality, separated from matter."

I nodded. "Yeah. I've never studied magical philosophy either. I guess I should have, at some point."

"Is it important?"

"Yes."

She looked a question.

I touched the Morganti dagger at my belt and said, "These things destroy souls. It would be very useful right now to know exactly what they destroyed, and how they did it, and what it all means. I'm trying to avoid being embarrassed at a critical moment."

"I see. I'm afraid I can't help you."

She had already helped. I leaned against the wall next to her and pondered the soul.

"Boss, why is it you always get philosophical just when—"

"Shut up, Loiosh."

He snickered into my mind; I ignored him.

To think of the soul as a field of sorcerous energy usually anchored to a living body might be incomplete, but also might be close enough to be useful; at least, to the best of my knowledge, that was how a Morganti dagger treated it. It said nothing about how such a nebulous thing as a personality could be contained in a field of sorcerous energy, but Morganti weapons are notoriously unconcerned with personalities.

If it was good enough for a Morganti dagger, it was good enough for me.

Heh.

Teldra was looking at me.

I cleared my throat. "I assume you want to be let in on what my plan is."

"That's up to you, Vlad. If you think I should know, tell me. Otherwise, not."

I stared at her. "You really do trust me, don't you?"

"Yes," she said.

"By the Halls of Judgment, *why?*"

"Because you keep surviving, Vlad."

She said it so matter-of-factly that I was almost convinced. "Heh," I said. "I'm just being saved for some spectacularly awful death."

"If so," she said, "I'm sure you'll comport yourself with dignity."

"Dignity? Me? Not bloody likely. If I go down swinging, it'll be because I think swinging is more likely to get me out of it than running. If I go down running, I won't be surprised."

She gave me a smile as if she didn't believe me and said, "I hadn't meant to turn the conversation morbid."

"Oh, don't worry about that, Teldra. Most of my thoughts are morbid. I think it comes of having spent so long killing people for a living. Strange way to live, when you think about it, so I try not to, but I can't help it. On the other hand, you work for a guy known for sacrificing whole villages, so I guess I'm a bit of a piker by comparison."

"More like hamlets than villages, Vlad. And he *was* at war against them at the time, you know."

"Oh. Actually, I hadn't known that. I just chalked it up to another example of how charming my dear Goddess can be."

"It was while he was consolidating his power and retaking his ancestral homelands. They worshiped Tri'nagore, a God you don't hear from much anymore, and had overrun Blackchapel, killing everyone in it. Morrolan returned the favor, and sent their souls to his Patron Goddess."

"I see. They don't tell that part of the story."

"The Lord Morrolan refuses to be put in the position of defending his actions. He considers it undignified."

"So he'd rather everyone thought him a bloodthirsty butcher?"

"Yes."

"Yeah, I guess he would at that."

To the left, I reflected, he could be bloodthirsty enough, however much Teldra downplayed it. I recalled an incident at Castle Black. I wasn't paying much attention, being involved in some rather nasty squabble with another Jhereg at the time, but I remember him challenging another Dragonlord to a duel, and then doing everything to the guy except making him unrevivifiable—I mean he dismembered the poor bastard, and seemed to take great joy making the fellow's death as slow and painful as he could. This was a memory I didn't care to dwell on; I don't enjoy such scenes. But it was certainly impossible to deny that that side of Morrolan existed. I wondered—

"Teldra," I said suddenly. "Do you recall a certain Lord Vrudric e'Lanya whom Morrolan fought a few years ago?"

She looked at me quizzically and nodded.

"Can you tell me what that was about?"

"You don't know, Vlad? Vrudric was casting aspersion on Adron's character."

"Adron? Adron e'Kieron?"

"Yes."

"That's it? Morrolan did that to him because he was casting aspersions on the character of the guy who was either so greedy, or so incompetent, or, at best, so misguided that he destroyed the whole Verra-be-damned Empire and dissolved Dragaera City into amorphia? *That* guy?"

"Adron is one of Morrolan's heroes. I thought you knew that."

"No," I said. "I hadn't known that. But Adron . . . okay. It's strange, but I guess I can get used to it. Hmmm. Morrolan e'Drien. Who was Drien, anyway?"

"A contemporary of Kieron the Conqueror, perhaps the first Shaman who was a warrior, or the first warrior who was a Shaman. From what I gather, he or she was brilliant, fiery, talented, creative, powerful, and emotionally unstable."

" 'He or she'?"

"As I understand it, Drien was born female but transformed herself into a man around the time of the founding of the Empire. Or it may have been the other way around. I don't know if the man or the woman had offspring, or both; and perhaps the story isn't true, but that is the tradition."

"I see. Hmmm. But then . . . never mind. What about the other story? I mean the one about Morrolan charging up to Dzur Mountain when he found out that there was someone in his domain who hadn't paid him tribute."

"Oh." Teldra smiled. "Yes, that one is true."

I chuckled. "Oh, to have been there to witness that conversation. I don't suppose you went along?"

"Hardly."

"Did he ever say what happened?"

"No. But it can't have been anything too horrid; they've been friends ever since."

"Oh yeah? Does she pay him tribute?"

"I don't know," said Teldra, smiling.

"I'll be sure to ask him. Sometime when we're not in the middle of trying to batter our way out of a trap set by demigods. Which reminds me, I had an idea about that. I'll give you the rough outline of—"

"*Boss!*"

I spun around. Morrolan and Aliera were back, both holding their swords in their hands, and looking like I felt—that is, full of the desire to kill something.

"Welcome," I said, "to our temporary abode. I'm afraid our hospitality may be—"

"Where are they?" said Aliera.

I shrugged. "They forgot to say where they were going when they left. Actually, I forgot to ask them. I was napping at the time, as I recall. Oh, by the way, Morrolan, I'm curious about whether you get any tribute from Dzur Mountain."

"Vlad," said Morrolan, "do you have any idea what we had to do to get back here? To even find the place, much less break through, required the Necromancer to spend twelve hours pulling memories out of Blackwand—memories she didn't know she contained. After that—"

"How long has it been, in your world?"

"Not long. A couple of days. A very busy couple of days, I might add."

I nodded. "A few hours, here. Did you bring any food? Jerky and gammon are getting old."

Morrolan and Aliera looked at each other. "No, sorry," said Morrolan.

"Perhaps it would be best to get going, then."

"Yes," said Aliera. "That's the idea." Morrolan was frowning his frown of concentration—I hoped and believed doing what was necessary to get us out of there.

"That is," I added, "if the Jenoine will let us. Do you think they will?"

"Perhaps not," said the Lord of Castle Black, looking up suddenly. "But we are prepared for them to attempt to stop us. Unfortunately, the gate has shut again. I'm going to try to open it." He did that thing with his hands again, and he was once more holding his thin, black wizard's staff. This time I noticed something: a blue ring that he always wore on his left hand was no longer there, yet I had been certain he had been wearing it an instant before. Okay, it was a nice trick, and it had some flash. I could always respect flash, if it didn't conflict with practicality.

I looked at Morrolan, as if seeing him for the first time, with all that Teldra had told me buzzing around in my head. Adron? He certainly was far more complex than I had ever thought him.

It suddenly flashed into my head to wonder if he and Sethra were currently or ever had been lovers. Now *that* was an inter-esting thought, and one that would probably come back to me on many cold nights—assuming, of course, that I would have the opportunity to have many cold nights.

Which brought me sharply back to the present. I said, "Sethra is in on this, isn't she?"

"Yes," said Morrolan. "And she's at Castle Black, in the Tower, waiting to assist us."

I nodded. "Knowing, I'm sure, that her help is likely to be either insufficient or unnecessary."

"Yes."

I felt myself scowling, and my stomach growled, just to make sure I understood how it felt, too.

"Got it," said Morrolan suddenly. "Over here, quickly."

There was a shimmering waviness in the air, gold colored, about six feet behind Morrolan.

"Very well," said Aliera, walking toward it. "Let's do it; the gate won't remain open forever. Teldra, you first. Hurry, Vlad."

"They're late, Boss."

"Seems like."

Teldra and I took a step toward her.

Sometimes, things are so close—almost this, or just barely that; one thing and another, balanced just so, that there seems to be an instant where they are both happening, and neither happens, and each path is fully realized, like a psiprint, held in place by the strength of mutual impossibilities. Sometimes lives—your own or another's—depend on decisions that come within a whisper, a hair, a fraction of breath, of going one way, or the other. Have you the strength of will to do what you know—*know*—is the right thing, or will your appetite rule the moment? Will you allow the anger of an instant to command your tongue, and make a breach that can never be healed, or will you manage to hold ire in check for just long enough—a tiny portion of a second—to escape?

Sometimes it is so close, so very close.

I took a step forward, and—

—as my footstep faded, I could almost hear—

—an infinitely extended moment, nothing happening, taking forever, but much too fast—

—was instantly aware—

—voices whispering in the silence, with the silence, not disturbing it—

—a foot almost descending, simultaneously in one place and another—occupying two places at once, but that's what movement is all about—

—that Loiosh was no longer with me. Even before—

—leaving perception, without the awareness of whence it sprang except—

—all life is movement, which is to be here and not here and the same time, or here and there simultaneously, or to deny time, or to deny place—

—I realized that my surroundings had changed, that I was uncertain where I was, that—

—that it came from outside of self, if such a distinction is valid without time or place to hang it from, and the voices—

—is to be, in fact, nowhere, and nowhere is—

—Teldra and Aliera and Morrolan had cross-stepped while I lunged, I knew—

—came with eyes, and ears, and other things that—

—everywhere is here and there and there ought to be a way—

—that I was out of touch with my familiar and it—

—gave me the feeling that I was being studied, scanned, analyzed, and ultimately—

—to seize control, or at least to act, or at the very least to make a decision—

—had been years since I had come so—

—discarded, and permitted—

—to be holding a chain of gold light, in my mind if nowhere else, so that in and through the shield of swirling gold which suddenly—

—close to panic—

—to stop, or resume—

—seemed to me to be a *place*, not a thing, that I could—

—but that, like so much else, is self-defeating, so I—

—the interrupted pace, the walk, the step, which in turn permitted—

—enter into and go through and be changed by—

—tried not to think about it, but trust in him and me, and just do—

—a junction of thought and a resonance of experience, so that I managed, or thought I managed, or almost managed—

—spinning corridors of gold that were within and without, and then through once more, leaving me—

—and I guess it worked because what was before me became behind me, and here became there, which was all right, because I—

—to make contact, once more, with my familiar familiar.

—somewhere real at last.

—was back.

"Well," I said or thought, lying against the cold stone floor. "If it isn't one thing, it's another."

"Are you all right, Vlad?" It took me a moment to realize the voice belonged to Teldra, and even longer to understand that the question begged an answer. What the answer ought to be was beyond me.

"Vlad?"

I turned my head and made eye contact with her, looking up at her impossibly tall form, hoping she would see that I was at least somewhat sensible.

"*You okay, Boss?*"

"*Ask something easier, it'll take me some time to figure that out.*"

"*Where did you go?*"

"*That's what I was going to ask you.*"

Around then, I realized that we hadn't actually gone anywhere—we were still in the Jenoine's prison.

"Vlad?" This was Morrolan's voice. I managed to turn my

head and see that he and Aliera were still there, as well. So nothing had changed, but everything had.

Story of my life.

I found my voice and managed, "How long?" In my own ears, my voice sounded weaker than I actually felt.

"How do you feel?" asked Aliera. Why can't anyone just answer a Verra-be-damned question?

I started to say something snappy, but it was too much work, so I said, "Dry."

Morrolan held a flask to my lips, and I drank some water. Damn, but it was good. I was going to ask him where he found it. Water. Wonderful stuff. Who knew?

"What happened, Vlad?" asked Morrolan. Yeah, like I was the right guy to ask.

"How long has it been?" I repeated. It was easier to talk now. I opened my eyes, not sure when I had closed them. Aliera and Morrolan were directly over me, staring down. Teldra was out of sight. Loiosh stood on the floor next to my left ear. Being the center of so much interest wasn't as pleasant as I would have expected.

"As far as I can tell, you've been unconscious for around nine hours."

"More like ten," said Aliera.

Morrolan said, "My judgment—"

"Doing what in the meantime," I said.

"Failing to reopen the gate," said Aliera, with a look at Morrolan that the latter ignored.

"Okay," I said. "Would someone like to help me up?"

Morrolan reached a hand out. With his help, I was able to stand up, and after a moment I was able to remain standing on my own. The room spun, then settled out, and—

"What the—?"

"What is it, Vlad?"

"Where are we?"

Silence greeted the question, which meant the answer couldn't be anything I wanted to hear.

Aliera said, "Vlad, we're in the same room we've been in all along."

Yeah, that was one of the things I hadn't wanted to hear.

Teldra was now looking at me, too. "What is it?" said Morrolan.

I took a deep breath and blew it out slowly. Where to begin?

"There is more to this place than used to meet the eye," I said. "Either we've all been taken in by an illusion, or I'm being taken in by one now."

Aliera closed her eyes momentarily, then opened them. "I detect no illusion," she said. I shrugged.

"Perhaps," said Morrolan, "you could describe what you are now seeing."

"There is a large rock, or stone, in the middle of the floor— right there." I walked over to it, but didn't touch it. "It's about three feet high, maybe five feet long, and a foot and half wide at its widest point, but very irregular and jagged; it is mostly a dark shiny grey, with pink veins running through it."

I glanced over at them, they were looking at me, not the rock. *"I don't see it, Boss."*

"Figures."

"That way," I said, "against the wall, are four large jugs or vats, pottery of some kind, green with black geometrical patterns near the neck. They're just a bit under five feet high and—" I walked over to them. "One seems to be filled with sand, another with ash, this one with, I don't know, looks like water but I wouldn't count on it, and this last one with something that looks like very tiny seashells."

I turned my head. "Over this way—right here—is the doorway that Teldra and I found earlier; it is now plainly visible."

Morrolan and Aliera looked at her; she shrugged and said, "Yes, we did find a doorway there."

They turned back to me. "What else?" said Morrolan.

"The shelves are all filled."

"With?"

"That one," I said, gesturing, "has weapons. I mean, things

that are obviously weapons—that look like weapons even to me. Swords, knives, daggers, lances, pikes. Things like that. There must be a hundred of them, all in all. The one over there has—I wish you could see it—it's full of crystals. Some of them the size of the end of my finger, some of them fist size, a few of them the size of a lormelon. They're a bit scary. And the colors vary from a mild pink to a deep purple, almost black. The big ones are both of the black color. Like I said, they're a bit scary."

I cleared my throat. "The shelf over at the far end has things I don't recognize. Mostly metal, and peculiar shapes—some wheels, some devices made of several pieces riveted together, some partly made of leather or something else. Some that remind me of that strange object Sethra has. I would assume they are sorcerous devices of some kind, but I don't know. I don't feel like touching any of them. And the last shelf, this one, has more odd contraptions, but I recognize manacles among them.

"Okay," I continued. "So much for the shelves. The walls are all painted with designs—black paint against a background that doesn't look like I thought it did—more like a greyish blue. And the designs are, well, probably sorcerous. All geometrical shapes. The walls are covered with them, top to bottom, and there are various symbols scrawled in amongst them. I can draw them for you, if you'd like."

"Yes," said Aliera, at the same time Morrolan said, "Perhaps later."

I grunted. "There is also a table at each end of the room, and chairs around it. All metal, all much larger than any furniture for either you or me. Go figure, huh? Oh, and the ceiling looks the same as it did before, except that there are more lighting devices than I'd thought.

"So, that's about it. It's obvious that they've done something to my head during this last—how long? eight hours?—or I wouldn't be seeing this stuff. I'll leave it up to you clever people whether I'm now being taken in by illusion, or all the rest of you are. If we go by majority, I'd guess it's me that's seeing things. And there's also the fact that Teldra and I never tripped over any of that stuff earlier. And the fact that I can't imagine why they would have messed with my head to allow me to see what's really here. Chances are, while I was gone, they did other things as well, to make sure I'd carry out whatever plan they have. But I do want all of you to admire how calm, cool, and collected I am while discussing the fact that my head has been messed with. Okay, your turns."

Aliera addressed Morrolan. "It's the rock that interests me most."

"Yes," said Morrolan. "Does it sound familiar?"

Aliera nodded. I felt ignored. Loiosh nuzzled my ear. Teldra came over and stood next to me, not saying anything or even looking at me, but it was nice of her.

"I think," I told her quietly after a moment, "that you ought to leave me out of your plans."

"Do you feel as if your mind has been tampered with?"

"No."

"Or probed?"

"No. But it seems likely, doesn't it?"

"It is possible. But it seems more likely that a glamour has been removed from your eyes than one placed there."

"Sure. But why? And how, for that matter?"

She shook her head. Meanwhile, Morrolan and Aliera had finished their conference. Morrolan said, "Vlad, we will not be telling you of our plans until we can ascertain whether your mind has been tampered with."

"Hey," I said. "Good idea. I should have thought of that myself."

He answered me with a Morrolan look. I went over and sat down against the wall; I didn't feel like using the Jenoine's furniture.

"*Okay, Loiosh. You know how we do this.*"

"*Right now, Boss?*"

"*Right now.*"

Aliera approached. "Vlad, I'm wondering if that rock you describe has any—"

"Not now, Aliera. I'm busy."

She raised an eyebrow, I suppose wondering if I were kidding.

"I'm having my brain examined. It should only take a few minutes."

She glanced quickly at Loiosh, then nodded and walked away to continue her conference with Morrolan. I let my head rest against the wall, closed my eyes, and tried to think of nothing. I've never been good at thinking of nothing.

Loiosh had done this maybe half a dozen times, and he was starting to get good at it; I felt the invasion, but there was less of that rattling, jangling sensation, like being hit on the numbing point of the elbow except in the brain. I sat still and waited it out, thinking of nothing but what was going on inside my head. Thinking about what is going on inside your head is a good way to make yourself miserable, if you haven't any other methods handy, but there was no way around it. As he sniffed and poked through the nooks and crannies of my thinking gear, I'd get flashes, unbidden, of moments of my past. I remembered the descent into Deathgate, the sight of my hands gripping the ropes, their feel against my palms, and sometimes I'd look down and see the top of Morrolan's head below my feet, the roar of the falls in my ears. I remembered the feel of Cawti's breath, fast in my ear, my hand in the small of her back as we explored each other. I remembered the feel of a ship's deck beneath my feet, the creaking of the sails, and the endless blue-green of the sea. I remembered the Necromancer's cold, cold fingers on my soul, the edge of Blackwand against my throat, the voice of the Imperial Inquisitor as the Orb circled my head and the Empress looked on, and the laugh of the Serioli who led me by circuitous routes to the Wall of Baritt's Tomb.

It indicated how much better Loiosh was getting that so few of these memories were unpleasant.

Presently he said, "*All right, Boss.*"

"All right?"

"*All right.*"

"What do you mean, 'all right'?"

"I mean 'all right.' "

"All right, as in, all is right?"

"That's the all right I meant, Boss."

"Okay, I think I got that part. Now the tough one: How certain are you?"

He hesitated. "Pretty sure."

"Pretty sure?"

"Pretty sure."

"What do you mean, 'pretty sure'?"

"I mean 'pretty sure.' "

That wasn't exactly the answer I wanted. I've found I often don't get exactly the answers I want, but I keep asking questions anyway.

"And, Boss—"

"Yes?"

"Now I'm seeing it, too."

"Well, that's something then. Either I'm not under a glamour, or you are as well."

"Heh. I'm a jhereg, Boss. The being hasn't been spawned that could put a glamour on me."

"Cocky little son-of-a-bitch, aren't you?"

"Damn right."

"I'm back," I announced to the room in general. No one cheered immediately, but I got a smile from Teldra. I said, "Loiosh believes my brain has probably not been tampered with, for whatever that's worth."

"Probably?" said Aliera, frowning.

I shrugged. "Best I can do; take it for what's it's worth. And he's now seeing the same thing I am."

"Which means," said Aliera, shrugging, "that perhaps he is under a glamour as well."

I said, "He's a jhereg. The creature hasn't been spawned that could put a glamour on him."

Aliera frowned, looked over at Morrolan as if to see if he was convinced, then shrugged.

Loiosh said, "*Thanks, Boss.*"

"*No problem, chum.*"

I said, "Now, Morrolan, can you tell me what happened?"

"What happened?" asked Morrolan. He was leaning against the wall near where we'd been chained up, arms folded, looking cool and imperturbable.

"The attempt to get us home."

"Oh. Nothing happened. They sealed the gate."

"Then we're stuck here?"

"For the moment, yes."

"I see. Is sealing your gate, uh, easy to do?"

"No."

"Why would they want to keep us here now, when they could have kept us here the first time?"

"I don't know," said Morrolan. "And I should very much like to. Is this all part of a plan of theirs, or are they improvising as much as we are? You perceive it is a rather important question."

"I'm glad I'm not the only paranoid in the room," I said.

"It isn't paranoia, Vlad, if they really are—"

"So I've heard. Okay, so we can spend all our time wondering if they have all this planned and every step we take is according to their wishes, and when they have us good and ready, they'll crush us like bugs. Or, alternately, we can stop worrying about what moves they're going to pull on us, and start thinking about what moves we're going to pull on them."

Morrolan sniffed and said, "Good idea, Vlad. How do you plan to go about it?"

"Nothing fancy," I said. "I had just planned to kill them, and go from there."

Aliera shrugged. "Couldn't hurt," she said.

10

"Tell me about this rock," said Aliera.

"All right," I said. I walked over and stood in front of it. "The edges are all jagged. It looks like a large piece of something that was once even larger, if that gives you any idea. I told you about the colors, but there's also a very thin sort of purplish vein running along one side."

Aliera said, "Does it seem at all crystalline?"

"No, not . . . well, yes, I guess sort of, if you look at it right."

Morrolan nodded. "Well, Aliera?"

She nodded and said, "Trellanstone."

Morrolan nodded.

I said, "If you don't mind—"

"Trellanstone," said Aliera, "is what the Imperial Orb was fashioned from."

"Oh," I said. "Well. And here I thought it might be something interesting."

About then I caught something in Aliera's eyes, and then in Morrolan's, and realized that they were both a lot more excited about this than they were willing to let on.

"I don't suppose," I said, "that either of you have studied Orb-making? I can see where having an Orb might be useful right around now."

"Certainly," said Aliera. "Then all we'd need would be a source of amorphia."

"Oh, we have that," I said, enjoying dropping it into the

middle of the conversation, like, "Oh, the Easterner? Yes, he's the Empress's consort."

I certainly got Morrolan and Aliera's attention quickly enough. "What are you talking about?" said Morrolan.

"Lady Teldra and I went for a walk while we were waiting for you. It's a lovely place, really, except for the air and how heavy you feel. There is a river of amorphia just outside of that door."

They both glanced over at Teldra. You could see them thinking, "That's it. Poor Vlad's mind has snapped at last."

But Teldra nodded and said, "He is quite correct."

"A river of amorphia," repeated Morrolan, almost reverently.

"Impossible," said Aliera. She turned to Morrolan. "Isn't it?"

He shook his head. "I can't imagine how such a thing could be. We need to look at this."

"Yes," said Aliera.

"I'll wait here," I told him. "If the Jenoine emerge, shall I ask them to wait, or suggest they return when it is more convenient?"

Aliera snorted. There was a lot of that going around. Having made her statement, she turned and headed toward where I told her the door was, stopped, and turned back.

"Where is the bloody door?" she said.

I managed not to chuckle, started to answer, but Morrolan said, "One thing at a time, please. I, too, wish to observe this thing, but I wish first to address the issue of why Vlad can see what we cannot, and what, if anything, we can do about it."

I could see that Aliera wanted to argue with him, but apparently couldn't find any good pretext, so she clamped her jaw shut, and returned. I found I was enjoying this: two sorcerers, who had to be dying to investigate one of the most remarkable discoveries in the history of magical philosophy, and they were just going to have to wait.

To add some more confusion into the mix, I said, "Excuse me. This rock-that-turns-into-Orbs. Would you mind telling me about it?"

"It's magical," said Aliera dryly.

I glanced over at Teldra, but she was just standing, near the wall, the epitome of patience. I turned back to Aliera and said, "Thanks loads." She started to speak, but I cut her off. "Look, there's too much I don't understand here, and neither do you. If we're going to work this together, I'd like to have some idea of what this stuff is we're talking about. We're paralyzed until we have at least a reasonable guess about what is real and what isn't."

"I have never," said Aliera, "had any particular problem knowing what is real."

"Oh, no? Think about it. Morrolan is right. Why do I see what you don't? Whose mind has been tampered with? What is the illusion? And, more important, *why*? That's the part that really bothers me. I can understand casting an illusion in front of all our eyes, but why then remove it from one of us, or some of us, whichever it is?"

Aliera frowned. "All right," she said. "Granted. I don't know."

Morrolan cleared his throat. "It is possible," he said, "that removing the illusion was an error. We still don't know exactly what happened while you were gone. Did you, for example, use your chain?"

I was suddenly very aware of Spellbreaker, wrapped around my wrist. "Yes," I told him. "As it happens, I did. At least, in my mind. I thought about it. Could just invoking Spellbreaker in my mind have broken the illusion?"

"Perhaps," said Morrolan.

"Perhaps," I agreed. "Then again, perhaps not? How can we tell?"

"Let me think about that," he said.

"Okay," I agreed. "While you're thinking, could you fill me in a little?"

"On what?"

"For starters, just what is that rock?"

"Well," said Morrolan, "you know, basically, how sorcery works, right?"

"I know how to do the simple stuff, if that's what you mean."

"No, I'm talking about how it works. The theory."

"Oh. No, I'm proud to say I haven't a clue."

"Oh," said Morrolan, with a look that indicated he was suddenly stumped. I took a perverse pride in that. I guess I was in a mood.

Aliera came to his rescue. "The basic idea," she said, "is simple enough: Everything is made of matter, or energy, which is the same thing in a less organized form. Amorphia is the opposite of matter. The purple vein in that rock is necrophia. Necrophia is a substance which can control amorphia, and which responds to the human—or Eastern—brain. Sorcery is the art of learning to manipulate necrophia, as Elder Sorcery is the art of learning to manipulate amorphia."

She stopped, as if she were done. Heh. I said, "And necromancy?"

"The art of using necrophia, and amorphia, to control the energy levels of different life-states."

Oh, well, now I understood everything. Heh. I said, "And witchcraft?"

She looked at me, blinked, then turned to Morrolan.

"Witchcraft," he explained, "is something else again."

"Ah," I said. "Well, good. That helps." Before they could respond, I remarked, "I've never heard of necrophia before."

"Your education," said Aliera, "is sadly lacking."

Morrolan said, "Witchcraft is a process of understanding and changing—the more you understand a thing, the more you can change it, and the more you work to change it, the more deeply you understand it. Sorcery is a process of correspondence—the minute amounts of energy generated by the mind must be made to correspond to the Orb, which in turn permits the release of the energy contained in the Sea of Amorphia, and this energy thus becomes available to use to manipulate the world."

"You should have been a teacher."

He ignored me. "That rock you describe contains an ore that has the property of resonating with amorphia, and with our minds; that is why the Orb was constructed from it."

"All right, I can see that. Mmmm. I imagine it is rare?"

"It only appears as a gift from the gods."

"Okay, that would be rare. Is it sentient?"

"How could it be sentient?"

"You're right," I said. "Stupid question." I don't know if he caught the irony, but I'm fairly sure Aliera did; she smirked. I continued, "All right, I think I see a bit of how the arts fit together. Now: Why would the Jenoine put us in a room with this in it?"

He didn't have an answer for that one. Morrolan has always been better at understanding how objects work than how other beings are thinking.

Teldra said, "They don't think the way we do." Because it was Teldra, I didn't make any remarks. She continued, "They don't consider us enemies in the same way we consider them enemies; nor do they see us as threats. They worry about our escaping the way one might worry about a pet greeterbird making its way out of its cage; and they worry about our damaging their artifacts the way one might worry about a pet kitten getting into the jewelry box. By sealing the area against necromantic gates, and laying a mild glamour on us so that we cannot see the objects in the room, they believe they have done enough."

There was a moment of silence; then Morrolan cleared his throat. "How long have you known this?" he said.

"I suppose, in a way, since I spoke to them. What I have just told you, my lord, only occurred to me this instant. I am still considering the matter and trying to understand, but it seems to me that they spoke to me—insofar as I could perceive tone—in the tone one might use to, well, a greeterbird. They were amused that I could form any sort of coherent thought; they think we're cute."

"Cute," said Aliera e'Kieron.

"Cute," said Morrolan e'Drien.

"*I* am *cute*," said Loiosh.

I said, "And that didn't, uh, annoy you at all?"

"I thought it interesting," said Teldra. "Actually, I didn't put it together in exactly that way; I've been thinking about it since the conversation, and that is my conclusion."

"Hmmmm," I said.

"Cute," repeated Aliera.

"All right," said Morrolan. "I think we can accept that. So, what do we do?"

"Kill them," said Aliera.

Morrolan rolled his eyes. "Of *course* we're going to kill them," he said. "I meant, *how?*"

"I wonder," said Aliera, and her voice trailed off.

Morrolan waited, then said, "Yes?"

Aliera hesitated, then finally said, "Do you suppose, if Vlad were to strike us with Spellbreaker, it would break the glamour on us?"

Morrolan frowned his thoughtful frown. I contemplated giving Morrolan and Aliera a good, hard whack apiece, and tried to refrain from smiling. Morrolan said, "I believe it would be less likely to remove the glamour than to, uh, damage many of the items you and I carry about with us, if you understand what I mean."

Aliera nodded. Oh, well. I wouldn't have enjoyed hitting Teldra anyway.

"But," said Morrolan, "I do want some way to remove the glamour; that stone could be very useful. And, perhaps, some of the other things in here could be useful as well. Have you any ideas, cousin?"

She shook her head. Then Lady Teldra cleared her throat; conversation stopped and we all stared at her. It would have been terribly embarrassing if she'd had nothing more than the need to clear her throat. But, no, she said, "It is just possible that the stone itself could help."

Aliera frowned. "I don't understand. If we can't even see

it . . . ?" She was a lot more polite than she'd have been asking that question of Morrolan or me.

Teldra said, "Vlad can see it."

Morrolan scowled. "The air in this place must slow my brain down. You're right, of course."

I cleared my throat; quite a different effect than when Teldra did it. "Uh . . . what exactly does this involve?"

"Nothing you haven't done before," said Morrolan.

"Heh. There are many things I've done before—"

"You must let me see through your eyes," he said. "It is a simple enough spell, as you recall."

"Yeah, I know that. But there's a no sorcery here. Can we do it with pure psychic energy?"

"Not reliably enough," he said. "But we have no need to."

"Oh? Without sorcery, what do you use as a link?"

For answer, he drew Blackwand. I recoiled instinctively from the assault on my mind—the feeling, something in between hearing and smell, of a hungry animal; a feeling that has to have been built into me at some level of instinct or below, that made me aware of the sweat in my armpits, and how hard it was to breathe, and made the room, however large it was, seem too close.

Suddenly I wasn't having fun anymore. "I'd rather not touch the blade, if it's all the same to you," I said.

He seemed amused; maybe it was his turn to have fun. He said, "Well, I'm certainly not going to let you hold her."

"I—"

"Don't worry; she doesn't bite."

I stared at the dark, dull grey blade, then back at Morrolan. "Yeah, right."

"Do it, Vlad."

"I—"

"Do it."

I took a deep breath, hesitated, then laid my palm on the blade quickly, before I could think about it too much. It was faintly warm, which metal isn't supposed to be. And it almost seemed as if it were vibrating, or trembling, just a little.

"Okay, dammit, do it before—"

"Keep still, Vlad. I have to concentrate."

I tried to keep my growl inaudible.

Loiosh's feet shifted on my shoulder; he wasn't liking this either. I can't say why, and it doesn't make sense, but that made me feel a little better.

The most terrifying things, in some ways, are those that catch us off guard—a shock out of nowhere, danger unanticipated, all that. And yet, in other ways, to see something coming, know it is about to happen, and be unable to prevent it has its own special terror. But there are times—rare, but they happen—when you see the danger before you, it builds up, you brace yourself—and then it's over, before you had time to really get a good scare going, much less the unpleasantness that you were scared of.

This was like that.

Morrolan said, "Okay, I'm done."

"You're done?"

"Yes."

"That's it?" Even as I questioned him, my hand was free from that blade, jumping off as if of its own volition.

"That's it," said Morrolan.

"Uh . . . did it work?"

He nodded and turned to Aliera. "All right, cousin. Your turn."

"I don't feel any different," I said.

They ignored me. Loiosh said, *"Boss, it would be Morrolan who feels different."*

"Oh," I said. *"Yeah, I knew that."*

Now Aliera drew Pathfinder, but she swung it over toward Morrolan; it no longer had anything to do with me, so I was free to back away. I did so.

Presently, Aliera turned to Lady Teldra. "This will be trickier," she said.

Teldra nodded and came forward; I didn't want to watch, so I walked over to Morrolan. "Well?" I said.

"Well what?"

"Are you now seeing—"

"Yes."

Creep.

"So, how was my description?"

He glanced around the room, and grunted; I imagine so he wouldn't have to tell me how good a job I'd done. Teldra, by this time, was blinking rapidly and looking all about.

"Okay then," I said. "We've gotten this far. What next?"

No one answered me directly, but Aliera looked at the door that she could now, evidently, see quite clearly. Then she looked an inquiry at Morrolan. He winced. It was obvious that he wanted to go exploring, and was damned curious to see our river of amorphia; it was equally obvious that he didn't think it was what he should do just then.

"All right," said Aliera, who could read him as well as I could. "We'll wait on that." She went over to the rock, and began studying it; her hands reached out as if to touch it, stopped, drew back. She frowned.

"Yes," she said. "It is trellanstone." She smiled suddenly, "And a nice, big, juicy one, too." Her eyes were green, and looked alarmingly catlike, and I would have gotten worried if I hadn't been worried already.

"All right," I said. "Let's hear it."

"It's simple enough," said Aliera. "The trellanstone will permit us to break through whatever is blocking—"

"No," said Morrolan.

"What do you mean, no?"

"That isn't how we're going to do it."

"Oh?" said Aliera. "It isn't? Then, pray, how *are* we going to do it?" She let the irony drip from her lips onto the floor and crawl over to rub against Morrolan's leg.

My eyes rolled up of their own accord. I walked to the far side of the room, pretty much out of earshot, because listening to Morrolan and Aliera yell at each other was already getting old; I found it was not one of the things I missed, although it had never bothered me before. I wondered if being away from people had changed me, made me less patient with minor annoyances.

"*No, Boss, it's just made you introspective.*"

"*Shut up, Loiosh.*"

"*Impatient, too.*"

I sent a psychic growl in his direction, then sat down against a wall and leaned my head back. Morrolan and Aliera, after an instant of conversation, walked out of the door Teldra and I had found. I blinked. Well, I suppose they figured if they were going to argue, they might as well investigate our story at the same time.

Teldra came over and sat down next to me.

I said, "Well, whatever happens, it has been a pleasure having the chance to speak with you."

"Thank you, Vlad. I feel the same way."

I wondered if she really did. That's the tricky part about the Issola; you can never be certain how they are feeling. Maybe it doesn't bother Dragaerans, not knowing how someone is actually feeling, but we Easterners aren't like that. I wondered if it bothered Teldra to know that, when she really, actually liked someone, that person would always have to wonder how much was genuine, and how much was show.

After some time, Morrolan and Aliera came back through the door, approached us, and Morrolan said, "All right, we have a plan."

"That's lucky," I told him.

His eyes narrowed, but he must have decided to let it pass. Best for him.

"*Worked yourself into a mood, haven't you Boss?*"

I mentally grunted at my familiar. Morrolan said, "We're going to attempt something with the trellanstone. We're going to—"

ISSOLA 161

"Use it to break through whatever is blocking you from opening the gate?"

He closed his eyes, then opened them again. Then he slowly and carefully explained the plan to me. Teldra gave nary a twitch of an eyebrow, and Aliera's eyes had turned blue. When Morrolan was finished, he said, "Are there any questions?"

I hardly knew where to begin. I said, "How did you come up with *that* idea?"

"In part, because of your river of amorphia. The fact that they have it changes everything. And, moreover, this is something that—I believe—lies within our power."

I grunted at him and muttered, "If all you've got's a stick, everything looks like a kneecap."

"Beg pardon?" said Morrolan.

"Never mind; old Jhereg saying."

He graced me with a look of distaste and turned to Lady Teldra. "You are clear on your role?"

"Yes, my lord."

"Aliera?"

She rolled her eyes, which Morrolan and I took as an affirmative.

"Then let's begin."

"He didn't ask if I was ready."

"And I'm not going to either."

Morrolan took a position next to the trellanstone, hovering over it like a goose over her goslings. Aliera stood in front of it, to Morrolan's left, and laid her hands on it, touching and feeling it as if looking for handholds. For this stage, Teldra and I were back and out of the way, watching. Aliera's hands came to rest, and she nodded to Morrolan. He licked his lips. I recognized that gesture—I'd been there often enough myself, just before trying something difficult and a little scary.

Sometimes it almost seemed as if Morrolan were human. He placed his hand on the stone, near Aliera's. Presently he said, "All right, I'm getting something."

"Yes," she said.

I couldn't see her face, but I saw the concentration in the muscles of her back, and in Morrolan's case, in the muscles of his jaw. They were working. It was nice to see for a change. They fell silent, I assume communicating psychically; Teldra and I waited patiently for them to finish. Or, rather, Teldra waited patiently; I waited. Presently my feet started to hurt; standing hurts more than walking. I shifted from foot to foot and tried to catch Teldra's eye, but she was watching the sorcerers work.

Abruptly, and for no reason I could see, the veins in the stone began to glow—not much, you had to be watching closely, but it was there, like a yellow phosphorus, if you can imagine such a thing.

Morrolan said, "Okay, Vlad. Get ready."

"I'm ready," I told him, which wasn't entirely a lie. I let Spellbreaker fall into my hand, and felt a very small, subtle vibration running through it, almost a tremble, as of eagerness.

"Boss—"

"Not now, Loiosh. I don't want to think about it."

Easier said than done, that not thinking about it business; but I really didn't want any distractions just then, because if Morrolan's plan worked, things were just about to get interesting. I touched the rapier at my side, started to check my daggers before remembering that most of them were lying in pieces around the room. My hand accidentally touched the sheath of the Morganti blade I still carried; my hand then returned to the hilt of my sword and remained there, so I looked like I was ready to draw in a hurry—like I was ready for action. Maybe Morrolan would be impressed if he glanced over at me. Maybe if the Jenoine showed up suddenly they'd see how ready for action I was and die of fear.

"I'm getting something," said Aliera. "It's opening." I happened to notice her hands, which now gripped the stone very tightly; her fingers were white. I looked for some change in the stone itself, but didn't see anything.

"All right, Vlad," said Morrolan, in that tone of voice he

uses when he's keeping tight control on his emotions—which is usually, now that I think of it.

I nodded, even though he couldn't see me, and, under my breath, I began an invocation to Verra. It was one of the old ones, one of the first I had ever learned, and I shan't repeat it here. At first, I was only going through the motions, but soon enough I felt Morrolan's presence, and, through him, Aliera's, pointing out to me the direction, as it were, in which to, well, direct my efforts. I recited the invocation over and over, trying for some sort of response, or at least the feeling that I was getting through.

It is strange, the things I've done to the inside of my own head. In one way or another, that is where all magic is; that is *what* all magic is, and that is why it is magic—you treat the contents of your skull as if they were a sort of world that you can walk around in, filled with objects that you can manipulate; creatures with whom you can communicate; landscapes that you can observe. This bit of witchcraft is a narrow stream, and you dip your feet in it and splash. This piece of sorcery is a lever you can move stones with, and you grunt and sweat until it moves and you feel the satisfaction of watching it roll down a hill. And the invocation was a chat with a Demon Goddess who bore only the most passing and coincidental relationship to the being I had met, who had from time to time aided me, and who had used and was using me for purposes I was only beginning to have a glimmering of.

The conversation was strictly one-sided; how could it not be, being a creation of myself with myself. One-sided, yet (and here is the magic) it must have done something, because as I stood upon that world whose air was nearly unbreathable, in that room whose contents were nearly unknowable, doing things to my head that are nearly indescribable, feeling a connection within me in a language almost untranslatable, there appeared before my real eyes a hint of red and golden sparks generated by nothing, that shimmered there for a moment, until they took shape, solidified, and became the Goddess herself, who appeared standing, tall, composed, and with a wry look, and she said, "Well, I'm here. Now you must tell me, are you traitors, or fools?"

11

DISAGREEMENTS WITH DEITIES

All sorts of replies came to mind, but I managed to hold them back. Letting Morrolan and Aliera deal with her would be more fun.

The Goddess stood taller than Morrolan, and glared down at him. He put on his supercilious look and seemed unimpressed with her glare; if it was an act, it was a good one, and if it wasn't he had a remarkable amount of confidence in himself. Or he was a complete fool, which I'd suspected for some years. Or, at any rate, a Dragonlord, which is much the same thing.

He said, "You believe they planned all this, Verra? That they wanted you here? Fine. So what? Sethra believes—"

"Sethra," said the Goddess scornfully.

It had never occurred to me that I might one day hear "Sethra" pronounced scornfully; that would have to count as the big shocker for the day.

Morrolan shrugged. Aliera said, "Sorry if you were inconvenienced, Mother, but we were tired of waiting around."

"It isn't a matter of convenience, my dear. It is a matter of permitting them to bring me to a place where they can destroy me."

Morrolan said, "Most of a day, I believe." I stared at Morrolan for a second, trying to figure out how that made sense in regard to anything, then decided not to try.

"I shan't let them," said Aliera.

Verra said, "You shan't let them?"

"That is correct."

"My darling Aliera—"

Teldra cleared her throat, and instantly had everyone's attention. She said, "Our apologies, Goddess, if we have been precipitate. But may I beg you to tell us, now that we have acted, what we ought to do?"

The Goddess smiled, as one might at a kitten rolling on the floor playing with a piece of string. She said, "Ah, my little Issola. How sweet. Well, I will answer your question. First, we—" She stopped in midsentence, stared at something over Teldra's shoulder, and said something that sounded like, "kyrancteur!"

At first I thought it was an exclamation in some foreign language, or else she'd suddenly recognized a friend who was invisible to the rest of us, but then Morrolan said, "Yes. Or trellanstone, if you prefer; that is the name we have always known it by."

"How could it have come to this place?"

"It is," said Morrolan. "With Vlad's help, using an old invocation," which, in case you didn't notice, made no sense at all.

Verra didn't seem bothered by the non sequitur. "I see," she said slowly. I looked up at her bony face, with its slightly askew forehead, and strange jawline, and deep-set eyes, and the thought suddenly came to me: *She's scared.*

I found myself thinking, *Dear Verra, protect us,* before I caught myself. She glanced at me, and a smile flickered briefly around her lips, then went out. She turned her eyes once more to the trellanstone. Presently she asked, "What was it, exactly, that Sethra said?"

Morrolan cleared his throat, started to answer, stopped, and finally said, "There was a great deal of military theory in it."

"That doesn't astonish me," said the Goddess.

"I might summarize it by saying that complex enemy plans are the easiest to defeat, and we shouldn't be afraid of walking into a trap."

"Uh huh. What else?"

"She reminded me that they can be killed."

"So can we all."

Morrolan shrugged. "I have never liked giving up the initiative."

"Nor I," I muttered under my breath, earning me a quick glance from the Goddess, who evidently had very good hearing.

"And yet, my love," said Verra to Morrolan, "we are here, on their world, and they can appear if and when they wish, so they have the initiative. And if little Sethra is that certain, why isn't she here herself?"

"Mother," said Aliera. "You know the answer to that very well."

Verra gave her an indulgent smile. "Perhaps I do."

"I don't," I remarked, but they all ignored me.

"Moreover," continued Aliera, "you also know, I am certain, that if you hadn't wanted to come, you wouldn't have. You are no demon to be summoned and dismissed, and no one here except perhaps our Easterner could take you for one."

"Could I have refused a plea for help from my daughter?"

Aliera snorted. "Easily."

Verra chuckled. "My darling child, you don't know me as well, perhaps, as you think you do."

Morrolan said, "It is the only means we have of learning," which made no sense whatsoever; I was starting to get used to that though.

Aliera herself didn't deign to respond. The Goddess spread her arms and gave Morrolan an exaggerated bow. "Very well, then," she said. "You have summoned me, and I am here. What, exactly, is your plan?"

Aliera and Morrolan looked at each other.

After an embarrassing moment, Verra said, "You don't have a plan?"

"Not exactly," said Morrolan.

"Plans are overrated," I said. "Let's just start killing things. If there's nothing else around, we can always kill each other."

"Don't tempt me," said Morrolan.

I snorted. Verra said, "Perhaps you should allow the three of us to confer, my dear Easterner."

"Sure," I said. "I'll just amuse myself by exchanging sarcastic comments with Loiosh."

"No doubt you will," she said.

Lady Teldra was standing across the room, as calm and patient as an issola, as if waiting for some call that hadn't come. She had taken herself away from the conversation while no one was watching. I reflected on what a fine skill it would be to know when you weren't wanted at a place you didn't want to be, so you could make everyone happy by going away. I walked over to her. She looked up at me, a slightly quizzical expression on her face. I said, "How do you do that, Teldra?"

She smiled and raised her eyebrows, and came as close to looking smug as I'd ever seen her.

I said, "So, all right, how do the laws of courtesy tell us we should handle this mess?"

"The laws of courtesy," she said, still smiling, "are strangely silent on the subject."

"I'm not surprised."

"In any case," she added, "I think you know them as well as I do."

"Oh, yeah," I said. "If there's anything I know, it's courtliness and good manners. I'm even better at politesse than I am at refining petroleum."

"I know little of petroleum, Vlad, but I do know that you are actually quite skilled in the arts of courtesy."

"Right."

Behind me, Aliera and Morrolan were continuing to speak to the Goddess, but I couldn't make out what they were saying. In the event, this did not displease me.

"It is the simple truth, Lord Taltos. It is how you survived for so long in the world you used to inhabit—or, more precisely, the worlds."

I bit back a smart reply and just waited. After a moment, she said, "The Jhereg has its own rules and customs, you know—

codes of appropriate behavior. You couldn't have survived
among them without knowing what all of their signals mean.
And I've seen you with my Lord Morrolan. That is another
different set of codes."

I snorted. "I've almost pushed him far enough to kill me.
More than once."

"I know that, too," she said.

"Well then?"

"What stopped him from killing you?"

"His strong sense of self-interest combined with iron self-
control."

"I don't believe that is entirely correct, Lord Taltos. I know
him rather well, I think, and there are severe limits to his self-
control, whereas there are no limits to his pride. Had you pushed
him far enough, you would have faced a mortal contest."

Morrolan, Aliera, and the Goddess all turned and walked
out the door. I guess if you put a pretty little stream outside your
door, people will want to look at it. I hoped the Jenoine would
feel gratified.

"Okay," I said to Teldra. "Look. I'll concede that, over the
years, I've learned that there's no point in making a bad situation worse, and that it's less work to talk yourself out of a tough
spot than to slice your way out, and that words, while potentially
deadly, are less deadly than Morganti daggers. But I don't think
that is quite the same thing as being courteous."

"I believe, Lord Taltos, that it is very much the same thing.
And you know more than those things, if I may say so. You
know when a casual insult is, in fact, courteous under the circumstances—and when it is not. You know when to make a
friendly gibe, and when the gibe is not quite so friendly, but still
called for. You know how to negotiate from a position of weak-
ness but make it appear to be a position of strength. These are
the sorts of things I'm talking about. And do you know how
many of our folk—and yours—never learn these lessons that
appear so simple to you?"

"Maybe, being an Easterner, I have a natural talent."

"You forget how many Easterners I have known, Vlad. Your people have no such natural talent. In fact, the conditions under which your people live tend to promote the opposite: an irritating obsequiousness, or an aggravating combativeness."

After a moment's thought, I said, "That's true."

She nodded. "It is really all a question of taking appropriate action for the circumstances. I'm sure you realize that I could have this conversation with few others—human or Eastern—that I know. Some it would embarrass, others it would merely confuse."

"Yes, I understand."

"You have learned, faster than some of my own House, what actions—and words are only a special case of actions—are appropriate to the moment."

"A survival skill, Teldra."

"Yes, it is."

"Ah. That's your point, isn't it?"

She smiled, making me feel like my grandfather had made me feel when I had managed the correct riposte after parrying a lowline cut.

Morrolan, Aliera, and Verra returned at this point, speaking in low tones. I gestured toward them and said, "And the Goddess?"

"What about her?"

"What need has she of courtesy?"

"Toward her peers, the same as you or I. Toward us? None. Many of the gods, I believe most of them, display a certain degree of courtesy even though none is needed. Those who don't acquire a reputation."

"For being, say, chaotic?"

"Yes."

"So it is all a question of courtesy?"

"It is all a question of doing the appropriate thing. Of acting as the situation calls for."

"Appropriate thing. You keep saying that, Teldra. When someone walks up to me and says, 'Out of the way, whiskers, you're blocking the road,' is it appropriate to bow and say, 'Yes, my lord?' Is it appropriate to suggest his mother was a toothless norska? Or to quietly step out of his way? Or to urinate on his boot? Or to pretend to ignore him? Or to put a knife into his left eye? Just what does appropriate mean, anyway?"

"Any of those things might be appropriate, Vlad, and I daresay there are circumstances where you might do any of them. But you are always, or nearly always, correct in which you choose. And this is not a matter of instinct, but of observation, attention to detail, and experience. Appropriate action means to advance your own goals, without unintentional harm to anyone else."

"Unintentional harm."

"Yes."

"By Verra's tits," I said, forgetting then remembering that the pair of them weren't all that far away, "you're as cold as Morrolan, aren't you?"

"Yes," said Teldra, "I suppose so. Or as cold as you."

"Me? I'm not cold. I'm the soul of compassion, understanding, and courtesy."

"Yes," said Teldra, dimpling. "You are indeed. But only when it is appropriate."

I chuckled. And, "Okay. I'm convinced. All problems are matters of courtesy, and I am the personification of tact. So, to return to the question, what is the appropriate thing for us to do now?"

"I have no idea," said Teldra, still smiling. "I imagine that is what our friends are discussing right now."

I glanced over at them: heads together, deep in conversation.

"Great," I said. "I can hardly wait to see what they'll come up with."

"I have no doubt," said Teldra, "that it will be entertaining."

I nodded. "Entertaining. Good. That's always been high on my list for the kind of plan I need to get out of a fix."

She didn't reply. I shrugged, gave her a hint of a bow, and

wandered over to the others. As I approached, they all stopped talking and looked up, like they'd been caught at something.

"Well?" I said. "Have we come up with the ultimate solution to all of our physical and spiritual problems? Have we saved the world, made sure the Empire is secure, and—"

"That will do, little Easterner," said the Goddess, giving me a look that made me question what Teldra had just been telling me. I restrained an insolent shrug, perhaps answering the question.

"What do you think, Loiosh? Am I the very soul of tact, discretion, manners, and courtliness?"

"Am I a three-legged tiassa?"

"Just checking."

"We have decided," said Verra, "that if the Jenoine are not polite enough to appear suddenly and force us into action, we will attack them."

"That took serious discussion?"

"Yes."

"Yeah, okay. I sort of suspected you might come up with that one. Have you worked out the details yet?"

"Some of them."

"Okay. How are you going to try to get me killed this time?"

"This time," said Verra, "we just might succeed."

"Heh. You should be so lucky."

Morrolan said, "We're trying to reach the Necromancer. We're hoping she—"

"The Necromancer!"

"Yes. We're hoping—"

"With you and Aliera and the Goddess and Sethra Lavode we don't have enough of a concentration of power? You need to bring the Necromancer in on this? How 'bout the Empress, for the love of V . . . something or other."

Morrolan waited for me to run down, then spoke again. "We're trying to reach the Necromancer," he said. "We're hoping she can find the Jenoine, and a way to get at them. Our problem at the moment is reaching the Necromancer."

"Why do you need the Necromancer at all? Why not have Aliera do it?"

"What are you talking about, Vlad?" asked Aliera a bit impatiently.

"Pathfinder," I said, and suddenly they were all staring at me.

Then, "Pathfinder," repeated Aliera.

"Damn," said Morrolan.

"How did I manage to not think of that?" said Verra.

"How did *I* manage to not think of it?" said Aliera.

"Pathfinder," said Morrolan.

"All right, all right, I'm a genius," I said. "Now we've thought of it. Can we get on with whatever we're going to do?"

"I've never met anyone so impatient to get himself killed, Boss."

"Shut up, Loiosh."

"Yes," said the Goddess, "I believe we can, as you put it, 'get on with it.' Aliera, your weapon?"

I involuntarily took a step back as Aliera drew, and, as the weapon cleared her sheath, I noticed something odd.

I had been in the presence of Morganti weapons a great deal more than I cared to in my brief life; and the same is true of the Great Weapons. I had become, if not used to, then at least familiar with the ugly and terrifying sensation of their presence—sort of the mental equivalent of finding sour milk in one's pitcher, combined with the feeling of waking up suddenly after a dream of being in a cave with a dzur blocking the exit while anklesnakes slithered around behind. But what was odd was that I suddenly realized that Pathfinder felt different from Blackwand. Not that it was at all pleasant, you understand, but it was as if I were picking up bits of personality from the weapon. I don't know, maybe what is strange is that I'd never noticed it before.

Exactly what the differences were was harder to say, except that Pathfinder didn't seem to be quite as, well, aggressive as Blackwand. Morrolan's weapon gave me the feeling that it would love to have the chance to swallow my soul if I'd just come a little closer; from Aliera's weapon I got the feeling that it would devour me without a second thought if I gave it the chance, but it wouldn't go looking for me, either. Also, Blackwand gave me a strong sense of a female personality, whereas from Pathfinder I got no clear indication of a sex. Aliera's sword, it seemed, was more patient, perhaps more protective, and there was a sense of inquisitiveness; while from Morrolan's blade I picked up feelings of arrogance, of strength, of the desire to get to smashing things. And there were other, more subtle differences, too, that I couldn't exactly identify but was now aware of.

I also became aware that Morrolan had said something. "Excuse me," I said. "I was distracted. What was that?"

"I said that is a good idea, Vlad. You may need it."

I almost said "Need what?" before I realized that I had allowed Spellbreaker to fall into my hand. It was dangling, inert, about a foot long, with tiny little links. For a second I stared at it; then I recovered and grunted something at him, and fingered it.

Aliera held Pathfinder out in front of her, the blade at about a forty-five-degree angle toward the ceiling. Her eyes were almost but not quite closed—reminding me, crazily, of how Aibynn looked when playing his drum. I waited, sort of expecting Pathfinder to start glowing or something, but nothing of the kind happened.

After a while, Morrolan said, "You need to find—"

"Shut up, cousin," said Aliera pleasantly.

Morrolan clamped his mouth shut, and Aliera returned to doing whatever it was she was doing. As I waited, I felt a stirring in my left hand, as if Spellbreaker were trembling a little.

"Something is happening with that thing, Boss."

"Noticed that, did you?"

"I'm not sure I like it."

"I just wish I understood what it meant. Any Serioli around to ask?"

"I wouldn't be surprised. We've got everything else."

"Okay," said Aliera suddenly. "I'm getting something."

Her eyes were a little more open now, and she was focusing in front of her, in the middle distance—I followed her glance, but there was nothing there, so she was probably seeing things not apparent to a regular pair of unenchanted human eyes. I happened to look at Verra, then, and she had an expression on her face of the sort you'd associate with any mother seeing her daughter pulling off a difficult task. If I'd let myself, I could have gotten very distracted thinking about just how bizarre that was.

Then I noticed that the tip of Pathfinder was trembling, very slightly. I don't know how much you know about the science of defense, or about Aliera's skill as a swordsman, but, believe me, that hint of movement at the tip of her blade bespoke more intensity of magic and power than a roomful of pyrotechnics.

"*Here we go,*" said Loiosh.

I wanted to be holding my rapier, or a dagger, or something, but I didn't know what, so I just waited.

"They aren't far away," said Aliera. "This world, within a few thousand feet, in fact. But . . . barriers. There are barriers of some kind. I don't yet know of what kind, or how strong. Stand closer to me."

We did so. I made sure Teldra was between me and the Goddess, not for any particular reason except that I didn't feel like standing next to her.

I said, "Does anyone know what we're going to do when we get there?"

"We're going to attack them," said Morrolan.

"Oh."

"We should have surprise working for us," he added.

"Do you really think so?"

He didn't answer. Verra said, "The theory, my little Easterner, is that they don't actually want to kill us, or they'd have done so already."

"What if what they wanted is to kill you, Goddess?"

"They may find that difficult."

Aliera was murmuring under her breath—the sort of mur-

muring one might expect of a rider urging his horse over a difficult jump.

"Can you get through them?" asked Morrolan.

"Of course," snapped Aliera. "Now let me concentrate. Be
ready."

Be ready.

They were always saying stuff like that.

Just exactly what does that mean, anyway? Be ready. Like,
have your eyes open? Be certain you've had a good meal and
used the chamber pot? Now is the wrong time for a nap? Make
sure you aren't sneezing when It happens? What, exactly? It
means nothing, that's what it means. An empty noise.

"I'm ready," I said.

"As am I," said Morrolan. "Yes," said Teldra. Verra did not
deign to speak, and no one expected her to, I suppose because
being a goddess means never needing to sneeze.

I was watching the trembling at the end of Pathfinder, so I
saw it when it happened: A tiny spark appeared on the very tip
of the blade. The trembling caused it to jump around, leaving
diminutive golden trails in the air; I couldn't tell if they were
really there or were just products of my vision. Not, I suppose,
that it mattered. There began to be a sensation of motion—the
kind of motion that happens in dreams, where nothing changed,
and my feet didn't move, but there was the feeling as if my
stomach had suddenly been left behind and needed to catch
up—not the wrenching nausea of a teleport, fortunately, but still
unsettling.

The sense of motion increased.

"Shallow breaths, Boss."

"Right."

Sometime in there, Morrolan had drawn Blackwand—it
tells you how messed up my senses were that I hadn't noticed,
still didn't feel it; all I was really aware of was the sensation of
motion, as if something had pulled me from the bottom of a hill
and I start up up up rolling and spinning and being everywhere
at once and no place at all happening at the same time and

time again you've been through this before you realize that you'll never forget everything you thought you knew about moving from one place to another flash of light flickering and still moving past and present and future filled with unknown dangers appearing from everywhere nowhere somewhere somehow what when where was I and how did I get here from there we are slowing down down down stop.

There were four of them; maybe two of them were the same ones we'd seen before, but I couldn't tell them apart well enough to say. Two were standing, two sitting on what appeared to be an uncomfortable-looking couch. I'd been among humans, Dragaerans, Serioli, cat-centaurs, and gods. One way or another, they were people—but these were *things*. They looked like things, and I thought of them as things, and I really wanted to put them away like things.

The first bit of bad news was, the things didn't seem startled by our presence. If we were counting on surprise, we could be in real trouble.

One of the sitting ones was holding something that appeared to be some sort of tube, with projections that fit nicely into its hand. If it was a weapon, we could be in real trouble.

It was clear that two of them, including the one with the tube, were looking at Verra. It was possible that their idea all along was to kill her, and now that we had brought her, the rest of us could simply be disposed of. If that was their thinking, we could be in real trouble.

I had no time, just then, to pay attention to surroundings—I think I noted that we were indoors, and that was about it. Things happened so quickly that I just had no time to note the sort of details that can save your life; we might be in the Jenoine equivalent of someone's parlor, or of a sorcerer's laboratory, or the weapon room of their Imperial Guard for all I knew. We might be surrounded by Jenoine food and drink, Jenoine books, or Jenoine death traps. If the latter, we might be in real trouble.

"I think we might be in real trouble, Boss."

"*It's possible.*"

"Let's do it," said Morrolan.

There was no time for any other remarks, so we all got to work.

12

EXERCISING DUE CARE FOR THE COMFORT AND SAFETY OF OTHERS

It's funny, but it didn't occur to me until much later to think of it in terms of four of them and five of us. None of the ways things could have gone had much to do with numbers. Morrolan and Aliera were the first to move, Great Weapons flashing. The Goddess strode forward, right behind them, leaving Teldra and me standing there for just an instant before I cursed, put my hand on the Morganti dagger, started Spellbreaker swinging in a slow circle, and tried to figure out something useful to do.

Nothing came instantly to mind.

The two who were sitting remained sitting. One of the others turned its hands over as if asking why we might want to disturb it—Morrolan and Aliera began moving at this one. That left the other one for the Demon Goddess, while Teldra and I were, I guess, just along as witnesses.

It seemed like the opening of some sort of dance—Morrolan and Aliera moved toward either side of the one, who stepped forward as if to place itself between them—in the worst possible position except for letting them both stand behind it. There was a strange grace to its movements. Was it an especially athletic one of its kind? Were they all like that? How can you tell when you're seeing something typical of a species, and when you're seeing an interesting individual of that species? Why does my mind always wander like that when I'm frightened and don't know what to do?

Verra, in the meantime, began to circle to her left with the

179

other Jenoine, who obligingly circled to its left, as if it had no qualms about turning its back to me.

"*Careful, Boss. The two sitting ones are watching you.*"

I acknowledged the warning. But, still, I had a Morganti dagger; if the thing were willing to actually show me its back, how could I resist? Offering a Jhereg your back is like offering a Dzur an insult or an Orca a free piece of merchandise: he'll find it hard not to take it even if he has no use for it. I kept my hand on the hilt of my dagger, watched, and waited.

Two things happened, then, so close together they were almost simultaneous—one was the sudden realization on my part that the room was shrinking in all directions; in other words, the walls were collapsing inward, very quickly. The other was that Verra laughed. I know that I flinched, I don't know if any of the others did, and then, just as quickly, the walls stopped collapsing.

"*Illusion,*" said Loiosh. "*Never fooled me for an instant.*"

"Yeah. Me, *either,*" I told him.

Spellbreaker was about a foot and a half long, with rather thick, heavy links; I kept it spinning slowly. Verra and the Jenoine facing her had both stopped. It was, unfortunately, just short of giving me the nice shot at its back I wanted. While both of their eyes faced forward, they were also wide-set—they had, then, better peripheral vision than humans or Dragaerans, and I needed to be aware of that when trying for a back shot.

We trained professionals notice stuff like that.

The Goddess and the Jenoine appeared to have locked gazes; I couldn't tell if they were engaged in some sort of massive, mystical, magical struggle happening on a level beyond my comprehension, or if they were just having a good old-fashioned stare-down.

Teldra came up to my side; perhaps to share in whatever protection Spellbreaker might give, perhaps just to back me up if I was attacked.

I said "Any ideas, Teldra?" and out of the corner of my eye I saw her shake her head.

"Shallow breaths, Boss."

"Check, Loiosh."

My thoughts were still on the Morganti dagger at my side, but I didn't draw it; wouldn't know quite what to do with it. My instincts told me to wait and see what happened, that this was not—yet—my moment.

Then Aliera lunged suddenly with Pathfinder, and Morrolan struck with Blackwand in a downward slanting arc at the same time. Their timing was precise, their coordination perfect. It ought to have been a deadly combination, the more so as the Jenoine made no effort to avoid either attack. It worked perfectly, except for the part where the Great Weapons were supposed to stab or cut the Jenoine; that didn't happen. Both weapons stopped what appeared to be a fraction of an inch away from their respective targets. Offhand, I didn't know anything tough enough to withstand the direct attack of a Great Weapon. Nor, in fact, did I want to know any such thing, or even think about it too hard.

Then I realized that whatever had neatly stopped Pathfinder and Blackwand had stopped Aliera and Morrolan as well—they were standing utterly motionless, as if frozen by their weapons' contact, or near contact, with the Jenoine. That was no good at all.

I get the shakes when I think back on that moment—Aliera e'Kieron and Morrolan e'Drien and Pathfinder and Blackwand held motionless by these things, while Verra, whether she was doing something or not, at least wasn't casually destroying them the way she ought to be, and, on top of it all, there were those two just sitting there, not even getting involved, as if it weren't worth their effort. That's how I feel now. But at the time, all I felt was irritation, especially directed at those two sons of bitches who were sitting on their superhuman godlike asses.

I really wanted to do something to get their attention.

Okay, I know how stupid that is, I should have been giving thanks to Verra—who was, after all, only a couple of feet away—that I *didn't* have their attention; but maybe I was tem-

porarily nuts or something. No, I won't say that. I won't plead
the excuse of being off my head. I remember clearly and coldly
making the decision, and putting it into action.

My right hand left the vicinity of the Morganti weapon—
which, powerful as it no doubt was, was certainly not going to
do anything Pathfinder and Blackwand couldn't do—and
reached into my pouch. I made my motions small and smooth
to avoid attracting premature attention and, almost immediately, my fingers found what I'd sent them after.

"Boss, do you know what you're doing?"

"More or less," I told him.

"Oh, good."

It was, in fact, something that, years before, I had been
warned in the strongest possible terms never to do again. But
the first time I hadn't had any choice. This time was different:
this time I was irritated.

What I was about to do wasn't like witchcraft: a focusing of
the will, a concentration on desire; nor was it at all like sorcery:
an almost mechanical application of known laws to achieve a
precise result. When I'd done it before, years ago, it had been
born out of anger, frustration, and desperation, and on top of it
I had had my link to the Orb to provide the power to get it
started. This time I had none of that—just the idea, which had
been in the back of my head since my walk with Teldra, and
the vague notion that I ought to do something.

But I did have a few things working for me: For one, the
simple knowledge that I'd done it once before, which was by
itself of incalculable value. For another, my memory, confused
and imprecise, but there, of how that had felt, and where I had
reached into myself, and how I had found those innate abilities
inherited through the connection of my spirit to ancestors
stretching back to when Sethra was young. And, for still another, I had the device in my fingers—a small, purple-blue stone,
smooth as a pearl, which would act like the rendered goose fat
that provides the basis of a good red pepper sauce.

I held it up.

Verra said, "Vlad!"

I remember her saying it, and maybe I was just concentrating too hard to permit myself to be distracted, or maybe I decided that this was a good time to ignore her. In any case, I reached into the stone, and into myself, and cut loose the moorings that held reality anchored to time that passes and the space that uses time, tried my best to give it some focus, and let it go.

I suddenly had the attention of all four Jenoine.

I smiled at them. "Hi there," I said.

The two who were sitting rose to their feet far quicker than I'd have thought they could. I moved Spellbreaker, which was still spinning, a little to the side so it would be out of the way of whatever I was about to do, if I could do it. Something seized hold of the unreality between my fingers, and I felt it start to dissolve.

The two Jenoine moved toward me. I concentrated on them, imagined them dissolving into the raw, eternal, basic matter—or non-matter—of the universe, all coherence vanishing in light and shadow and formlessness.

"Vlad!" said Verra. "Don't!"

So far, so good.

Suddenly, Aliera and Morrolan were free again—and I don't know what had been done to them, but they didn't like it much, because they both jerked back suddenly, as if simultaneously kicked in the chest. Morrolan sprawled on his back; Aliera managed to stay on her feet, but, to the extent that I could spare any attention for them, they didn't seem happy.

Verra had stepped back from the one she faced, and was looking at me; Teldra emitted some sounds that I knew to be in the language of the Jenoine—her voice was even and level as it chirped and croaked and squeaked. Verra's hands were up, and she was making gestures in my direction and Aliera and Morrolan were charging in again, and things got even more confused, as one of the Jenoine who had just risen said something in its own language, though it was hard to hear over the roaring sound that I realized had been steadily growing, and was coming from between my fingers, which was also the source of the reddish-golden light that was streaming out toward three of the Jenoine, who held their ground, their hands clasped together in front of them in a gesture of supplication, though no doubt it meant something else to them, and in the confusion, now that my little purple stone was entirely gone, and the light and the sound were fading, I drew the Morganti dagger to give them something else to worry about, but two of them were worrying about Verra, who seemed to have taken all the light into herself, or at least she was glowing, and she seemed taller as one of them lifted its hands toward her, and another, who was still holding that odd tube, lifted it until it was pointed directly at the Demon Goddess, who said, "That was stupid, little Easterner; she couldn't have hurt me with that thing."

"What was stupid?"

"*You okay, Boss?*"

"*What the—?*"

"Welcome back, Vlad," said Aliera.

"Back," I repeated, at which point things came into focus, and I said, "Sethra! What are you—?" Then, "How did I get back to Dzur Mountain?"

"Over my shoulder," said Morrolan.

"Damn," I said. "I missed it, didn't I? And I'll bet it was fun, too."

"It was successful," said Aliera. "That is, we're here."

"How long has it been?"

Aliera said, "About an hour," at the same time as Sethra said, "A week and a day." They looked at each other, both started to speak, then looked at me.

I managed to say, "Never mind. My fault. I—what happened to my arm?"

Sethra hesitated, then said, "We aren't exactly sure."

"My arm doesn't seem to be working," I explained.

"I know," said Sethra.

I felt my heart start to pound. Now was a hell of a time for it to start that. I took a deep breath, reminded myself that I shouldn't, then realized that it was all right after all. I made myself speak evenly. "I don't know if I'm more frightened that my arm doesn't work, or that Sethra isn't sure why."

"I hope to find out," said Sethra.

I nodded. "Well, why don't you tell me about it."

Of course, Aliera and Morrolan started speaking at once, glared at each other, and so on. I waited patiently. Finally, Aliera said, "Do you want the short version, or the long version?"

"Just tell me what happened, all right?"

"We attacked them. There was a skirmish. You unleashed pre-Empire sorcery, which succeeded in freeing Morrolan and me from whatever was holding us, and also, it seems, broke whatever was keeping us from our gate. No one was hurt except you—"

"None of them?"

"No."

"Hmmm," I said. "They're pretty tough, aren't they?"

"Yes," said Morrolan.

"Okay. What happened to me?"

Morrolan and Aliera looked at Lady Teldra, who nodded and said, "Yes, I saw it. You went forward toward one of them, holding the dagger—"

"—the Morganti dagger."

"Yes."

I nodded. "I don't remember . . . wait . . . yes, I do. I remember drawing it and moving in."

"Yes. Then one of them aimed some sort of weapon at Verra. You interposed yourself, and—"

"I *what?*"

"You interposed yourself between Verra and the weapon of the Jenoine, and were struck by it somewhere high on the left arm or shoulder."

"I didn't really."

"*You did, Boss.*"

"You did, Vlad," said Teldra.

"Why?"

Verra chuckled. Morrolan said, "I'd give my summer palace to know."

"You don't have a summer palace," I said.

"True, but I'd like one."

"I'd like my left arm back. I can't believe I did that."

"None of us can," said Morrolan.

I glanced at the Goddess, who was looking at me with an unreadable expression. I'm tired of unreadable expressions. I said, "Is that what you said was stupid, Goddess? I thought you meant my use of the Elder Sorcery."

"That too," said the Goddess. "You could easily have destroyed us all before I could contain it."

"I have confidence in your Godlike abilities," I said.

"You—"

She didn't finish the thought. I had left a Goddess speechless. I wondered how that would count when I reached the Halls of Judgment. I said, "Spellbreaker didn't help?"

"It isn't that kind of magic," said Verra helpfully.

"Then what kind is it?" I asked, more because I was annoyed than because I wanted an answer; which was just as well because the only answer I got was a slight smile from Verra. I turned to Sethra. "You don't know what happened?"

"Not exactly. Are you in any pain?"

"No."

She nodded. "I suspected you wouldn't be. It probably works directly on the muscle."

Verra said, "They had something like that when I knew them, for use on test subjects. But it was larger and clumsier."

"Test subjects," I repeated.

Aliera said, "Any idea how to effect a cure?"

"Not yet," said Sethra.

"I see."

After an uncomfortable silence, I said, "All right, then what happened?"

Morrolan said, "At about the same moment you went down, Aliera and I struck at two of them." He glanced at Aliera, then said, "I cannot speak for my cousin, but I put a great deal into that attack."

"Heh," said Aliera.

"They were able to avoid physical contact with our weapons—I'm not certain of the nature of their defense—but our attack that time nevertheless appeared to discommode them."

"Heh," I said.

Aliera shrugged. "At any rate, they were not able to paralyze us as they had the first time. We had both struck them once before, a coordinated attack—"

"I remember that," I said.

"I don't know what happened next," said Morrolan, "except that it was Verra who did it."

The Goddess said, "I did little enough. The Easterner's foolishness destroyed the devices that were keeping us on their world; I merely transported us off it, which you or Aliera could have done. I did take the opportunity to give them a few things to keep them out of the way. They still fear me," she added.

"I imagine they do," I said. "Then what?"

"I picked you up," said Morrolan, "as the gate began to open. That was, perhaps, an hour ago."

"An hour. That's all?"

He nodded.

I rubbed my left arm. There was no sensation in it, but neither did it feel cold or especially warm to my right hand, for whatever that was worth. It is odd touching a lifeless limb. My fingers felt my arm, but my arm couldn't feel my fingers. It's a strange sensation. Try it sometime.

"A very respectable escape," I ventured. "Well done."

"And yourself," said Aliera. "I must disagree with Mother; I believe your attack was worth the risk. At least, I don't know how we'd have gotten away otherwise."

"I do," said Verra, giving Aliera a stern look that made me want to giggle.

Aliera shrugged. "Well, we managed it, and without much harm. That's the important thing."

I glanced at my injured arm, and started to object to the "without much harm" business, but didn't.

"No," said Morrolan. "The important thing is that Vlad, however well intentioned, invoked powers he does not understand, and cannot control, and nearly got us killed."

"Sorry about that," I said. "It seemed like a good idea at the time."

"It was a good idea," said Aliera. "It was also necessary, after my cousin made such a clumsy strike at the Jenoine—"

"It was hardly clumsy," said Morrolan. "It was quite sufficient, or would have been, if the Jenoine had not succeeded in blocking it, as, in fact, he blocked yours. More easily, I suspect."

"Not likely," said Aliera. "In fact, as I recall, you were late in your—"

The worst part was, I was too weak to get up and walk away.

"I was hardly late," said Morrolan. "If anything, you—"

"Oh, stop it," I said.

They ignored me.

"If anything I *what*," said Aliera. "Pathfinder was—"

"*Stop it!*" I said, and for an instant they stopped. I rushed into the void like Sethra rushed her reserves into the breach at the Battle of Ice River Crossing (actually, I know nothing about the Battle of Ice River Crossing except that there was one and Sethra was there; but it sure sounded knowledgeable, didn't it?). I said "Can you two, just one time, give a tired and injured man a little peace? Besides, your arguments, as always, are stupid to begin with. Morrolan goes out of his way to be contentious toward Aliera because he idolizes Adron and therefore believes his daughter ought to not only be his equal in all matters, but ought to do and say everything exactly the way Morrolan imagines Adron would; and Aliera, of course, idolizes her big, powerful, brave cousin Morrolan, and so has a tantrum whenever he fails to live up to the Morrolan she's manufactured in her head. It's infernally stupid, and I've been listening to it for more years than a short-lived Easterner should have to, and I'm heartily sick of it. So shut up, both of you."

I ran down at last.

"My *goodness, Boss.*"

I was a bit surprised myself; I hadn't known I knew most of that stuff until I said it, and wouldn't have believed I'd have said it if I knew it. And now I got to sit there and wonder if, after all of Teldra's remarks about how tactful I was, I had finally stepped over the line.

I risked a look at the pair of them.

Morrolan was looking down, a self-conscious, maybe even embarrassed smile trying to fight its way past his facial control. Aliera was *blushing.* Actually blushing. This was as remarkable as having astonished the Demon Goddess. I don't know, by the way, how the Goddess reacted to my outburst, because I carefully avoided looking at her.

Morrolan cleared his throat, started to speak, then didn't.

Eventually, Sethra filled the silence with, "Well, my friends, it is certainly the case that Vlad could use a little quiet. Or, at least, less volume."

Morrolan grunted something that sounded like agreement; Aliera looked down and nodded. They hadn't even looked at each other. I hoped I hadn't made things uncomfortable for them. Except that part of me hoped I had.

Before anything else could happen, I turned to Teldra and said, "I'm glad you survived."

"I did," she said. "Thank you."

"What was it you were saying to them, right when I was doing whatever I was doing that created such a fuss?"

Teldra chuckled. "I suggested that it would be easier for them to resist the effects of the amorphia if they were to release Morrolan and Aliera."

"Oh. Was that all?"

"Almost."

"Oh?"

Lady Teldra blushed. "I'd rather not say, if you don't mind."

I felt my eyebrows rising. Aliera, and now Teldra. What was the Empire coming to? Morrolan chuckled and said, "A well-timed, properly delivered insult can unsettle anyone. I don't know exactly what she discovered that a Jenoine might find so offensive as to disrupt its concentration, but I am not astonished that Teldra knew."

"Teldra," I said admonishingly. "Was that polite?"

"It was," she explained, "appropriate."

Morrolan snorted.

"In any case, we're alive, and free. It's over," I said hopefully.

The Demon Goddess gave a small laugh. "Over? Do you really think so? Do you imagine that your escape has foiled whatever campaign the Jenoine have begun? Or that I will be satisfied letting them continue their mischief without making any sort of counter?"

I sighed. "No, I suppose not. But I'm injured; whatever you do won't include me, will it?"

I looked at Morrolan, Sethra, and the Demon Goddess, and sighed. "Well, can we at least have a decent meal before we do whatever it is we're going to do?"

Sethra nodded. "I think that is an excellent idea. I'll see to it."

She left to have food prepared, and my stomach growled and rumbled at the idea. I closed my eyes.

I heard the sounds of people sitting, and, wounded arm or no, enjoyed the feeling of being momentarily safe. The muscles in my shoulders and neck relaxed, and I took a big lungful of normal air that I didn't have to think about breathing.

Presently, a rough, high-pitched voice said, "Wine, my lord?"

I opened my eyes, saw Tukko, and closed my eyes again. "Yes," I said. And, "please," I added, because Lady Teldra was nearby. I sat up, discovering that it was harder than I'd have thought without being able to use my left hand, and took a glass of something red and sipped it. My tongue liked it—it was faintly nutty and had a bit of tang to it—but my stomach complained that it wanted something solid before I got too involved in this whole drinking business. I caught Teldra looking at me, and lifted my glass to her. "To survival," I said.

"Yes, indeed," she said.

Sethra returned and said, "Dinner will be ready in an hour." She smiled at me and said, "Will you survive that long?"

"I think so," I said. It suddenly occurred to me that, while Sethra was off giving the order for food to be prepared, Tukko, the only servant I'd ever seen here, was with us. Was there a staff of cooks I'd never met? If so, why, since Sethra's usual diet didn't feature anything that needed cooking? If not, had she gone off to arrange for some culinary ensorcellment? Of all the myriad mysteries surrounding the Dark Lady of Dzur Mountain, I knew that this one was going to bother me. Maybe I could bring myself to ask her. Sometime when Lady Teldra wasn't around.

I drank my wine, and Sethra sat down next to me. "Let's see that arm," she said. I couldn't show it to her because I couldn't move it, so I just shrugged my one good shoulder and looked away. Out of the corner of my eye, I could see her holding it, rolling my sleeve back, touching it; but I felt no sensation.

I said, "Evidently the nerves have been damaged, too; I can't feel your charming, cold, undead fingers."

"Mmmmm," she said. Then, "Yes, it *is* nerve damage, not muscle damage." She continued her inspection. I tried to think about other things without much success.

"Is it repairable?" I asked eventually, trying to keep my voice casual, as if I were asking if a blunted dagger could be resharpened.

"I'm not sure," she said in much the same way. Bitch.

"Good wine," I told her. "Thanks."

She smiled as if sharing a joke with herself and said, "You are most welcome, Lord Taltos."

She set my arm back in my lap and said, "We'll have to see."

I nodded. No one spoke. I cleared my throat and said, "So, all right, what's the plan?"

13

"It's too soon to talk about plans," said Morrolan. "I'm still trying to recover."

"Nonsense," I said. "It's never too soon to talk about plans. Making plans is one of the great joys of my life. Sometimes, on a lazy afternoon, I just sit around and make up plans. I've often said—"

"Be quiet, Vlad."

"Feel better now, Boss?"

"A bit, Loiosh."

"You know, Morrolan," said Aliera. "He has a point. It wouldn't hurt any to start thinking about how we're going to go after them."

"It's too soon to talk about plans," I said. "I'm still trying to recover."

Morrolan favored me with a disgusted look.

Sethra said, "Lady Teldra, I assume you will grace us with your company at table?"

"That is kind of you," said Teldra. "Yes, I should be delighted." For a moment that confused me, until I remembered that she was Morrolan's servant, which fact had somehow gotten lost in the last few days.

"Good," said Sethra.

"Let me see that arm," said Aliera abruptly. She came over and knelt down next to me, picked up my arm, and stared at it. "Nerve damage can sometimes be repaired," she said after a moment.

193

"Yes," said Sethra. "Sometimes, depending on the nature of the damage. In this case, I can't quite tell what they did." This, of course, made me feel great. What is it about physickers, or sorcerers acting as physickers, that makes them talk about the sick guy as if he weren't in the room?

Aliera turned to Verra and said, "Mother? Do you know how it works?"

"The one I remember worked on the muscle, not the nerve," she said.

"Well, can you help?"

"Perhaps," said the Goddess.

Perhaps. I liked that. What's the point of divinity if you can't help your devoted worshipers? I sat there, my arm hanging limp, and thought evil thoughts.

Sethra suggested I lie back down and relax until we were called to table, which seemed like a good idea, so I did, and I believe I actually dozed off for a while, to be woken by Loiosh, who is quite accomplished at waking me, explaining that he was used to surviving on scraps, but if I wanted any more than that it was time for me to be moving.

I grunted and struggled up to my feet, which, as I've already observed and now discovered again, is harder than you'd think when shy an arm, then followed Aliera and Teldra, who were having a quiet conversation and making their leisurely way to the dining room. I sat down with Teldra on one side of me, and Sethra, at the head of the table, on the other; Morrolan and Aliera were across from us. I said, "Where is the Goddess?"

"Is that a philosophical question, Vlad?" asked Morrolan.

"Yeah, I suppose."

"She has returned to her own domain," said Aliera.

"What, she didn't like the menu?"

Sethra smiled at that, but gave no response; nor was one needed, because Tukko came in at that moment, carrying a large silver platter in each hand. He set one of them down between Morrolan and me, the other between Teldra and Aliera.

"Oh," said Sethra, in a tone I'd never heard from her before.

I looked up, and she was staring at the food with a look of distress on her face. I tried to remember when I'd seen her distressed before.

"Vlad, I'm sorry," she said. "I didn't realize what was being prepared."

I looked at the food again, frowned, and then figured it out and chuckled. "Oh," I said. "That's funny, in a grim sort of way."

My father had never approved of what he called "half-prepared food," of which this was a sample. I don't have a problem with it, myself—it's sort of fun to put things together yourself, adjusting the quantities, and so on. But my father believed that a good chef made all the decisions about food; if the guest added even a bit of lemon or salt to something my father had built, then, he believed, there must be something wrong— either with the food or with the guest.

I think this says more about my father than about food.

The item before us consisted of treska leaves—fresh, green, and curly. One would spoon a tiny bit of plum sauce onto a leaf, add a minute quantity of dried kethna, a morsel of diced leek, a piece of lime, a slice of bitterwort, a sliver of ginger, and a dusting of dried red pepper. One then rolled the thing up and popped it whole into one's mouth. I'd had versions of this before—most of the islands had something like it, using dried seafood of some kind in place of kethna, as a lovers' snack. Cawti and I had once—but never mind that. The point is, you need two hands to prepare it, and Sethra had just realized that it was exactly the wrong thing to serve just then, and she was mortified. I was amused. Hungry, but amused.

The funniest part was that I caught Sethra glancing at Teldra. Teldra, for her part, said, "Here, I'll wrap one for you."

"That would be great," I said.

She put one together for me, her long, graceful fingers nimble and precise as she measured each ingredient out on the leaf that lay in the palm of her hand; then she rolled it up in a smooth motion, and handed it to me with the least hint of a bow. I smiled at her, took it, and ate it. It was very good; the bitterwort slid through the plum sauce, and then the ginger and the red pepper sort of burst in on your tongue along with . . . well, you get the idea. I had two more of them, making a point of eating slowly to give Teldra time to wrap and eat a couple of her own. Tukko came in with the next course, shuffling about and moving much quicker than it seemed he was. He gave us each what I thought was just a ball of rice, only the rice had been prepared with ginger, and saffron, and I swear a tiny bit of honey; it was quite remarkable.

"My compliments, Sethra," I said.

"Thank you, Vlad," which was just about the only conversation for some time.

The fruit was a selection of local berries, some of which I hadn't run into before, but they were all good, and served with ice and thick cream, after which came thin slices of beef, just barely seared and seasoned with pepper and parsley and calijo, and served with fresh, thick-crusted dark bread. I couldn't cut it with the knife, so I just set the meat on the bread and tore off bites of both.

It was very good.

I ate a great deal.

I noticed that I was sitting with my feet wrapped around the legs of my chair, which is something I've found myself doing when serious about eating. I stopped at once, of course; it's hard to look tough with your feet wrapped around the legs of a chair. Sethra picked at her food, as she had the other times I'd eaten with her. I knew she didn't eat much, for obvious reasons; I wondered if she enjoyed the flavors. Add that to my list of things I'll never ask her, but would like the answer to.

Eventually, I sat back, stretched out, and said, "Okay, Sethra. Give me a couple of hours to digest, and I'll take on every Jenoine you have, all at the same time."

"Careful what you promise," said Sethra Lavode.

"All right," I said. "Let me rephrase that."

Morrolan chuckled. So did Loiosh. I'm quite the jongleur when out of danger and with a meal inside me. Eventually we made our way back to the sitting room, and Tukko brought out a liqueur that was older than Morrolan and much sweeter, featuring the smallest traces of mint and cinnamon—an odd combination, but a successful one, and I'm pretty sure there was some honey in there, too.

I moaned softly. Sethra said, "Is the arm beginning to hurt?"

"No," said Aliera. "That's his moan of contentment after a good meal."

"Now, how would you know that?" I asked her.

She gave me an inscrutable smile that she must have learned from Morrolan. I grunted and drank some more, and enjoyed the transitory sense of contentment I was feeling.

Sethra looked at my arm some more—and when I say she looked at it, that's what I mean. She stared at it so hard I'd say she was looking right through the skin, which is probably what she was doing, at least on some mystical level that I'll never understand.

After several minutes, she said, "I don't know. I'm not sure if I can do anything about it, but it looks like I may not have to."

"How, it'll fix itself?"

"I think so. It seems like it might be a temporary condition. I've been watching the signs of activity in the nerves, and it now seems clear that it is getting better rather than degenerating."

"Degenerating," I said. "Okay. What would that have meant?"

"Paralysis, then death, probably from suffocation when you became unable to breathe, unless your heart became paralyzed first, which would have killed you more quickly. But, as I say, it isn't going that way, it is repairing itself."

"Hmmm. Okay, that's good news. Any idea how long?"

"I can't say."

"Remember, we Easterners don't live more than sixty or seventy years."

"I doubt we're talking about years."

"Good. Then I imagine you're not going to ask me to do anything until I have two good arms, right?"

"I'm not sure we can wait, Vlad."

"Oh? You mean, after two hundred thousand years, or whatever it's been, things suddenly got urgent? When, yesterday?"

"Yes," said Sethra. "I believe things have become urgent. They became urgent when Morrolan and Aliera were taken. Everything is at a new level now, and developments are taking place quickly."

"But—"

"More important," she continued, "I doubt they will give us time to do anything at all."

"They wouldn't attack Dzur Mountain again, would they?"

"I hope so. Anything else they might come up with would be worse, because we haven't any preparations for it."

"Hmmm," I said, because that always sounds wise. "Have you spoken to the Empress?"

"Yes."

"Well then—wait. You have?"

"Yes."

"Oh," I said. "And, uh . . . what does she say?"

"She wants me to deal with it."

"She wants you to . . . with all of her resources, she has no one else to call on except—"

"Me? And Morrolan e'Drien, and Aliera e'Kieron?"

"Uh . . ."

"Go ahead, Boss; talk yourself out of this one."

"Shut up, Loiosh."

"I was referring to myself, Sethra," I said.

"Ah. Well, she is calling on me, and I am calling on you."

"You are—"

"Traditionally, this is exactly the sort of thing the Empress has called upon the Lavodes for; it is what we were created for. Now, as it happens, I am the only Lavode left. Well, there's one other, but he isn't ready yet."

"The Lavodes were created to fight the Jenoine?"

"The Lavodes were created to handle threats or potential threats to the Empire that were fundamentally non-military."

"I see." I thought about it. "But I thought the Lavodes were disbanded before the Interregnum."

"That is true, but I always thought that was a bad idea. The Empress, as it happens, agrees with me."

"Ah. She agrees. Well, how nice. And evidently the Demon Goddess agrees with you, too. And Aliera agrees, and Morrolan agrees. And Teldra, of course, can't help being agreeable. So I guess you've got agreement all the way around except from the Verra-be-damned Easterner who'd really like to have his left arm working again before doing anything stupid."

"You might have a choice," said Sethra. "But most likely you won't."

"Great. So we're going to be in for it, whether we want to or not. What do we do?"

"Do you have any suggestions, Vlad?"

"For handling rampant Jenoine? No, that has never been a specialty of mine."

"Then, perhaps, you'd care to shut up and let us figure something out."

"Ouch," I said. "All right. I'll just sit here like any good weapon, and wait to be pulled from my sheath, blunted edge and all."

"Good," she said. "That's just what I want."

That hadn't been the answer I was looking for, but I decided to be content with it before I encouraged something worse. I fell silent, just sitting there with my left arm hanging limp and useless in my lap.

"I wish," said Aliera abruptly, "that we could find a way to carry the war to them."

Morrolan looked at her. "Since that is such an obvious observation that you could not possibly have any reason for making it, I must assume you have an idea as to the particulars."

She smiled sweetly at him, and suggested where he might put his assumptions, but caught herself, glanced at me, and eventually said, "No, as it happens, I was musing. I can't think of any way to do so."

Morrolan nodded. "If we're speaking of wishes, I wish we understood them better."

"I have a few guesses about them," said Aliera, "based on what we've just been through, and what I've picked up from Sethra and my mother."

"All right," said Morrolan. "Keep talking."

Sethra leaned forward attentively; I pretended to be bored with the whole thing.

"My first guess is that, whatever their long-term plans are, their next objective is Verra. We know that she has been their enemy for her entire existence, and everything that has happened can be seen that way—even the nonsense about trying to convince Vlad to kill her might be second-level deception, or even a straightforward attempt to convince him to do so."

"Yes," said Sethra. "I agree with your reasoning. Go on."

"All right," said Aliera. "My second guess is a little more daring."

Morrolan muttered something under his breath.

"I believe," said Aliera, "that their second target is the Orb."

Sethra stirred. "The trellanstone?"

Aliera nodded. "The best way to attack the Orb would be with a device with similar properties."

"Then why," said Morrolan, "were we allowed to see it?"

"You think you were allowed to?" said Sethra. "I thought you had managed to penetrate their illusions, and see it in spite of them."

"That's what I had thought, too. But if the trellanstone is important, then why, of all the places in the Universe, would they put us near it, illusions or no? In fact," he continued, "there's been too much of that going around with these things. Too many coincidences. Too many times we have to ask ourselves, 'Why would they do that?' All the way from asking Vlad to kill Verra, to doing nothing while Vlad broke us out of the manacles, and doing nothing again while he broke himself and

Teldra out, and then allowing us to see the trellanstone, and—"

"My Lord Morrolan," said Lady Teldra suddenly.

He stopped, and turned to her. He'd forgotten her, as had the rest of us. Her eyes were just a trifle wide.

"I know that look, Boss. She just got something. You get the same look when you finally figure out the obvious."

"How would you know what I look like? You're on my shoulder."

"We have ways."

Meanwhile, Teldra was holding up a finger, asking us to wait, making little nods to herself as pieces fell into place. Then she said, "If I may be permitted to express an opinion."

Morrolan nodded impatiently.

"I think, perhaps, you do not understand the Jenoine."

He chuckled. "That, my dear Teldra, is hardly news."

Her smile came and went like a straight shot of plum brandy, and she said, "I learned something of the Jenoine years ago, most especially their language. I'm sure you are all aware that language holds the key to the thinking of a culture. And, of course, one cannot spend time in such illustrious company as my Lord Morrolan, Sethra Lavode, and such gods as they come in contact with from time to time, without learning more. And then, I spoke with them."

She paused. I wondered if she got her sense of drama from Morrolan, or if he hired her because of it. "When you speak of place, you are speaking in terms that would not make sense to them. They have a concept of 'place,' but it is used in their mathematics, not in their daily lives."

"All right," said Aliera. "You have our attention."

"I have heard some—including you, Aliera—speak as if the Jenoine had come to our world from another place. This is not entirely true. I—please bear with me, this isn't easy to describe." She hesitated. "The clearest way to say it is that they do not move as we do, nor do they remain stationary as we do. That room in which we were held captive is, in an important sense, the only 'place' they have. At least, as we would use the term 'place.' The world that Vlad and I explored was, to them, the same place as the room. When we shattered the enchantment that kept us from seeing some of what was in the room, what we did was the equivalent of breaking out of that room and exploring other places in the structure. When we physically left the room to explore the world outside that room, we were, in their view, spirit-walking. Well, that isn't exactly right—it isn't such a perfect reversal, but it is something like that."

"Well," said Aliera. "That makes everything clear."

Teldra frowned. "Let me try again."

"Take your time," said Morrolan, giving his cousin a dirty look.

"Think of them this way: They are to us as amorphia is to normal matter. To them, our world and the place where we were held captive are the same place, differing only as states of being. I . . ." Her voice trailed off.

"I'm sorry to say," said Morrolan, "that I don't understand."

I was glad I wasn't the only one.

"The Necromancer," said Sethra suddenly.

"Ah," said Teldra. "Yes."

Morrolan said, "Shall I summon her?"

The mere mention of her name explained some of it—it meant we were dealing with the sorts of mind-bending things that are beyond the powers of normal people to understand.

"I'm not certain," said Aliera, "that I could survive that just now."

I thought about making a comment about Aliera's delicate emotions, but good sense prevailed. A lot of my best wit is shared with no one except Loiosh and you, so I hope you appreciate it; he usually doesn't.

Teldra took her comment seriously. "It requires an adjustment in thinking that doesn't come naturally. I began to get glimpses of it when I studied their language, but I didn't actually understand it until speaking with them. Yes, the Necromancer must necessarily understand these things, and I'm certain she could explain it better than I."

Morrolan cleared his throat. "I don't suppose," he said, "that you could explain the, uh, practical ramifications."

"I believe I can," said Sethra Lavode.

Teldra shot her a look full of gratitude. Meanwhile, I was thinking, "Wait a minute; how is it Teldra knows this stuff and Sethra doesn't?"

She answered the question before I could decide if I wanted to ask it aloud.

"What you are saying, my dear Teldra, makes sense of many things I have almost understood. Yes. It explains why they were able to achieve access to Dzur Mountain just when they did. It was not, as I thought at the time, a failure of my mundane defenses, nor of the magical ones. It was an attack from a direction that was unexpected, because, if you will, I didn't know the direction existed."

Teldra nodded. "To themselves, they would say they redefined your defenses."

"Yes."

"Okay," I said. "Good. Now I understand everything."

"In practical terms," said Sethra, as if I hadn't spoken, "it explains at least some of the peculiar behavior you witnessed while confined. In particular, the place they kept you is, as you said, the only place they have. The world the only world, the building the only building, the room the only room. They were, in that sense, in there with you the entire time. You didn't see them or hear them when their attention was focused elsewhere. They—"

"Rubbish," I said.

"Excuse me, Vlad?" said Sethra, who I imagine wasn't used to being addressed that way.

I repeated my remark, then amplified. "I don't care if they consider it a place, or a state of mind, or, well, or whatever they consider it. They are real beings. They have bodies. They have places those bodies are."

"What is your point, Vlad?" said Sethra, who seemed to be doing me the courtesy of taking me seriously.

"You don't sit a bunch of prisoners down in front of a pow-erful object, even concealed, unless either you *want* them to find it, or . . ."

I stopped, considering what I had been about to say.

"Yes, Vlad?" said Morrolan. "Or?"

"Or unless you have no choice."

Sethra said, "How could . . . oh. I see. Yes, that makes sense."

Morrolan and Aliera were already there. Morrolan said, "It was the trellanstone that was holding us in place, that was keep-ing that gate shut. Yes, I can almost see that."

"Almost?"

"Well, it needs something to work with."

"You don't think there is enough amorphia on that world?" I said.

"Oh, right," said Morrolan.

Sethra looked at us. "Amorphia? How could there be amor-phia there? It only occurs on our world. They cannot duplicate the conditions that gave rise to it without, in all probability, destroying their entire world."

I said, "I don't suppose there is a quick explanation for that remark, is there Sethra?"

Morrolan and Aliera looked impatient, but Sethra said, "The Catastrophe that created the Great Sea in the first place resulted from several fluke occurrences, as well as some nasty scheming and plotting on the part of Verra and others with her. But the fact that it failed to entirely consume the world is the biggest fluke of all. Amorphia is not something that is contain-able, by its very nature. To create it is to end everything."

"But Adron's Disaster—"

"Very nearly destroyed the world again," said Sethra, "but the one advantage the gods had in containing it was the exis-tence of the Great Sea. Had the Great Sea not been there, the Lesser Sea might well have destroyed all life in the world." She shook her head. "I simply cannot conceive of the Jenoine finding a way to produce amorphia."

"Well, they did," I said. "Or else found another way to get it, because they've got it."

Morrolan and Aliera told her about the river of amorphia we had found, Teldra and I making the occasional murmur of agreement. When they had finished, Sethra said, "I didn't think they could do that. I still don't understand how they can do that," which was followed by an unpleasant silence, during which we all, I suspect, contemplated the powers of the Jenoine.

"Are they gods?" said Morrolan suddenly.

Sethra shook her head. "I do not believe so. Teldra?"

"Not in any meaningful way, at least as far as how they see themselves."

"Well, that's something," said Morrolan, which was much like what I was thinking. "So, then, how do we approach them? How do we defend ourselves against them, beyond that we've been doing for thousands of years?"

"Don't forget the weapons," I pointed out.

"Weapons?" said Sethra.

"They had whole racks of weapons. Mundane weapons, the sort of thing I think of as weapons. Things that cut, and stab, and make nasty gouges. If those bastards are so bloody magical, what do they need with weapons?"

"Good question," said Morrolan. "He's right, they had quite a collection of them. What are they for?"

"That," said Sethra, "I think I can answer. I believe that, after establishing themselves here, they intend to subvert a portion of our citizens and use them as a mundane army."

"How can they subvert them?" said Aliera.

"If they can, indeed, attack the Orb, then they can, at least potentially, gain access to the minds of those who are linked to it."

That thought made me shudder. For one thing, I was linked to the Orb myself.

"Well, let's see," said Aliera. "Consider what we know about them. They are after my mother, and perhaps others of the gods as well. It is the gods who are protecting our world—I think I now understand a little how they are doing it. But what the Jenoine want is full access to our world. What prevents them from having it are the Lords of Judgment, the Orb, the power of Dzur Mountain. They attacked Dzur Mountain once before, and failed to take it."

"Barely," said Sethra under her breath.

"Therefore, our defense of these things—"

"Defense," said Morrolan like it was something foul. "Why not attack them instead? I've always preferred attacking to defending."

"I know," said Sethra. "But you are still young, and may yet learn."

He glared at her. She ignored it and said, "Go on, Aliera."

Aliera continued, "Our defense of these things has to happen on several levels at once. We require the assistance of the Lords of Judgment, in the first place, and I should think we really ought to consult the Necromancer after all."

"Yes," said Sethra. "But whatever we're going to do, we ought to do it quickly. We don't know how much time they're going to give us. And worse, we don't know where they're going to attack."

"Yes, we do," said Morrolan suddenly, sitting upright, and staring off into space.

We all looked at him.

"Trellanstone," he said. "It all revolves around the trellanstone, or kyrancteur, in the language of the Serioli. They managed to find some, and they are using it. They wanted Aliera and me out of the way to—"

Sethra figured it out first. "Oh," she said. "Yes. I should have seen it at once."

Then Aliera got it, and nodded slowly. "Foolish of me. One of them was able to stop a simultaneous attack from two Great Weapons. It should never have been capable of stopping even one of them. I was so annoyed, I didn't stop to wonder how it managed it. Yes. There is only one way it could have done that. How annoying."

Of course, I could have sat there for the rest of my life and never figured it out, but Sethra realized I was confused and took pity on me.

"Trellanstone," she said. "It is useful for manipulating amorphia—raw chaos. So far as I know, there are two places in the universe where one can find amorphia, and both of them are on this world. The Great Sea of Amorphia is protected by the Orb, which is protected by the Empress, who is protected by the Lords of Judgment, by Dzur Mountain, and by the Orb."

"Ah," I said. "And so now we know, I'm sure, where they got the amorphia from in the first place."

"Yes," said Sethra. "We used the power of the Greater Sea to protect the Orb, and used the Orb to protect the Greater Sea. It never occurred to me that they might tap into the Lesser Sea, because it isn't connected to the Orb. But they have somehow tapped into it. They have been draining it, and learning to control it with the trellanstone, and that could give them what they need to attack the Orb."

"The Lesser Sea," I said. "Well. Can't we just cut it off from them?"

Sethra nodded. "Yes. And we will. I can do so myself. But then what?"

"Then," said Morrolan, "they will use their trellanstone to attempt a permanent link with it, much as the Orb is linked to the Great Sea. If they achieve that, they will, in effect, have the seeds of their own Empire on our world."

I nodded. "Yes. And after that things could get all kinds of difficult, couldn't they?"

"They could indeed," said Sethra. "We must act at once. Every moment that passes, they draw more energy, and become stronger, and it will make it harder to resist them. We must cut off their flow, and then be prepared to make certain they cannot re-establish it. That means facing them down right there, at the Lesser Sea of Chaos."

"Adron's Disaster," said Morrolan.

Aliera nodded. "I was afraid Daddy would cause trouble sooner or later."

14

I was glad Teldra and Loiosh were there, because I didn't want to be alone.

Morrolan, Sethra, and Aliera had left us, continuing their discussions as to who should speak with whom about what—Morrolan to speak with the Empress, Aliera to talk to the Necromancer, and so on, and what they should tell them. Dzur Mountain is a big and lonely place, and some of that feeling rests in each chamber, no matter how small and warm; with little effort I could imagine the nightmares from my childhood creeping out of the corners—especially since this was a place where some of the nightmares were real. And it didn't help that it required very little imagination to see Jenoine appearing out of nowhere; from all evidence, that was a very real possibility.

Teldra and I spoke for a while about the meal, and the furnishings of Dzur Mountain, and other things. I wanted to ask her about Cawti, but I refrained. Instead I said, "Do you think I was out of line, Teldra?"

"My lord?"

"My, uh, blowup at Morrolan and Aliera. Was I out of line?"

"I don't believe it is my place to say, my lord."

"Heh. In other words, yes."

She shook her head. "No, I simply mean it is not my place to say."

"All right."

She hesitated, then said, "I think you, being wounded, had the right to request respect for your injury."

"Mmmmm. But you wish I hadn't said it?"

"I'm not certain, Vlad. Certainly, everything you said is true. Not exhaustive, but true."

"Not exhaustive?"

"I mean your insight was well taken. But, there is still much you don't understand about my Lord Morrolan. For all of his skills and strengths of character, Morrolan is still a young Dragon. He knows this. It is why he wanted me as his seneschal. To know and take steps to counter one's weaknesses is praiseworthy, in my opinion. Also, rare."

"I see. Other than having the desire from time to time to slaughter a few hundred helpless peasants, what does it mean to be a young Dragon?"

"It means seeing the world with one's self as the center."

"Really? I've never considered Morrolan to be self-centered."

"He isn't," said Teldra. "Not as the term is usually meant. There is a subtle but important difference, Vlad, between thinking only of yourself, and seeing the world as it affects you." She smiled suddenly. "And the difference, by the way, is exactly what courtesy is all about."

"You'll have to explain that to me."

"Do I, Vlad? I somehow doubt that."

"Oh?"

"Oh. But, very well. Morrolan is generous, and self-sacrificing, and always glad to be of help to a friend, but sometimes he sees things first from how they affect him. It means he will sometimes go into a situation wondering what he should do, rather than wondering what needs to be done."

"That's pretty subtle, Teldra."

"Not as subtle as you might think. Or, rather, it is a case where subtleties can become very large. Sometimes, for example, you step into a situation where the thing that needs to be done is nothing at all; someone looking at it from his own perspective is unlikely to realize this."

I made a noncommittal sound, trying to work it all out.

"I know of one case late in the Interregnum—because my

Lord Morrolan told of it himself—where he was a division commander under Sethra. He was, he says, an effective commander, but he had the bad habit, when given an order, of sending back suggestions to Sethra about what she should do with the rest of the army to support him, not quite able to realize that she might have thought of these things, and that it was she who had the best view of the entire picture, and was placed to make those decisions. The result was a small increase in friction among the staff, and a series of delays in carrying out her orders. His intentions were good, but he was seeing everything from his own perspective."

"Hmmm," I said. "Okay, I see your point. And, yeah, Morrolan is like that, sometimes. So is Aliera, for that matter."

"Yes, she is also a young Dragon."

"Which, of course, is part of why they keep knocking heads, notwithstanding my juvenile outburst earlier."

"Of course."

I shrugged. "Well, okay, I'm glad we settled that. What are young Issola like?"

Teldra flashed me a smile. "Obsequious to the point of irritating, or else timid to the point of invisibility. What about young Easterners?"

"Brash, cocky, and convinced we can beat anything that walks, flies, or swims, and that we know all the answers to everything."

"Rather like Dzur, then."

"I guess. I'm generalizing from one example, here, but everyone generalizes from one example. At least, I do."

That earned an actual chuckle; I felt very proud.

I added, "Of course, by Dragaeran standards, all Easterners are young Easterners."

"Yes. Which is only one of the reasons Easterners are treated the way they are by humans."

"Morrolan is an exception; he deserves credit for that. As are you, by the way."

"Thank you," said Teldra. "In my case, I can't help it, it's how I was raised." She smiled.

There were footsteps in the hall, and I knew it was Sethra before she appeared, either because I recognized her footsteps, or because of some subtle psychic awareness of her that I was developing. She nodded to us and said, "Have you two solved all of our questions of grand strategy for us?"

"No," I said, "but we've solved a great deal of the mystery of the mysterious Morrolan."

"I'm impressed," said Sethra, sitting down in an oversized chair to my left. "That's much more difficult." It seemed to me, watching her sit, that she was tired. I guess she'd been busy enough while we were away.

I said, "You reached the Necromancer?"

Sethra nodded. "She'll be along directly."

I tried to say, "Good," but couldn't force the word past my lips, so I settled for the old brusque nod. Sethra glanced at my arm and said, "Any change?"

"About five or six minutes ago it twitched a little. Hardly anything; I was talking to Teldra and barely noticed it."

"Very well," she said. "That's probably a good sign. The muscles are coming back to life, which means, among other things, that they aren't entirely dead."

"You thought they might be?"

"It was a possibility."

"Why didn't you tell me?"

"What good would it have done you?"

"It would have given me a good excuse to have a hissy-cow, right when I badly wanted to have one."

"A hissy-cow?"

"Uh . . ."

"No, no, Vlad. Don't explain." She chuckled. "A hissy-cow. I think I like that."

I had gotten a chuckle out of Teldra and Sethra within the same hour, and that after making Teldra and Aliera blush, and before that I'd managed to shock the Demon Goddess. My life was now complete. I decided this was a good time to quit, so I leaned back and closed my eyes, only to be interrupted by the sound of more footsteps. I didn't want to open my eyes, for fear that the Necromancer would be there, so I did and she was.

You must understand, it isn't that I'm afraid of her. I've spoken with her, and, if you can get past the fact that she's undead, and that her mind is perfectly comfortable living in places that would drive me mad, and that for her the distinction between the living and the dead is just a matter of which way she's facing, she's a perfectly decent sort, as Dragaerans go. It's just that her showing up just then meant that things were liable to start moving, and I was very happy sitting on a couch in Dzur Mountain, feeling relatively at peace with the world, and luxuriating in the notion that no one, just at that moment, would be able to kill me.

"The technical term is 'self-pity,' Boss."

"Did I ask for the technical term?"

"Hello, Vlad," said the Necromancer, in that strange, almost hollow-sounding voice of hers, with her eyes looking more through me than at me.

"Hello," I said, resisting the urge to growl.

Aliera was standing next to her, and nodded me a cool hello. "How's the arm?" she said.

"It twitched."

"Good," said Aliera. "I was hoping it would do that."

Bloody great.

Sethra said, "Have you explained what we require of the Necromancer?"

"No," said Aliera. "I thought I'd leave that to you."

"Very well. While I do so, I think you know what your next task is."

"Yes," said Aliera. "I shall attend to it at once."

Sethra nodded, and Aliera took two steps forward, one step to the side, and vanished as if she had stepped through an invisible doorway.

Sethra Lavode turned to the Necromancer, and I suddenly

had the feeling that I was present at one of those great historical moments that you read about, wishing you were there. Here was the Enchantress of Dzur Mountain explaining to the Necromancer the plan of campaign against the ancient enemies of the Dragaeran race. This might be one of the great turning points in the history of the Empire. It seemed incumbent on me to say something to undercut to the whole significance of it, but nothing came to mind.

The two pale, black-clad undead women regarded each other—thin faces, ancient eyes; sort of a strange mirror image. Sethra was perhaps a little taller, and her hair was a bit darker and longer; the Necromancer gave the appearance of a little more age, though this was illusory. In addition, though I knew Sethra was a vampire, the Necromancer looked like one—so pale, wasted, drawn; like someone in the last stages of some horrible disease.

"We are expecting an attack from the Jenoine," said Sethra.

"Where?"

"The site of Adron's Disaster."

The Necromancer's eyebrows went up. "Is it unprotected?"

"Yes. The other has been protected all along, almost by accident, as it were. And it never occurred to me to look for an attack that way."

The Necromancer nodded, closed her eyes for a moment, then opened them. "Nothing yet," she said.

"Are you certain?"

The Necromancer frowned and said, "What do you mean?"

"Look again. Look for anything that doesn't belong."

"Very well," she said. Then, "Oh."

"They are tapping it?"

"Someone is. It will take a while to find out where it is going, but it certainly seems like their workmanship."

Sethra nodded. "I suspected it, from what Vlad told me. They are evidently collecting it in quantity."

"Collecting it? Raw?"

"So it would seem."

"How are they keeping it unstable?"

"They have found a large piece of trellanstone, and use it to keep the amorphia flowing, rather like a stream, from what Vlad and Teldra said."

"I see. Yes, that might work, if you had someone monitoring it at all times, and if it was physically near the trellanstone."

"The stream ran within a few hundred feet of it."

The Necromancer nodded. "This could be a real problem," she said, almost as if she cared. "Have they stirred?"

"They have indeed. Morrolan and Aliera were taken, Verra threatened—yes, they are stirring."

"Then they are ready with their stroke."

"So it would seem. Except that we have freed Morrolan and Aliera; I don't know how that will change their plans. But we have to assume they're still going ahead with it."

"Very well," said the Necromancer. "What do you require? I can cut their access easily enough."

"Insufficient," said Sethra. "Can you keep them out of the area?"

The Necromancer was silent for a moment; then she said, "I don't know. It's so large. Thirty-five or forty square miles, the last time I looked."

"Yes," said Sethra. "The Empress will almost certainly be willing to help."

"Then perhaps," said the Necromancer.

"If you cannot keep them out, do you think you could, perhaps, keep them in?"

The Necromancer frowned. "One of them, certainly. Ten or twelve of them, all with access to the power of the amorphia, impossible. But the same set of enchantments can be used in both directions."

"All right," said Sethra. "Good. You ought to start your preparations at once. In the meantime, I need to be there, along with Morrolan, Aliera, and whoever else we can gather together quickly. How much time will you need?"

"I don't know. I won't know until I start. Certainly, several hours, even with the Orb. Possibly a day or two. I wish you had told me sooner."

"I wish I had realized sooner what they were up to. We cannot wait a day or two before cutting off their link. I'm nervous about waiting even another hour."

"I shall hurry as much as I can."

"Yes. We will move as soon as we can, and, if you aren't ready, then we will endeavor to hold the place until you are."

The Necromancer nodded and said, "I'll get started, then." She turned away without ceremony, took three steps, and sort of faded away in midstride, leaving a trail of golden sparks behind her; possibly for effect, though that didn't seem like the sort of thing she'd do.

She left the room just as Morrolan returned—he coming in by the door—according to some sort of law of conservation of wizards. The Necromancer left in a shower of sparks; Morrolan appeared with a flapping of wings. Jhereg wings, to be exact. Rocza's wings, to be precise. Loiosh left my shoulder and flew toward her, the two of them doing a sort of midair dance of greeting, then flying around the room once together before landing on my shoulders, and continuing the reunion with neck and face rubs behind my head. It was all very cute.

"*I told you I was cute.*"

"I thought you might be missing her," said Morrolan.

"I was, and so was Loiosh. Thank you from both of us."

He nodded to me, then faced Sethra and announced, "The Empress agrees."

"Good," said Sethra. "So does the Necromancer."

"I love it when a plan comes together," I remarked to no one in particular.

Morrolan shrugged and said, "Here, Vlad." He reached into his cloak and emerged with a bag, which he emptied on the table near my elbow. It contained half a dozen daggers of various sizes. "I thought you might like to restock," he said, "so I grabbed these from my armory. I don't know exactly what you like, but one or two of these must be all right."

"Yes," I said. "That was very thoughtful of you." I inspected them, then placed all of them about my person in various ways. It took some work, with only one hand to work with; but this reminded me to make sure they were all accessible to my right hand. That put one behind my back, one between my shoulder blades, one in my right sleeve, well, you get the idea. Having them there made me feel better at once. I stretched my feet out in front of me and leaned back. Sethra said, "You look like a man who isn't going anywhere, Vlad."

"Well, I don't plan on leaving here any time soon. Am I mistaken about something?"

"I had planned to bring us to the site of Adron's Disaster right away. We don't know when they will appear; I'd just as soon anticipate them."

I looked at my left arm, then at Sethra, with what I hoped was an eloquent expression.

She nodded. "I take your point. But Spellbreaker could still be useful, if you can manage to wield it right-handed."

I sighed. "Very well," I said, and made it to my feet. "I assume Aliera will be joining us soon?"

"I should imagine. Morrolan, if you will please reach your cousin when she becomes available, and let her know that we are leaving now, and give her our precise location."

He saluted, with, I think, a touch of irony. I imagine he was still annoyed about her "young Dragon" remark earlier.

I drained off the remainder of my wine and said, "Do you ever get tired being the general-in-chief, Sethra?"

Sethra gave me a wry smile. "This is half of a general's dream, Vlad: a campaign with no need for a quartermaster. The other half, of course, would be a campaign with no subordinates to keep happy. If I ever have both of those at once, I'll consider my existence fulfilled and become part of the rock of Dzur Mountain again."

"*Again?*" said Loiosh.

"Again?" I said.

She shrugged and didn't answer, damn her.

I carefully set down my wineglass and said, "Well, shall we be about it, then?"

"Yes," said the Dark Lady of Dzur Mountain. She turned to Teldra and said, "If we have the chance to negotiate with them, we will take it, but the difficulty will be knowing if they are deceiving us. Do you think you can tell?"

"I don't know," said Teldra. "I hope so. I will certainly try."

Sethra nodded. "All right. Let's make an end to this."

"Do you think," I said, "that this will really be the end?"

"If we're lucky, it will end this gambit on the part of the Jenoine."

"That's good enough for me," I said, trying to sound like I was all kinds of excited to be part of it. My arm hung there, limp and useless, and Spellbreaker unraveled. I took it in my right hand, and managed, after too much effort, to get it around the wrist. It felt funny there. It also felt funny to be carrying a Morganti dagger. And not having a working left arm felt funny as well. I was a walking joke.

"*Shut up, Loiosh.*"

"*I didn't—*"

"*I know. It's what Sethra would call a preemptive strike.*"

Morrolan said, "Is there anything we need?"

Sethra touched the hilt of Iceflame at her side and said, "No, I believe we have what we need."

"Do you have the location?"

"I will in a moment. Bide."

Teldra came up next to me. I said softly, "Do you know know what she meant by 'becoming part of the rock of Dzur Mountain again'?"

"No," said Teldra, just as softly. "I was wondering myself."

"She was probably speaking metaphorically."

"Probably."

I wasn't convinced; I'll bet Teldra wasn't either.

Teldra took a moment to construct me a sling out of a dark grey linen towel she procured from somewhere. She set my arm in it carefully, and I grunted a thank-you.

"Let's go," said Sethra, and we gathered around her. I touched my grandfather's amulet, just to reassure myself that it was still there, and it occurred to me suddenly that I'd been wandering about without any of my protections and hadn't even noticed—this could be dangerous habit. On the other hand, if I were killed by the Jenoine, I would have no need to worry about the Jhereg. You take your consolations where you find them.

I had gotten to about this point in my reflections when the walls abruptly collapsed and opened up to the outdoors—or that's what it seemed like. We stood now on a small rock ledge, overlooking the Lesser Sea of Amorphia, where the greatest city of the Empire used to be until Aliera's daddy had a hissy-cow at the Emperor. I must make a point of telling Sethra not to underrate the power of the hissy-cow.

I looked out upon the raw, seething amorphia below us— the quintessence of chaos, crying out to be organized, and defying anyone's ability to do so. Some of those with me knew what it took to create order out of chaos; those we were expecting also knew. Some wanted to use it for one thing, some another, and therefrom sprang conflict mortal. Me, I'd just as soon let the damned stuff be.

The old city of Dragaera had grown up in what once, I'm told, was a fertile plain, fed by several streams and rivers coming down from a range of mountains that has more names than peaks. The mountains, which were west of the city, were now behind my left shoulder, except for bits of them that spread out in the form of sharp, ugly bits of greyish rock, one of which I now stood on. There were no signs of any rivers from where I stood, and what had been the city and most of the plain was a swirling mass of colors—browns, greens, and oranges, mostly—murky in places, sparkling at times, occasionally even pulling back to show what appeared to be brown dirt beneath. It did, indeed, seem very much like an ocean, if you can imagine an ocean with no tides, but instead with random waves that lash out up to two hundred feet from the "shore"—

waves with the charming property that the merest touch will not only kill you, but cause you to instantly dissolve into nothing. It was not my favorite place to be; especially here, about fifty feet away from it.

To be fair, I should add that being above it was rather safer. Not safe, but safer.

"Now what?" said Morrolan. "Spread out, or remain together?"

"Remain together," said Sethra. "And settle in; we might be here awhile."

"Should have brought some chairs," I said. Morrolan gave me a Look.

So I squatted down. My arm gave another twitch. Maybe, if I were lucky, it would start working again before I needed it. I massaged the arm through the sling for a bit and couldn't even feel it.

Sethra drew Iceflame and pointed it out toward the middle of the Sea, staring intently after it. Then she sheathed Iceflame and said, "All right. Any time now."

"That was it?"

"That was it. I have broken their link. Now we wait. If the Necromancer can seal this place off from them before they arrive, then we can all go home. If not, then we get to fight them. If we are lucky, they will be unable to re-establish a link right away, so they will be fighting without the advantage of sorcery, and a good strike with a Great Weapon will kill them. If we are not lucky, things could be more difficult."

"Here's to luck," I said.

"There they are," said Sethra, and my heart jumped into my mouth. I stood, and tried to let Spellbreaker fall into my hand, but missed the grab and it slithered onto the ground. As I groped for it, I following Sethra's gaze until I spotted a shimmering in the air not fifty feet away from us, on the same ledge.

"Okay, here we go, Loiosh."

"Boss, it's Aliera and the Demon Goddess."

"Oh. So it is."

"Sethra," I said, "you did that on purpose, didn't you?"

"No," said Sethra, as she took her hand off the hilt of Ice-flame.

Getting the chain wrapped around my wrist again gave me something to do while I recovered. Aliera and the Demon Goddess came up to us, and looked out over the sea. There was an expression on Aliera's face that I'd never seen before. Was she actually staring out at *that* and thinking of her father? How could she? Then again, how could she not?

The first words out of Aliera's mouth were "What did the Necromancer say?"

"She's working on it," said Sethra. "But she says it may take a while."

I said, "Well, we have the Goddess here; maybe she can do something."

"Not quicker than the Necromancer," said Verra, in that oddly echoing voice of hers.

"Why not?"

"Because," said the Goddess patiently, "she's better than me."

I stared at her, wanting to say, "But you're a Goddess!," only that would have sounded stupid, so I just swallowed and said, "Okay."

Sethra said, "Very well, then, Verra, I will keep my attention focused the other way." I'd run into people who were hard to understand; the Demon Goddess is the only being I have met who makes those around her incomprehensible. There is something very wrong about having that effect.

Aliera drew Pathfinder; I took an involuntary step back. Aliera pointed her blade out generally toward the Sea, and swung it back and forth a couple of times, then she made some sort of indefinite grunt under her breath. "Nothing yet," she said.

Morrolan said, "I could reach the Necromancer and—"

"Disturb her while she works," finished Sethra.

Morrolan scowled, then chuckled. "Yes," he said. "That was my intention. You don't like the plan?"

"As much as you like waiting," said Sethra.

Morrolan looked at her. "You don't mind waiting, do you, Sethra?"

She laughed. "At my age, one gets used to it, little Dragon-lord. I spend more time waiting than doing anything else."

Morrolan shook his head. "I can't imagine getting used to it."

"You see? You have more in common with our friend Vlad than you ever thought."

I opened my mouth to protest, then shut it again. Morrolan had nothing to say, either. We stared out over Adron's Disaster, which did the dance of amorphia: colors shifting, shapes appearing and vanishing, and always something faintly enticing, the way a tall cliff is enticing to someone afraid of heights. I kept my eyes above it as much as I could, because I didn't want to look at it, but didn't want anyone to know I was afraid to actually watch it.

"You want to look useful, Loiosh?"

"You mean just to impress them? Of course."

He and Rocza took off from my shoulder and began flying around the area in opposite directions. I said, *"Don't get too close to it."*

"We don't intend to, Boss."

Sethra said, "Are we going to get any help from the Empress?"

"Yes," said Morrolan. "She's sending the Court Wizard."

"Ah."

That was irony—Morrolan had been Court Wizard for some years, since an unfortunate incident involving Sethra the Younger, who had held the post previously.

The Goddess said, "I believe we will be ready for them."

Aliera said, "If you missed that, she said we will have aid from Barlen, and several of the other Lords of Judgment."

This brought up several questions, such as why in blazes they needed *me* here; but what I said was "Aliera, why is it that whenever the Goddess your mother speaks, everyone hears something different? It seems—"

Sethra broke in suddenly, "The Necromancer says they are coming. She can't stop them, but she hopes to be able to hold them here."

Loiosh and Rocza returned to my shoulder. Aliera, Morrolan, and Sethra all drew their weapons. I managed to unravel Spellbreaker without dropping it.

I was disappointed.

I'd really been hoping Aliera would answer my question.

15

I wondered if Sethra was happy about having guessed right. Myself, I'd just as soon she'd been wrong.

"I see them," said Aliera.

I followed her gaze, and spotted them almost at once, about fifty yards from us, standing right next to the Sea—closer than I'd have gotten to it for any reason, ever.

"They've spotted us," said Morrolan pointlessly, because they were obviously staring at us.

"What are those things they're carrying?" I asked.

"Probably something magical," said Aliera.

"Thanks," I said.

"Loiosh?"

"I can't tell from here. Should I get closer?"

"No."

In the course of moving away from the rampant Great Weapons, I discovered I was next to Teldra. "Okay," I said to her in low tones. "I've got a plan. First of all, are you secretly Mario?"

"No," she said.

"Oh. All right, so much for that plan."

She laughed more than it was worth; maybe she was scared too.

As far as I could tell, the Jenoine were doing nothing except looking at us; Aliera, Morrolan, Sethra, and Verra spread out a little, leaving Teldra and I just a bit behind them.

I said to her, "Perhaps you should have a weapon."

She shook her head. "I hardly know which end to hold."

I nodded, thinking that I'd still feel better if she were armed. But why? What did I have to offer her that could hurt them? And then, for all I knew, she could be armed; you never know about an Issola. Hell, maybe she was secretly Mario. It would certainly solve a lot of problems if she were. I looked at Spellbreaker. It was long this time—almost three feet—but the links were very, very fine. I set it swinging slowly.

I took a step forward, then, and Sethra said, "Wait, Vlad."

I stopped. Maybe she had a plan. I'd like her to have a plan. I'd like any reason not to get any closer to those things.

"Sethra, are we going to attack?"

"Bide, Vlad. I'm not yet certain."

I bit back more questions, and waited.

"There!" said Sethra, suddenly.

I looked where she was pointing, and saw a dark figure standing, about as far from the Jenoine as we were, but on the opposite side.

"*It's Barlen,*" said Loiosh.

"*He should help.*"

I glanced at Verra, and saw her locking eyes with Barlen briefly. I felt smug, as if I'd caught her at something; supposedly they were ancient enemies and lovers. That's the sort of thing gods do, you know. It's all in the legends. If this thing continued, I was going to have to start believing in legends.

Then the other Lords of Judgment appeared. Four . . . six . . . maybe ten of them, spreading out over the area. Some I might have recognized from the Halls of Judgment if I'd been closer. Some of them appeared to be more or less human from this distance, others not—I recognized one figure that seemed to be nothing more than a burning stick; another took the form of a cat-centaur; there was a thing that reminded me a little of that chunk of trellanstone, only with legs and spindly little arms; yet another seemed like a walking prism, at least, there were a lot of colors, and my eyes couldn't focus on it; and there was even a dragon which, from across a long distance, seemed almost to catch my eye for an instant, as if it knew me. I stared back. Could it be that one from the Paths of the Dead? No, for some reason, it didn't seem like that dragon. Eventually it looked away, leaving me wondering.

"Sethra," I said. "Is this it? I mean, is this going to be the cataclysmic battle between the gods and the Jenoine? And, if so, may I please be excused?"

The Enchantress of Dzur Mountain didn't look at me, but said, "I sincerely hope not, Vlad. This would be a bad place for such a battle; the results would be unpredictable. But it might happen. My hope is just to keep them away from the Sea and unable to use it, and to inflict enough punishment on them to discourage them from trying again. And to answer your other question, no, you may not. We may require that artifact you're carrying, and someone who knows how to use it."

Wonderful.

The Jenoine were looking around them, and, as far as I could tell, did not seem unduly disturbed.

"All right," said Sethra. "Let's move in."

Just exactly what I wanted to do. But they all just nodded, so I did too. They all started closing in on the Jenoine, so I did too. They all put expressions on their faces like they were ready to conquer or die, so I did too.

"Do you do everything they do, Boss?"

"Sure."

"If they all jumped into the Sea of Amorphia, would you do that, too?"

"Not again."

"Heh."

Rocza shifted on my shoulder, and I caught the psychic whispers of Loiosh telling her something—she probably didn't like the place much. Well, who did?

We moved closer to them—so did the gods. If I'd been attuned to more levels of magic, I have no doubt I would have detected all sorts of powerful enchantments swirling about above the place that was itself the most powerful of enchantments. I set Spellbreaker spinning a bit faster.

"*I'd really like to be somewhere else, right about now.*"

"*Oh, c'mon, Boss. Where's your sense of history?*"

"*I like to read about history, not make it.*"

"*You see, Boss? It's because of attitudes like yours that there are so few human heroes.*"

"*And so many humans.*"

"*Heh.*"

Rocza shifted again on my shoulder.

"*How is she doing, Loiosh?*"

"*She'll be fine, Boss.*"

"*Are you sure? She seems nervous.*"

"*Right, Boss. As opposed to you and me?*"

"*Good point.*"

We continued on, another step, two, three, closer to where the Jenoine stood, on the very edge of the Sea.

"*Boss, does this remind you at all—*"

"*No. It doesn't. Shut up.*"

I realized that I was still avoiding looking at the amorphia—sort of skirting it with my eyes. I didn't want to look at the Jenoine, either, but I made myself. I watched them, and tried to keep an eye on our Divine allies. This really was shaping up to be one of those battles they write songs about. I wondered if I'd get mentioned—the Easterner, Jhereg, outcast, walking around unarmed except for a length of chain that was useful for blocking magic of a kind that I wasn't going to encounter here. Maybe Teldra and I could find a quiet spot and continue our discussion of the philosophy of courtesy. I had enjoyed that. In fact, on reflection, I had enjoyed that more than I had enjoyed anything for several years. Strange, isn't it? I hadn't even realized it at the time, but trapped on a world not my own, perhaps in a universe not my own, held by godlike beings intent on some ineffable evil, Teldra and I had sat back and had the sort of discussion that I most enjoyed, the sort that Cawti and I had once had.

Bugger. This was not precisely the right time to start feeling maudlin. But those were my thoughts as I moved toward destiny or whatever it was I moving toward. Destiny, a spot in a ballad, or a quick death, maybe, if the Jenoine noticed me, or if I slipped a little and fell into *that*.

As deaths go, that one wouldn't be bad.

I mean, dying in pain has never been high on my list of desires. But, on the other hand, I'm not real fond of the death that comes on you out of nowhere, not even giving you time to realize that you're going. When I had thought about it—and, in my line of work, I had found my thoughts often straying toward that most morbid of all subjects—I had often felt that I wanted to go peacefully, while awake, not in pain, but aware that I was going—with time to say goodbye to life, so to speak, even if it were only to be a temporary goodbye until an awakening in the Paths or in a new incarnation. But then, I wondered, what if I got that, and, in the event, proved craven? The last moments of life have always seemed to me to be a good time for a last mental balance sheet—a chance to say to yourself: Okay, how did I do? How terrible to arrive at that point reasonably happy, only to find that in your last extremity you lost your dignity with your life, and that your whole image of yourself was proved to be only a lie! Rather than that, I'd prefer to go in my sleep, which I've always dreaded; or even by the sudden hand of an assassin, as has seemed most likely for the past several years, or perhaps by a wrong step into amorphia.

Sorry to drag you along for all of this, but, as I say, those were my thoughts at that moment, and if I had to live through them, you have to as well. Deal with it.

Ummm . . . would you be mad at me if, after all of this buildup, nothing much happens? Heh. Don't worry about it. Stuff happens.

Distantly, in the back of my head, as it were, I was aware of Loiosh communicating with Rocza, who seemed to settle down a bit.

We were walking directly toward the Jenoine, but the Lords

of Judgment weren't—they were instead spreading out, as if to protect against a retreat. Myself, I was all in favor of permitting the Jenoine to retreat if they wanted to. But why did *we* have to be the group that moved toward them? Two answers popped into my head at once: first, we had the Great Weapons, and, second, I had no doubt that it was Sethra Lavode who was giving the orders.

There was even someone or something above the Jenoine— at least, there seemed to be a hovering sort of darkness about fifty feet up that appeared thick enough either to contain something sentient, or perhaps even to be something sentient, though if it was it was nothing I wanted to get to know personally.

Aliera said, "Sethra, look."

We all stopped and looked, and discovered that we were, in fact, not the only ones moving directly at the Jenoine: the dragon was, too.

"Well, that is hardly surprising," said Sethra.

"Who is it?" asked Aliera.

"You don't know?"

"No, should I?"

"Yes."

"Well then, who—"

"Not now," said Sethra. She frowned, and finally said, "Very well. Leave her alone, we'll adjust."

I wasn't sure I liked the sound of that, but it wasn't my decision. There is a certain relief that goes with knowing that someone else is making the decisions. Maybe if I were to live two or three thousand years I might get to the point of liking that feeling. Watching Sethra, I got the impression that she was in psychic contact with someone or other, maybe with all the gods at once, so she could direct the battle. I don't know.

The closer we got, the bigger they looked. And the scarier. They didn't look so large out here as they had when surrounded by walls; but they were big, and so bloody *alien*. Their arms were awfully thick, and their hands looked capable of crushing a human skull without too much work, and even from this distance their eyes seemed to glitter with intelligence, and with powers beyond my comprehension. I guess the problem was, I just had too much time to think about things. In my own line of work it was different—either it was an unexpected attack, in which case I was too busy to be scared until it was over, or, preferably, it was something I had planned out to begin with. This was just all wrong.

Sethra turned to us suddenly and said, "She did it."

I was about to ask who did what, but Aliera said, "The Necromancer?"

Sethra nodded.

"Good," said Morrolan.

"I don't get it," I said. "They're already here. What's the point of—"

"She has blocked their passage out," said Sethra. "They have no choice now but to flight."

I looked out over the Sea of Amorphia, then looked away. "Good place for it," I said.

"Yes, in some ways it is," said Sethra. "In spite of the unpredictability of the results, if they fail to achieve their link, then they have an additional threat, with no compensating advantage."

I had been being ironic, but I didn't explain that to her.

At that point the Necromancer herself shimmered into existence a few feet away, walked over, and joined us, as if she were taking her constitutional. She nodded to Sethra and ignored the rest of us. Apparently she was the one being in existence who was immune to Teldra's powers.

We continued our stroll toward the Jenoine: Teldra, me, Aliera, Morrolan, Sethra, the Demon Goddess, and the Necromancer. We kept getting closer, and they still didn't act, though now I could hear them jabbering away in their own language, probably deciding which of them got to eat which parts of which of us. There was no indication that they were worried.

"Dammit, Loiosh. I wish they wouldn't just stand there, waiting. I wish they'd do something."

"Sure, Boss. What would you like them to do?"

"Well, jumping in the Sea would be nice."

"Heh."

"Or they could even surrender to us. That would be fine."

I probably shouldn't have said anything, because it was right about then that they went into action. Well, okay, it probably had more to do with the Necromancer, and even more with the fact that we were barely twenty feet away from them, but it seemed that way.

The way things had developed, there's no way I should have been caught by surprise, but I guess that's one of the problems with surrendering the initiative—they moved very fast, and for a second I froze—Spellbreaker flopped there, swinging back and forth a little. From their position, facing out in all four directions, they moved suddenly, and as if they'd trained for the maneuver for years. They seemed to grow larger, and one of them reached out for us, as if to grab and crush us, though more likely he was going to—

"Vlad!" said Sethra sharply, and I started Spellbreaker swinging again.

"Left!" said Loiosh, and I moved to the left, though I'm not sure what I was avoiding. I bumped into Teldra and we both stumbled. Teldra kept her balance, but I ended up on one knee, automatically raising my hand so I could keep Spellbreaker spinning. Spellbreaker obligingly shortened itself—I felt it vibrating in my hand, looked at it, and saw the links become larger. When I looked back up, my view was blocked by Morrolan and I don't know what happened, but Sethra was holding Iceflame up above her head, and there was lightning and flashing and all that sort of stuff going on somewhere in front of me—it was really shaping up into one of those big sorcerous battles they always talk about. What was I doing here?

I wasn't even aware of how loud things had gotten until I saw Aliera shouting but realized I couldn't hear her—not that it mattered, she was probably yelling some sort of Dragon war cry or something. She was also moving Pathfinder around in some sort of pattern—I wanted Pathfinder to be emitting flashes, sparks, lights, but whatever Aliera was doing with it didn't show.

Blackwand, on the other hand, was doing everything I could have wished—he would point it, and it would flash, and he'd point it somewhere else, and it would shoot out something black and scary-looking.

Verra was writhing and gyrating, as if possessed by something that made her arms flail and her body twist from side to side.

The Necromancer stood very still, her arms at her sides.

The noise, I eventually realized, was a sort of constant, rolling thunder; it seemed to come from everywhere. I concentrated on keeping Spellbreaker moving and tried to stay aware of what was going on, and watch for anything that might come at me, though it was hard, because Morrolan was in front of me blocking my view—and he may, of course, have been blocking more than my view.

Then Morrolan stumbled and went down in front of me, and I realized that one of the Jenoine was close. Very close. Too close. Way too bloody close—like maybe ten feet away. I wanted to look at Morrolan, to see if he was bleeding, or showed any apparent signs of injury—but I couldn't take my eyes off the Jenoine.

Well, okay. Score one for their team.

As far as I could tell, the Jenoine wasn't looking at me; it was concentrating on Verra. Frankly, I'd be more concerned with a God than with a one-armed Easterner too. Aliera knelt down next to Morrolan, Sethra turned away, I guess concentrating on one of the others, and there was a tremendous flash of light from directly overhead that left me seeing spots just as I was wondering if I should get involved somehow. I kept seeing flashes out of the corners of my eyes and couldn't tell what was from the Sea and what was caused by our friends and what was caused by our enemies. The air had that queer tang it gets after a heavy thunderstorm.

"What was that, Loiosh?"

"Something from that guy overhead, I think, Boss."
"Good. Did it accomplish anything?"
"I don't know. But one of them is down."

I saw it, then—one of the Jenoine was down indeed, and wouldn't be getting up again, and there was no mystery about what had taken it out: the dragon was holding it down with two paws and tearing chunks out of the thing with its teeth, and scattering it in all directions, as if to tell us that good, old-fashioned gore did, indeed, belong in a battle of gods, demigods, and wizardry.

Well, okay. Score one for our team.

Aliera turned her back on Morrolan and took two steps, which brought her next to the Demon Goddess her mother— the two of them stood facing one of them—perhaps the one that had laid out Morrolan. I watched, motionless.

The three of them began moving in a circle, and as far as I could tell, not doing anything else. I glanced around, trying to get an idea of what else was going on. Another of the Jenoine stood on what I have to call the shore for lack of a better term, staring out over it with its hands extended—probably, I suppose, doing whatever it was they came here to do in the first place.

I supposed I should do something to stop it. Heh.

Another continued to be dismembered and gutted by the dragon, who wanted to make a thorough job of it, and the re- maining one stood with its back to the one on the shore, making sweeping gestures with its arms while the gods stood around it, trying to close but unable to—Barlen, in particular, was scraping his huge reptilian feet in the dirt as if scrabbling for a purchase. It is not every day that one gets to see the gods stymied; I might have even enjoyed it if I weren't part of the whole thing.

Judging from the sparks and flashes that occurred in front of the Jenoine, the gods were throwing all sorts of things at it that didn't get through, and there was that god overhead, dominating everything, making flashes of light that made the daylight seem brighter than bright. It was all very magical and stuff.

I tried to watch everything at once. I was conscious, once

more, of how relaxed I was now that the time for action was at hand. My fear was somewhere behind me—I recognized it, but it was as if it were someone else's fear. I don't know, maybe that's how heroes feel. If I ever meet a hero, I'll ask.

Teldra knelt down next to Morrolan and bent over him. The Jenoine facing Aliera and the Demon Goddess moved to-ward Verra, and she moved toward it, and there was a flurry of activity, and Aliera gave a yell or a scream that I saw more than heard. Sethra turned toward Morrolan and Teldra, as if noticing them for the first time, and yelled something to me that I couldn't hear over the other sounds, which had done nothing except gotten louder—the roaring was almost painful.

Then Sethra pointed Iceflame at the Jenoine that was tus-sling with Verra and moved into the maelstrom. Aliera took a step in that direction, fell, stood up, took another step, fell again, stood up again, and fell once more. The Jenoine stood over Aliera, both of its hands raised in fists over its head, looking like it wanted to pummel Aliera physically, which couldn't pos-sibly have done her any good. The dragon, which had finished its meal and was now trying to get at the Jenoine who was holding off the Lords of Judgment, turned toward us, then, its mouth open, showing teeth the size of Blackwand, and began to move in our direction.

Then, just as if things weren't weird enough, Morrolan's right arm, still holding Blackwand, raised itself until it was pointed at the Jenoine—apparently without any direction from Morrolan himself, who gave every appearance of lying senseless on the ground, Teldra still kneeling next to him, bent over him. It was downright disconcerting.

Blackwand gave out some sort black flash, and the Jenoine reeled for an instant and took a step backward. Aliera rose to her feet and pointed Pathfinder at its breast. Maybe Morrolan was alive after all. The dragon, for no reason that I could see, stopped as if it had struck a wall, rolled over—something that big does a lot of rolling over when it rolls—and then came to its feet once more, and shook its head in a very human gesture.

I took a step closer to Morrolan, so I could get a clear view of his face.

"He looks dead, Boss."

"I think so, too. I hope it doesn't discommode him."

Then Teldra stood up and looked at me, and if there had been any doubt about Morrolan's condition, Teldra's expression would have removed it.

If you ever feel like torturing yourself, playing the "if only" game is a good way to go about it. If I had heard what Sethra had been yelling at me, or had managed to guess it. If I had known what they were doing. If I had moved a little quicker—or a little slower. If, if, if. You can kill yourself with ifs.

Or you can kill someone else with them, I suppose.

I looked up at the Necromancer, hoping maybe she could do something, but she hadn't even noticed Morrolan fall, and I dared not disturb whatever she was in the middle of.

One thing I know about revivification is that time is critical. I stood there, Spellbreaker spinning, and tried to think of something I could do that would get this over with fast, so Aliera or Verra or Sethra could start working on him. My arm twitched again in its sling, just to let me know that it would probably be useful again when it was too late. I would have liked to have at least dragged him away from the fight, but I couldn't with one arm.

Then Aliera went flying backward, tumbling backward like a seed bag without the seed, landing next to the dragon. I thought she was dead, or at least injured, but she put her hand on the dragon's head, and, using it like a handhold, rose to her feet at once, shook her head in a gesture terribly reminiscent of the dragon's, then turned back toward the battle.

It was terrifying to think that one of those things was entertaining the Demon Goddess, Sethra Lavode, the Necromancer, a dragon, and Aliera e'Kieron—after having killed Morrolan e'Drien. Quite terrifying. And another one was holding its own against the Lords of Judgment, against the gods themselves. I just didn't belong here at all.

Aliera didn't seem too worried—she raised Pathfinder, gave a scream that was so loud I heard it over the roaring, and charged.

The Jenoine noticed her, flung the Demon Goddess away, and faced Aliera.

Pathfinder seemed about to take it in the neck, but it held up a hand and, just as before, Pathfinder was held motionless, as was Aliera.

Evidently, they had succeeded in re-establishing their link with the Sea. I wondered if that meant we could retreat now, call it a lost battle, and go home.

I guess not.

Verra jumped on its back, biting and scratching at it like a tag in a brothel who just discovered that someone has borrowed her favorite gown and gotten a wine stain on it.

The Jenoine spun quickly, striking Aliera with the Demon Goddess's feet—the whole thing suddenly looked more like a tavern brawl or a scene in a farcical play than an apocalyptic battle between the forces of Good and Evil. Aliera was knocked backward again, while the Goddess fell from its back, landing at its feet, leaving its back to us. There was the perfect backshot I'd been looking for before, but I will confess to you that never for an instant did it occur to me to take it.

It did occur to someone else, however.

I felt a pluck at my side, as if a clumsy cutpurse were operating against me. I reached down to grab the wrist, forgetting that that hand didn't work. Before I could do anything else, Teldra was past me, holding the Morganti dagger she had pulled from its sheath at my belt.

Before it could turn around, Lady Teldra struck it, hard and low in the back.

No matter how powerful the Jenoine, a Morganti dagger between the shoulder blades will seriously cramp its style.

I guess it was the surprise, the unexpectedness of the attack that did it, but, of all the sorceries and Great Weapons and gods and dragons and necromancies, it was that attack with that weapon that got through.

The Jenoine jerked and tensed, spun around, and its face, insofar as I could make out an expression on its alien features, seemed twisted into a grimace.

For a moment that, in my memory at least, stretches out forever, I felt hope; could it actually be that after Iceflame, Blackwand, and Pathfinder had failed, that thing had succeeded? Teldra had stuck it deep, that was for sure, and maybe, just maybe.

Time stretched out, and everything took a horribly long time.

The Jenoine reached behind itself, and when its hand came back into view, it was holding the Morganti dagger, which it neatly and smoothly buried in Lady Teldra's breast.

16

Funereal Customs

The Jenoine, having destroyed Teldra, turned away; obviously still in pain, and, it seemed to me, maybe even a bit disoriented. Well, I suppose if you've just had a powerful Morganti dagger plunged into your vitals, you are permitted a little disorientation. Aliera shook herself and started to stand, the Demon Goddess rose to her knees, Sethra lowered Iceflame and turned toward Teldra. The Necromancer stood there, apparently oblivious. Morrolan remained dead, but not as dead as Teldra was or I felt.

I was close to her; I took a step and knelt down beside her, suddenly as oblivious as the Necromancer to both my friends and to the Jenoine. The expression on her face was one of mild astonishment. Her eyes were opened, but sightless, vacant; there was nothing there. It was all gone. Teldra was gone.

The Morganti dagger was deeply buried in her, and still leaking blood—with a blade that long, it must be nearly all the way through her.

I reached for the dagger to draw it out of her, though I knew it was already too late. Maybe I was thinking of saving her, maybe I was planning to attack the Jenoine with it; more likely I was just not thinking.

It was hard to get a grip on it with Spellbreaker still in my hand; I was unwilling to drop the chain, and I had no other hand to use. I managed to wedge the end of the chain between my palm and the hilt of the blade, and got a sort of weak grip.

A tingling began to run up my arm, mild but unmistakable. It was different from the tingling I was used to feeling when

Spellbreaker intercepted some nasty that was aimed at me—it was sharper, for one thing, and it didn't stop. I kept hold of the weapon and the chain, and the tingling increased, becoming almost painful.

"Boss, what is it?"

"I don't know. There's something—"

Spellbreaker stirred in my hand, twisting against the smooth hilt of the dagger. I watched, fascinated, as it twisted and curled up and around, doing its snake imitation. I'd seen it before, at odd moments, and never understood why. Nor did I now; I just watched.

The links, already small, were becoming even smaller—they shrunk as I watched, which was creepy. At the same time, the end of the chain touched the blade, and then ran up its length in what was almost a caress. The other end, the end I was holding, was almost moving, though at first I didn't feel it through the tingling that was still running up my arm.

Spellbreaker's links kept getting smaller, almost vanishing entirely as distinct links, and it seemed to be getting longer overall. Was it, somehow, trying to rescue Teldra? If it was trying, did it have a chance?

I watched, fascinated. If the Jenoine had wanted to, it could have crushed my head without really trying, because between the death of Teldra and the strange things Spellbreaker was doing, I had forgotten it was there; but I guess it was distracted by Sethra and Aliera and Verra, the way I was distracted by—

—The links were entirely gone now, leaving Spellbreaker looking almost like a thin golden rope, and as I watched, it began to wrap itself around the hilt—it really was trying to save Teldra. I realized I was holding my breath.

It continued slithering around, more snakelike than ever, covering the hilt as if it were a hangersnake trying to strangle it; I had moved my hand to get out of the way, keeping contact with the blade only through the pommel. The tingling continued, and then I realized that the weapon was actually vibrating in Teldra's breast.

If there was, as I suspected, some sort of battle going on within the Morganti blade, then continuing to hold it was a bad idea.

I should let go.

I really should let go.

"Boss—"

"I can't. I just can't do it."

Well, if I couldn't get away from the fight, maybe I could help.

"Boss, do you know what you're doing?"

"Not a clue, Loiosh. Be ready to pull me out."

"I don't know if I'll be able to."

"I know."

There was a battle raging around me—gods and demigods and wizards and undead battling; but I might just as well have been in my old office, in the quiet space in the basement, where I used to perform witchcraft when I had nothing to worry about except how to find the guy whose leg I wanted to break, or how to get the most out of the new brothel I'd just opened.

I miss the days when I used to be nostalgic.

Lady Teldra was inside the dagger, somewhere, somehow, and I was going to go get her or . . . well, I was going to go get her.

I should have been surprised by how easily my awareness entered the chain, but even the action seemed normal, natural, inevitable—sending my consciousness spinning along inside Spellbreaker was the easiest thing in the world, and I could have done it at any time, if I'd ever thought to try. I was moving, flying even, through corridors of gold; endless corridors, with side paths and trails leading everywhere and nowhere, with a warm, almost hot breeze caressing my face.

I felt Teldra all around me, from everywhere—a sort of friendly reserve, giving the gold a reddish tint, and in that moment, I think I discovered her secret, I learned how she could manage to be so friendly to everyone who entered Morrolan's keep for whatever reason: She liked people. She just plain liked them. It was strange. My grandfather was like that, too, but I couldn't think of many others. Cawti, perhaps, when she let herself. It was strange, knowing someone like that; I guess it was why I had never been able to understand her, and why I always, even to myself, made ironic remarks about her courtesies, and tried to find hidden motives in everything she did; it is hard to be comfortable around someone who just likes you for no reason, when you've always—

No, there wasn't time for that. I needed to find her—find the center of the Teldra-ness amid all the confusion of gold and movement and corridors whipping past.

I called her name, but got no response, and yet I could feel her presence; her personality, which I'd had so much trouble defining, was overwhelming. But it was static, too: that is, she didn't seem to be feeling or doing anything, she just *was*.

As I hunted for her—moving, it seemed, in part because I desired it, and in part pushed along by some power of which I was only dimly aware—I began to notice, here and there, what seemed to be nondescript greyish threads hanging haphazardly among the corridors through which I sped. I grabbed one as I passed; it seemed the right thing to do. The thread came with me easily, and as I held it, Teldra seemed closer—the feeling of her presence stronger. I grabbed another, and another, one of them with my left hand. Okay, here and now, I had two good hands. Why not? Each time I saw a greyish strand hanging from a wall or ceiling, I grabbed it and held it, and if I missed one, I reached back without even looking and got it, too. I pulled the threads in and tied them together, holding them.

I was no longer aware of the tingling sensation that had been running up my arm, but now, instead, it seemed as if that entire tingle was filling my body, leaving me feeling strong, alert, even powerful; it was a heady sensation, but not an unpleasant one. I wondered if I should be worried.

"*Loiosh, should I be worried?*"

There was a long, long moment before he replied, which was unusual, and when the reply came, it was faint and distorted, as if from a distance. *"I don't know, Boss. I don't know where you are, or what you're doing, or . . . everything is heating up here, the Demon Goddess and Sethra and Aliera are . . . I'm scared, Boss."*

When your familiar is scared, it's a good time for you to be scared, too.

But—

I didn't feel worried. The whole idea of having a familiar is to tell you when to be frightened by something that doesn't appear frightening—a familiar is your other self that watches to make sure nothing is being done to you while your attention is elsewhere, and this was just such a situation, but my instincts were telling me to push on, to keep searching for Teldra, to keep grabbing at whatever those strands of power were.

If Loiosh had told me to pull out, I would have, but he wasn't certain, which left me to make the decision. It was close. But one thought just wouldn't go away: If it were me in there, and Teldra had decided to look for me, she wouldn't have stopped while there was any hope left.

Okay, the decision was made: Press on.

A famous Iorich once said that the difficult part of being a Justicer was sounding one hundred percent when you felt fifty-one percent. I knew what he meant: I tried to put the doubt behind me so I could continue my psychic, or necromantic, or mystical journey through Spellbreaker, but it wasn't easy, because doubt is less easily dispelled than illusion, and with doubt come tentative half-measures—and nothing worthwhile has ever been accomplished by tentative half-measures.

There was a keen sense of traveling along with me, almost an ache for Teldra, but it was a distraction—as were my uncertainties about whether I was controlling or being controlled by the forces I was playing with, and my knowledge that, while I was sending my consciousness through the links of the strange artifact I called Spellbreaker, all the time the battle was going on around my physical body—but then, there wasn't a lot I could do to influence that anyway, was there? I couldn't do them any good, and it was pointless of them to have brought me to this place. If only I had—

If only I had—

Oh.

Maybe you've had it all figured out all along and have been waiting for me to catch on—those of you who have been following my path, walking beside me through sorceries, deaths, pain, betrayal, and wizardries beyond human comprehension—but believe me it is much easier to figure out when you are sitting back watching it unfold before you than when you have your awareness spinning through strange, mystical corridors while outside of you rages a battle in which the very gods are only holding their own. In any case, it was only at that moment that I understood what I was doing, what I was creating.

Half-remembered conversations, half-heard remarks, bits of folklore, years of observations without comprehension—so the Serioli had simply been telling me the simple, unvarnished truth in the most straightforward way it knew how; and that was why the Goddess had been so ambivalent; and that's how Pathfinder had saved Aliera's life—all came together into the explosive epiphany that I had been, all unknowing, doing just exactly what I should be doing.

Yes, now I understood.

And with that understanding came confidence, and with confidence came decision.

Teldra was gone, and yet not gone. She was there, but it was pointless to find her. What mattered were those greyish strands of power. What mattered was completing the transformation, that would save as much of Teldra as could be saved.

Fine, then.

By an act of will I stopped, and I summoned the greyish threads to me until I held all of them in my grasp—an instant it seemed, and I think it was. I wrapped them around my left wrist. The next one, and the next one. I had all the time in the world, so I could be careful and thorough, and I was; as careful as an Issola is of every nuance of tact; as thorough as a jhereg is at extracting every morsel of food from a corpse. I took my time, and did it right: pulling in the tiniest threads and securing them, making sure they were woven so close to me that we could never be separated; there was no longer a Spellbreaker, or a Lady Teldra, or a Morganti dagger, or even a Vlad; we were all something different now. The Jhereg? Heh. Let them come after me with their pathetic Morganti weapons. Just let them.

Almost as an afterthought, I repaired the trivial damage in my left arm, which had been repairing itself anyway. I both knew and felt that what I was wrapping the links around was, in fact, my soul. My conversation with Teldra about the nature of the soul came back to me with a sort of gentle irony; Teldra was like that. My own irony was harsher—maybe she'd exert some influence on me. I didn't think I'd mind. I wasn't seeing anything anymore, nor was I hearing anything, I was just being, and doing, and then I was done.

I came back to myself, to the real world around me, and found that I was still on one knee, next to Teldra's lifeless body. She lay with an arm up over her head, her eyes open, glassy, and sightless, her long hair all scattered about. She'd never have permitted her hair to look that way. Her mouth was open a little, in that moronic way you see from time to time on derelicts who gather in the evenings near Barlen's temple near Malek Circle. It was all wrong on Lady's Teldra's face. I looked away, and at what was in my right hand—a long Morganti dagger, with a hilt like a very fine golden chain. It fit my hand like an additional finger, like it should have been there all along, or maybe it had been there all along and I'd never been aware of it.

It?

Her. It was, after all, Lady Teldra.

I stood up and faced the Jenoine, which was moving at an impossible speed, fending off attacks from Sethra and Aliera and Verra—Aliera had some blood on her, and seemed both dazed and determined; the Goddess had grown larger, and her eyes flashed with hate. Sethra, like the Necromancer, who still hadn't moved, had no expression on her face at all, but moved in and out, looking for openings in the Jenoine's defenses—which were, in fact, rather formidable: there were lines of power flowing from its fingers, which formed glittering patterns in the air that left no room for anything to get past, but through which it could strike at will, lines that I knew must have been there all along, but which I could now see for the first time. Lines keeping Path-finder and Iceflame, and Verra with the power she embodied just by being who she was, completely absorbed in coping, be-cause to do otherwise would court destruction of those who wielded the Great Weapons, and permitting the wielder to be destroyed was something a Great Weapon would not permit, because beyond any practical considerations—far, far stronger than any practical considerations—there were bonds of love: Pathfinder loved Aliera, Iceflame loved Sethra. Blackwand loved Morrolan.

And Lady Teldra loved me.

The defenses the Jenoine had formed were, as I said, for-midable, but the defenses were also, at the same time, laughable. Of course Iceflame and Pathfinder and Blackwand would be stopped by them; powerful as those weapons were, they had not been made for this. As I attacked the Jenoine's defensive spells I felt the same tingling I used to feel when Spellbreaker used to intercept something aimed at me. I cut through them as if they were paper.

The Jenoine felt its defenses fail. It turned around and, quick as a striking Issola, I thrust Lady Teldra up under its chin and into its head.

It roared and spasmed as if every muscle in its body had contracted at once, and then I felt rather than saw Iceflame and Pathfinder join the party, and a sense of power, energy, and well-being flooded through me, and I understood the reason for that now, too.

It collapsed into a heap at my feet; I felt as if I could take on all the Jenoine in the universe with one hand tied behind me. I heard myself laughing as I turned to face the remaining two, but at that moment, the Necromancer gave a cry and fell to her knees, and, just that quickly, they were gone, leaving only half the gods in the world, one very large dragon, and our little group standing on the spot of Adron's Disaster, next to Morrolan, who was dead, and his seneschal, who was more than dead.

Or perhaps less than dead.

The sudden silence was shattering; I basked in it, feeling as if I could emit sparks, and would if I weren't careful for those around me. It was so quiet, I could hear my companions breathing; I realized then that the Sea made no sound, not even ocean-type sounds.

"Doing all right, chum?"

"Grand, Boss. And Rocza is fine, too. And so are you, by the way, though I was worried there for a bit."

"Yeah, me too."

"I think I'm jealous, though."

"Bite me."

He did, but in the nicest possible way.

Sethra knelt next to the Necromancer, who stirred and shook her head as if to clear it—positively the most human thing I had ever seen her do.

"They broke the Necromancer's block, didn't they?"

"Brute force and desperation," said the Demon Goddess in her strange voice, made even stranger by the awful silence. "But for some reason, they released their link to the amorphia."

"So we won?" asked Sethra, sounding surprised.

Verra looked at Morrolan and Teldra lying on the ground, and nodded.

Aliera said, in the strangest voice I'd ever heard from her, "Daddy did it. Daddy took their link from them."

Sethra stared at her.

Aliera nodded and said, "I asked him to, and he did." Well, it was nice to know they were doing something while I was distracted.

Sethra looked out over the Sea and said, "Adron is out there?"

"Yes. I suspected he would be."

"Conscious? Aware?" said Sethra.

Aliera shrugged. I understood that shrug. "Consciousness" and "awareness" aren't always clear-cut concepts, as I had just learned. There were tears in Aliera's eyes. Well, there was plenty to cry about, I suppose, and there'd be more if we didn't get to work on Morrolan soon. I looked over to where the Jenoine had been, but there was no trace they had ever been there; the gods and even the dragon were gone as well. It was only Sethra and Aliera and the Necromancer and the Goddess and me; and Morrolan and what had been Teldra. Morrolan's sword had returned to his side, still gripped by his dead hand; I'm not sure when that happened.

"We need to get to work on Morrolan," said Aliera, her eyes still glistening.

Sethra stood up and nodded to her. "Yes," she said. "And quickly." She looked at Teldra's body, lying on the ground, then at the weapon in my hand, then at me.

"Well done, Vlad," she said.

Aliera, standing dazed and bloody behind her, but with a grim expression on her face, nodded. The Demon Goddess, however, had eyes only for the blade I carried.

Well, who could blame her? "You can put that thing away now," she said at last.

I looked into her eyes and chuckled. "Very well, my Goddess."

Verra scowled.

I cleaned her on the Jenoine's body—some customs must be observed, after all—then sheathed her, with some regret, my hand trailing over the smooth, gold hilt that had once been Spellbreaker. I was delighted to discover that sheathing her did not diminish the sense of her personality.

I watched Verra, who was looking back at me, but she had nothing more to say. With an aimless gesture of farewell, she turned into shimmering sparks and was gone. Sethra, mean-while, had lifted Morrolan in her arms.

"Come, stand next to me," she said.

Aliera looked out over the Sea, I suppose saying farewell to her father. Then Aliera, the Necromancer, and I took positions next to Sethra, and then we were gone from that place, and we were once more in the heart of Dzur Mountain.

17

TAKING ONE'S LEAVE OF FRIENDS

They laid Morrolan on a couch, and Aliera and the Necromancer began working on him. I watched for a while, then turned to Sethra. "So we won."

She nodded. "Yes, I'd call this a victory. They wanted to establish their own link to amorphia. That is, a permanent link, on our world, with which to challenge us. They failed to do so. And we destroyed two of them, which is no small feat."

"Good."

Sethra shook her head and murmured, "Adron."

"Yes."

"It's hard to believe. Sentience is, well, I don't know."

"Yeah, sentience is a strange thing, isn't it?"

She glanced up at me, catching my tone of voice, and said, "I shall miss her."

"Yes," I said. Then, "Did you know?"

Her eyes widened. "You mean, what was going to happen?"

"Yes. Teldra, the weapon—all of it."

"No, Vlad. I had no idea. If I'd had any idea, I should never have—no, I didn't know."

"What was it you yelled to me, in the middle of it all?"

She gave me an ironic smile. "You don't want to know."

"Probably not, Sethra, but tell me anyway."

"I told you to watch out for Teldra. It looked like she was contemplating doing something foolish."

"Yeah, I guess she was."

"But I suppose it is best for all of us that it turned out that way."

"All of us, except for Lady Teldra."

"Yes. Well, you are now a member of a rather exclusive club, Vlad. You are one of those the gods have cause to fear. Congratulations to you, and to Godslayer."

"Lady Teldra," I corrected her gently.

She shrugged. "As you prefer."

I touched the hilt and it was almost as if I could feel her fingers touching mine. I said, "Do you suppose the Jenoine knew?"

"No," said Sethra. "They would never have put the weapon into your hands if they had suspected. They wanted you to kill Verra, just as they said."

"You mean, that was it? They really expected me to just go and kill her?"

"Yes, which would have allowed them access to the Lesser Sea, where they could have established their own link—that is, a permanent one, with, in essence, their own Orb. It would have been a powerful blow against us. Although, knowing that Adron is still, in a sense, in there, I don't know what effect that would have had."

I shook my head. "But Sethra, all kidding aside, I was never going to kill Verra. I mean, I never even thought seriously about it."

"Yes, I know."

"It doesn't make sense."

"It doesn't make sense to us, Vlad."

"If they have so little understanding of us, Sethra, I'm not sure how worried about them we should be."

"Whatever their understanding, they have a great deal of power."

"But still. With such intricate plans, how can they be that far off?"

"They don't understand us, that's all. They never have. Talk to Verra sometime; that's been their flaw from the beginning."

"I don't think the Demon Goddess wants to have a lot to do with me these days. And that's fine with me."

"Yes, I suppose it is. And Vlad—"

"Yes?"

"Should I happen not to be around when Lady Teldra wakes up, you will not forget to give her my regards?"

"Wakes up? What do you mean?"

She smiled. "I think I'd rather not tell you."

Damn her.

Aliera, still bloody and dazed-looking, stumbled over and sat down next to us. I looked over at Morrolan, and saw the gentle rise and fall of his chest.

I nodded to Aliera. "Congratulations," I said.

She nodded and closed her eyes.

Sethra said, "Good. Now let's see to you." Aliera was, evidently, too exhausted to argue; she struggled to her feet, and accompanied Sethra out of the room.

The Necromancer walked over from Morrolan's side and sat down opposite me. We looked at each other for a while, and then she said, "I can bring you wherever you'd like."

"Thanks," I said. I looked over at Morrolan. "Who gets to tell him about Teldra?"

"Sethra, I should imagine."

"Lucky Sethra."

"What are you going to do?"

"Same thing I've been doing."

"You have rather less to fear from the Jhereg now—at least, Morganti weapons shouldn't frighten you as much."

"That's true. But I've recovered a bit from the bravado I was feeling, uh, earlier. I'd just as soon not give them a chance."

She nodded. "Where then?"

"Perhaps I'll visit my grandfather."

"I'm certain he'd like that."

"Or else I'll head East."

"Your ancestral homeland?"

"Yes. I was there once before, and rather liked it. Maybe I'll organize a defense there, in case Sethra the Younger decides to try to conquer it. I beat her once, maybe I can beat her again."

She studied me for a little. "When did this idea come to you?" she said at last.

I shrugged. "I don't know. Just now, I guess, while I was talking to you. Why?"

"It sounds a little public-spirited for you, Vlad."

"Maybe it's Lady Teldra's influence," I said ironically.

"That's what I was thinking," she said, without irony.

"Oh," I said. "Well, maybe I'll do something else."

"Is Lady Teldra's influence that bad a thing?"

I thought about that. "No, I suppose not."

"I shall miss her," said the Necromancer. "And you," she added.

I almost made an ironic remark about that, just out of reflex, but I refrained.

Maybe my reflexes were changing, but I didn't care to examine them too closely to find out.

I said, "Has anything exciting been happening in Adrilankha lately?"

She smiled a little. "I'm afraid I don't keep up on such matters."

I nodded. "All right," I said, deciding suddenly. "Here's what I'm going to do. I'm bloody well going into Adrilankha, and I'm bloody well going to have a meal at Valabar's, and if the Jhereg find me, fine, and if they don't, I'll figure out what I'm going to do next while I eat. If there's one thing I've missed—"

There was a soft moan from the couch. As I looked, Morrolan's eyes fluttered open. His mouth opened and he tried to speak, but couldn't manage.

"We won," I told him. "It wasn't pretty, but we won."

No, I wasn't going to be the one to tell him.

"Boss, your stomach is going to be the death of us all."

"Very probably, chum. But don't complain, you get the scraps."

"Oh, I'm not complaining. Just observing." Rocza shifted on my other shoulder; I imagine Loiosh had given her a hint of what was coming. For a wild jhereg, it hadn't taken her long to develop a taste for civilized food.

"All right," I told the Necromancer. "Let's go, then."

"Now? You don't wish to wait for Sethra and Aliera?"

"Please give them my farewell."

"You sure, Boss? Right now?"

"I don't want to be here anymore."

The Necromancer stood up. I said, "Can you put me right in front of their door?"

"Easily," she said.

"Good, then."

"What are you going to have?"

"I don't know, but it will start and end with klava."

Morrolan cleared his throat, tried to speak, then exhaled loudly and lay back.

"I'm sorry," I told him.

He looked at me, eyebrows raised.

I shook my head. The Necromancer put her hand on my shoulder, I put my hand on Lady Teldra. Loiosh and Rocza took their positions, and Dzur Mountain was gone, and I was outdoors, facing the familiar sight of Valabar's, which, of all things, hadn't changed a bit. I smelled onions and garlic and broiling kethna. There were no assassins waiting to kill me, at least yet.

I removed my amulets from their box and put them back on, just out of reflex, and stepped inside.